The Tattooist

The Tattooist

Louise Black

A Cutting Edge Press Hardback

Published in 2012 by Cutting Edge Press

www.CuttingEdgePress.co.uk

Printed and bound by CPI Group (UK) Ltd, Croydon, CR0 4YY

HB ISBN: 978-1-908122-16-2
E-PUB ISBN: 978-1-908122-17-9

For Julie, Jays, Jae;
the 'others mothers' of 2005 – Jennifer, Anne, Julia;
and Peter 'the Good'.

Introduction

Xanthe's fingers were sea slick and there was dried puke under her nails. She was sprawled naked in an explosion of scarlet sheets. Her skin looked cadaverous in the heavy silence of three a.m. Her long blonde hair coiled like serpents around her neck.

Xanthe was drunk. Not the kind of drunk that makes you louder and brighter and funny with friends. Xanthe was numb drunk. Her eyes were stones. Her cheeks were livid. The bottle of gin nestled close to her hipbone, its cap lost on the floor somewhere.

'Miz,' she told the empty room, raising her head a few centimetres and breathing hard with the effort, 'piss.' Xanthe giggled and collapsed back onto the stained pillows. She ran her swollen tongue around her lips and tried to brush the fringe from her face. Grabbing the bottle, she heaved herself into a seated position and swung her legs over the edge of the bed. One foot was tangled in the sheet. She kicked out irritably, knocking something onto the carpet. She knew what it was, and that she was absolutely unable to lean over and pick it up without crashing flat on her face.

Xanthe sat, gathering her thoughts and her uncoordinated limbs. She needed to pee. It was not the first time she had

1

tried to get to the bathroom. She had resurfaced hours ago with a sharp pain in her bladder, but there was some gin left, which she had gulped down and slipped straight back into unconsciousness again. Xanthe shook the bottle. Empty. Anger flared: a match in the dark. She knew there was none but she had to check anyway. Exhaling stormily she levered herself upright, holding on to the bedpost.

When Xanthe stood, everything she had drunk that night clamoured at once for expression. Utterly inebriated, exhausted and confused, Xanthe swayed, eyes closed, a golden trickle snaking down her leg.

Time slips in the dead of night. Xanthe was dandled in the fraction of a second it took for her bladder to open and the warm flush of urine to begin its precipitous descent. She gripped the furniture and smiled suddenly into the darkness . . . Relief . . . Xanthe felt comforted, like a great weight was slipping from her. At this point on the elastic limit of perfection, Xanthe was actually happy. But the urine cooled as it passed knee and ankle. Her eyes flicked wide white.

It was an ungainly dash to the bathroom, throwing off streaks of piss and crashing into doors. Bruises bloomed on Xanthe's body, mysterious as orchids overnight. Such strange growth had begun years ago, in the time she could not remember, before the time she wanted to forget. She hurled herself onto the toilet and rested her head against the basin. The noise of it sliced up the silence in her flat. She began to hiccup. The kitchen sink was still crusted with vomit from earlier, when she had been shovelling tortilla chips into her mouth along with the gin. Xanthe choked back the bitter tide. She took deep, laboured breaths. Her forehead was slick with sweat. Her legs were damp and cold. She began to shiver.

'Fuck,' Xanthe muttered. It was one of her favourite words. She wiped a hand over and between her legs and stood up again, using the basin to steady herself.

Painfully awake, Xanthe wandered into her living room. When she had moved in four months ago, the place had been a pristine box. She had liked that: white walls, white tiled floor, a smell that was not her own. A fresh start. Now a plastic carrier bag spilled rubbish all over the place. Dirty clothes erupted from the washing machine. Caked dishes towered around the clogged sink. The treacherous red eye of the stereo blinked. She would have to get up and go to work in three hours.

Xanthe groped around for her headphones, not out of consideration for her neighbours – whom she did not know – but because she could crawl inside the music that way. She jammed the cumbersome object over her hair and was joined as if on a leash to her stereo. She fell onto the sofa, aimed the remote and waited. It was one of the mix CDs she had made after the move. The pounding bass went straight to her heart. She began to rub the back of her neck. With her chin collapsed on her chest, Xanthe mouthed the words. Her voice sounded childlike in the pre-dawn hush.

'Hey Paul, hey Paul, hey Paul, let's have a ball.'

Xanthe's nose began to run. She smeared her face against the rough upholstery. Her skin was pricked with cold. Music was not what she wanted. Xanthe ripped off the headphones and stumbled back to her bedroom. She groped a yellow pill out of a plastic bag, swallowed it dry and dropped down onto her hands and knees. When she had found what she was looking for, she hauled herself into bed.

Xanthe warmed the new glass dildo against her chest, rolling it backwards and forwards between her breasts. It was shaped like a prehistoric goddess with a narrow head and ample swell of hips. Xanthe dug into the mess of her bed. She had bought the sheets when she moved. They had never been washed. Xanthe closed her eyes and slipped the glass over her stomach, then played the tip against her clitoris. Her mind was a blank screen.

Masturbation was one of the simple pleasures of her life now, like eating cereal straight from the packet instead of cooking dinner, and falling asleep on the sofa. Xanthe brushed her fingertips against her nipple, which became stiff as a seed pearl. Simultaneously the glass was becoming hot and slick between her thighs. Xanthe bit her lower lip and arched her back, her hair tangled beneath her. She moved both hands between her legs. The glass slipped deep inside. As she plunged it in, she also rubbed the sticky bud of her clit. Xanthe moaned as the pleasure built inside of her. The orgasm, when it came, was pulled from her body like cheap scarves in a conjuring trick.

'An Exposition Upon Sir George Ripley's Vision' by Æyrenaeus Philalethes, Anglus, Cosmopolita (1677)

When busie at my Book I was upon a certain Night,
This Vision here exprest appear'd unto my dimmed sight:
A Toad full ruddy I saw, did drink the juice of Grapes so fast,
Till over-charged with the Broth, his Bowels all to brast:
And after that, from poyson'd Bulk he cast his Venom fell,
For Grief and Pain whereof his Members all began to swell;
With drops of Poysoned sweat approaching thus his secret Den,
His Cave with blasts of fumous Air he all bewhited then:
And from the which in space a Golden Humour did ensue,
Whose falling drops from high did stain the soyl with ruddy hue.
And when his Corps the force of vital breath began to lack,
This dying Toad became forthwith like Coal for colour Black:
Thus drowned in his proper veins of poisoned flood;
For term of Eighty days and Four he rotting stood
By Tryal then this Venom to expel I did desire;
For which I did commit his Carkass to a gentle Fire:
Which done, a Wonder to the sight, but more to be rehearst;
The Toad with Colours rare through every side was pierc'd;
And White appear'd when all the sundry hues were past:
Which after being tincted Ruddy, for evermore did last.
Then of the Venom handled thus a Medicine I did make;
Which Venom kills, and saveth such as Venom chance to take:
Glory be to him the granter of such secret ways,
Dominion, and Honour both, with Worship, and with Praise.

When busie at my Book I was upon a certain Night,
This Vision here exprest appear'd unto my dimmed sight:

I

There was very little in the outward appearance of the shop that announced its line of business. It was crammed in halfway along rue Biot, between the dilapidated convenience store and a Lebanese restaurant. The narrow street straggled like an appendix scar beneath the pendent belly of Place de Clichy. Traffic was constant but not unbearable, subdued somewhat by the forgotten air of the place. The plain glass frontage of 109 shone in the spring sunshine. A symbol hung above the door: a circle with a dot at its centre and a series of lines radiating like an arrowhead from the top right quadrant. Fabrice brought his mug of tea from the back kitchen and bent to pick up the post.

Two giant pots of bamboo flanked the doorway to his world, in part obscuring what was going on inside from curious passers-by. A waist-high counter divided the cramped space. At the front, two wooden folding chairs were set facing each other. Tucked against the wall behind the counter was a Japanese paper screen. Taking up most of the remaining room was an imposing black leather chair and, beside it, a smaller leather and chrome stool. The floor was of polished black boards. The walls were painted white and decorated with a series of framed posters. A recessed set of shelves was stuffed with books.

Fabrice flipped most of the letters straight into the bin and took a sip of his sencha tea. His shaven head and slow, deliberate movements brought to mind a monk-like calm. His body was spare and strong. He was dressed in black kung fu slippers that whispered as he walked, a plain black collarless shirt with the sleeves rolled up, and khaki combat trousers hanging loosely from his narrow hips. Perhaps it was the atmosphere of the shop, but his brown eyes seemed to have an almost Asiatic aspect. They shone with a bright intelligence. His skin was old gold, stretched smooth over the blades of his face. He wheeled the stool in front of the bookshelf and placed his mug on the floor. His every gesture was measured, economical. He seemed in perfect harmony with his environment.

Fabrice sat, his posture graceful and correct, meditating with his stare fixed on the opposite wall where a woman was on her knees with her back to the camera, one hand scooping her lustrous black hair off her nape. Every working day began this way, in silent contemplation. A great indigo dragon writhed across the subject's body, its bulbous eyes and curved fangs following the contours of her buttocks. Its sinuous scales rippled up her spine. Its tail flicked over her shoulder. Nestled in the folds of its flesh was a serene goddess holding a peony. The design continued down one slender arm, becoming a complex web of indigo leaves and brightly coloured chrysanthemum heads. The woman's back and arm were entirely covered in ink. The tattoo would have been hand-poked by foot-long *tebori* needles in a traditional Japanese studio by a Japanese master. The master would have stabbed the pigment into the woman's willing skin over a number of sessions. The pain would have been intense. The woman would have borne it without complaint, perhaps slipping into unconsciousness from time to time. Fabrice smiled. A beatific light radiated from his features.

He loved working in his studio. Studying the poster would make him a better man. He was an artist, who took his work seriously. Always had. The thick plate-glass windows kept the sounds of the street at bay. His bamboo thrived in the polluted Paris sun. He had never hand-poked a tattoo but he had seen it done on his travels. It seemed so much more intimate and honest; the artist really transformed the flesh, which submitted to his efforts. There was none of the buzzing interference of the machine. You could hear your own breath flowing in and out, which gave life to the design. Inspiration. Illumination. Spiritual goals. He inhaled deeply.

Fabrice finished his tea, took the mug to the kitchen, rinsed it and washed his hands. A pale green door opened onto a dark and narrow corridor, which led to his bathroom and living quarters. He had been here for eight years. He had stumbled across the place on his way to meet a girl, and then had forgotten all about her as he called the vendor and arranged a viewing straightaway. You always know when you are coming home, even if the front door is shut and you have never been there before. It was exactly what he had been looking for: a rundown area, no chance of tourists dropping in on a whim, obscure but not out-of-the-way. He now watched the neighbouring streets with disgust as they became increasingly gentrified. Articles in *Zurban* instructed the *bobos* that Batignolles was a cool place to live, so they got on their scooters and flocked around its park, bars and brasseries. When the 17th got its first Starbucks, Fabrice would know it was time to move on. But not yet.

Fabrice had bought in the right place at the right moment. His grandfather would have been proud. The old man had been a cobbler, had spent his life in a little, dim shop just like this one. The inheritance meant that there was no mortgage to worry about and Fabrice did not care to develop his business. He lived simply. One or two clients a week, paying cash: that was all he needed. He did not advertise. He preferred people to come looking for him, as the commissions tended to be more interesting that way. The web of his creations spanned Paris and perhaps beyond.

Some of the ends of the bamboo leaves were looking dehydrated. Fabrice stroked a strong green frond between finger and thumb and tested the earth in the bulbous pot. He watered his plants, washed his hands and set to cleaning his work station.

Close to the chair was a mobile stainless steel unit. Clear plastic boxes on the lower shelves housed a rainbow of inks, grips, tips and needles. The top shelf was clear. Fabrice squirted some antiseptic spray and buffed it with a square of kitchen paper. Then he went to the autoclave in the kitchen to check the pressure.

Everything was ready. All he had to do was wait.

II

Yoshiko's building on rue Truffaut, just across from Square des Batignolles, had been braced with scaffolding since the week after she moved in. She was annoyed the estate agent had not thought to mention the extensive renovations that were planned. Green nets had been slung over the metal framework, which cast a perpetual deep-sea gloom on her apartment. She could not open her window because of the dust and the noise. At home she would not have put up with it, but here it seemed she had no choice.

Yoshiko looked down at her arms and felt trapped. She kicked at a pile of books, which toppled obligingly. Shiny French and English grammars slid all over the floor. She could still hardly tell the difference between them: wide-eyed *gaijin* questioning each other about their hobbies and holiday plans. She had applied herself diligently to her French lessons, got consistently good grades in school, but in Paris every time she opened her mouth to speak what came out was an incomprehensible babble. She should have been getting ready for class.

'Fuck that,' Yoshiko told the books. She had decided to go to the convenience store on rue Biot, the one that stocked dusty piles of *ramen* and instant miso soup. She longed for familiar things. Maybe slurping hot salty soup would cheer her up.

Yoshiko let her towel drop to the floor and went to the mirror to comb her hair. What would her father say if he knew? She could not imagine. Would he shout? Cry? Hit her? No, he would never hit her. He would be shocked. She saw his lips making a tight, pale line. Of course he would be shocked: that was why she had done it. She had been going through *juken jigoku*, examination hell; he had been working eighteen hours a day. She had just wanted to shake things up a bit.

She turned sideways and considered her profile: flat stomach, small breasts, short legs. She had known she was making a mistake about two minutes into the procedure. The shop had seemed all right from outside, with lots of sparkling chrome and mirrors, a long glass counter filled with trays of jewellery. She had made the two-hour trip into Shibuya seething with rage at her *chi chi*. He did not seem to notice anything she did. He had not noticed her marks, which were top of her class. He had not noticed, the night before an exam when she sat across the dinner table from him, her exhausted eyes gritty with tears. He had not noticed the lattice of paper cuts to her wrists and fingers. Well, he would notice this.

The tattooist had not looked much older than she did. He had had difficulty stretching the latex gloves over his sweaty hands. Following a brief conversation about what she wanted, he had begun. Did not even sketch out the design first. He could not seem to get her in the right position, either. He had tried her with elbow bent, then he had straightened the arm, then yanked it behind her, all the while inking in thick, wobbly lines. Rock music had been blaring from the stereo. He had sung along, off-key and oblivious. Yoshiko now wondered if he had been on drugs. People like that – weren't they all on something?

Yoshiko rubbed her right arm. The crooked spider web radiated out from her elbow. She hated it. Had never worn a T-shirt since. So her father had never seen. When he suggested she spend a year in Europe before attending Aoyama Gakuin University, she had jumped at the chance.

He would expect her to be fluent in French and English by the time she returned. Then she could follow him into a career in international marketing. Impossibly long days and family life skewed by the prism of jetlag. Yoshiko despised the Linguarama classes full of bored Korean housewives and young Chinese who were over the moon to be in Europe. She wondered if the school would report her to her father for not turning up. No. Of course not. Father was far away. She did not know if that made her happy or sad.

Yoshiko abruptly folded her arms over her chest. In the corner of the mirror she saw him, eyes wide, crouched on the bare planks suspended level with her window. It was not the first time. He was wearing a flannel shirt over ripped jeans, and a dirty white helmet. His hand went to the plastic brim in an almost gentlemanly gesture, like tipping his hat to her. Yoshiko turned around and dropped her arms by her sides. She shook her head slightly so that her long hair tumbled over her shoulders. She was as smooth and polished as a statue. The workman's tongue flicked around his lips, imagining kissing that sweet shaven pussy. Yoshiko moved one hand to cover her breast, fingers brushing the nipple. The other hand moved between her legs. Yoshiko knew she was getting wet. The man edged closer to her window, which was securely locked. She could see tiny bubbles of saliva at the sides of his mouth. Surreptitiously, Yoshiko hooked two fingers over her aching cunt. The man's palm slapped flat against the pane.

Yoshiko giggled, both hands rising to cover her face, and ran back to the bathroom, slamming the door behind her. By the time she came out again she knew he would be gone.

In the torpid excitement she forgot for a moment how lost and homesick she felt. Was it dangerous, flirting with the scaffolder like this? The first time, they had just looked at each other and smiled, two aliens making contact. It was Yoshiko who had decided to up the game. She needed someone to see her. Besides, the door and windows were firmly locked. Her rules. No problem.

III

Fabrice sat. His spine was as straight and strong as the bamboo, with its sharp leaves that seemed to pierce the stillness of his studio. A book was open on his lap but he had stopped reading. He was conscious of the creep of urban life outside. Saturday. The Quick hamburger restaurant near the Metro gobbled Parisians and soon disgorged them in a litter of greasy packaging and bad breath. Tight knots of tourists bent over the menu at Hippopotame, its distinctive blend of pungent steaks, low lighting and scarlet tablecloths seeming suitably French. On the steps outside the twelve-screen cinema on Place de Clichy, men and women waited for each other as they had done since the place was built in the 1920s, hungry for the distraction of a story told in light and sound. Fabrice's eyes went to the window as the precious volume weighed heavy on his thighs. It seemed as if there had always been a thick pane of glass between himself and others. It had been that way for so long, it felt natural. He glanced down at the dense text and then up again as a petite woman strode past wearing a tiny scrap of a dress, with bare legs, black socks pulled to just above the knee. Trying so hard. Wanting so much. Didn't she know she was just setting herself up for a life of suffering? Fabrice shook his head and tried again to concentrate.

The shop was an ideal place to further his studies. He had never been to university. It had not been an option when he was young. No one from his family, his school, could even think of spending three years without work. From what he knew of it now, all he had missed was the chance to run up debts and drink himself silly. And Fabrice did not drink alcohol. He had not met a graduate yet who impressed him. They wore their scant reading like a badge of honour, and mouthed second-hand opinions as if they were truth. University did not offer an education; it merely trained you to fit in with all the other suit-wearing salary slaves. Not that Fabrice was prejudiced. He loved passing a little time with academia's finest, when the opportunity arose. It was better than an anthropology degree for him.

A face appeared at his window. A stranger, shielding her eyes, was trying to see inside. Fabrice bent his head and focused on a footnote. Let her come to him. They had to find their own way in this world, all those lost and timid creatures. Fabrice became mindful of his breathing. He inhaled light and energy, letting them flood his body. A scooter sped past, the racket of its horribly tuned engine battering the worn facades. She moved to the other side of the door, peering over the top of the bamboo. She must have seen something that gave her the resolve to try the handle.

The woman pushed on the door and entered.

'I didn't know if you were open. There's nothing to say so.' Her voice trailed off as she took another hesitant step forward.

Fabrice looked slowly up from his book and smiled. 'I am always working.'

Silence spun between them. He would not help her. She had to say what it was she wanted. It was one of Fabrice's rules. He was painfully aware of the weight of his work: a tattoo was, after all, for life. The woman's eyes darted from the chair to the posters on the wall and back to the quiet tattooist.

'Um . . . you did a friend of a friend of mine, a year or so ago.'

Fabrice nodded encouragingly.

'I have this . . . thing . . . that I want to cover up.'

Fabrice leaned forward, glancing up and down her body, wondering where it might be.

'Do you have a list of charges?' As if you could put a price on everything in life.

The woman was tall and slim, with dark hair cropped close to her skull. Creole of some sort. Skinny-fit jeans. Very flat shoes. Self-conscious about her height?

'Bring a chair round,' he directed, indicating one with a nod of his head. He turned his back on her to replace the book on the shelf as she struggled to manoeuvre it around the counter. Fabrice ignored her question. 'So,' he said, as they were seated close together, 'what do you have to hide?'

'It was stupid really,' she began, right hand placed flat on her hip pocket.

Fabrice did not respond to her self-deprecation, not even a flicker of his thick, dark lashes.

'I had it done on holiday a few years back. I've always had this thing about Mickey Mouse. I love Mickey. Had Mickey Mouse blankets on my bed as a kid, a Mickey watch.'

The air in his studio was close as a confessional. She was already telling him her life story.

'Well, a few of us were in Florida for the summer break – after the Bac, you know, eighteen years old, exams over, blowing off steam – and we all thought it would be an amazing idea to get a tat, to kind of immortalise the moment.'

Fabrice stared at her hip pocket. She looked down, surprised.

'Oh! You want to see it?' She tugged at the waist of her jeans. Mickey's bulbous ears appeared. From what Fabrice could see, not a bad job. Clean outline. Evenly shaded. 'The thing is, I don't feel it's me any more. I still love Mickey, sure, but I have a proper job now. The cartoon character: it's just not serious.'

Their eyes met. Fabrice gave a slight nod and looked away again. She thought she was serious. 'What would you like instead?' His voice was even, authoritative, absolutely non-judgemental.

'Well, that's the thing, you see. I don't know. What would you suggest?'

'Ah!' Fabrice leaned back on his stool and smiled. It was such a beautiful smile that his features were irradiated. One tanned hand flew towards the open neck of his shirt and he thoughtfully stroked the dark tendrils of hair level with his heart. She smiled too and bent towards him. 'For that, I would need to know a little more about you.' But there was only one thing it could be: a tribal.

The woman liked his big brown eyes on her. They seemed very understanding and intelligent. Hardly missing a beat, she replied, 'My name's Zairah. I'm twenty-three years old.

My dad's a lawyer and my mum's an artist. I'm following in Dad's footsteps, but when I was younger all I wanted to do was paint. My mum comes from Martinique.'

And so it went on. Fabrice trained all of his attention on his garrulous client, reading the increasingly confident gestures of her delicate hands. He was in no way her usual type but there was something about the way he listened, so patient and attentive, that charmed her.

'I will need to see you,' he concluded at last, nodding towards Zairah's lap.

She seemed momentarily taken aback, as if she had forgotten why she was there.

'Stand up.'

Zairah did as she was told. She hesitated a moment with her fingers on the clasp of her jeans, and glanced over her shoulder towards the door of the shop.

'Don't worry. Nobody can see you. But if you would feel safer, we can pull the screen across.' Fabrice inflected the word 'screen' with the merest hint of disappointment.

'No, it's fine,' Zairah declared. She did not want him to think she was shy. She unsnapped her jeans and pulled them down to her thighs. There was Mickey, grinning inanely.

'May I touch?' Fabrice asked, scooting his stool closer. 'I need to know how it lies.'

She nodded.

'I have your permission?'

She felt he expected her to say something. 'Yes, of course.'

Fabrice laid a steady, smooth hand on her hip, his thumb brushing Mickey's ears. Zairah looked down at his stubbly black hair, resisting the urge to stroke it. She had never had a boyfriend with a shaven head. He looked like a *racaille* thug but he spoke like a gentleman. It was a new and tempting combination for Zairah. She normally went for the clean-cut type, someone her parents would approve of, young men with floppy fringes and a solid future. Fabrice ran his thumb along the curve of her hipbone, traced the line of Mickey's pot belly and stringy legs. Her skin was cold. The shop was silent. She held her breath and wondered what was going to happen next.

'What we can do,' Fabrice said, his voice now brisk and businesslike, 'is cover it up with a tribal design, something fierce to match your personality.'

Zairah was flattered. Fierce. Yes, in a way, she was, and he had known that after only a few minutes of conversation. Most people did not see the fire in her. She looked down at him.

'I will draw it out on paper first. That way you know it is absolutely unique to you.'

Zairah smiled. He had also realised she wanted something special.

'Sure. How much will this cost?' It was not that Zairah had to be too careful with money, it was just something she believed in: always fix your price. Her parents had taught her that.

Fabrice backed the stool away. He calculated what he imagined she would be willing to pay and added on a hundred Euros.

'Fine,' she said, buttoning her jeans. 'It's a bit steep, but I expect you're worth it.'

He sketched the tribal with a thick ink pen on tracing

paper, like he always did, its coiled edges resembling stylised flames. He did not speak as he was working. Zairah, on the chair beside him, was beginning to fidget.

'It's pretty big,' she commented.

Fabrice put down his pen. 'It has to be, to cover up Mickey.' He could tell she was losing heart.

She looked at her watch. She mumbled, 'Look, sorry, but I don't think I have time for this today. Can I think about it? Come back next week?'

Again Fabrice smiled at her. It was a warm, wide, reassuring smile. 'Of course. Come back whenever you want. I'm always here. Always working.'

Zairah got up to leave.

'I'll put your name on this, so you know it's waiting for you.'

He was sweet. Zairah gave him the correct spelling.

'See you soon, Zairah.'

She liked the sound of her name in his mouth. His top lip was full with a generous dip to it she could easily imagine kissing. He seemed like an interesting guy. But that design: it was a bit frightening.

A Toad full ruddy I saw, did drink the juice of Grapes so fast,
Till over-charged with the Broth, his Bowels all to brast:

IV

Xanthe bought her booze at a number of different places. She let the escalator carry her on the tide of commuters out of the station at Saint-Germain-en-Laye, glancing at the hulking château to her left. Its confection of crenulations, the leaded windows and flying buttresses, reassured her with their timeless strength. The bodies crammed around her dispersed as they left the RER and headed for home. Xanthe ducked down an alleyway between the kebab shop and a place where André Breton once took Nadja for the night. She had to walk the long way back, via Monoprix. It would have been easier to pick up a bottle at the convenience store close to her flat, but it was always the same man behind the till there. She pushed past packed café tables under the old arcade in the centre of town. Beads of conversation rolled at her feet. She ignored them. Everyone was enjoying the balmy weather in this clean and prosperous little town.

Metro – boulot – blotto. Xanthe's life had a regular rhythm. She travelled to work in the centre of Paris by train. She taught English to indifferent office employees. She drank a bottle of gin a night, more or less. It did not always used to be like this. It used to be chaos.

Xanthe entered the narrow passage that led to her building. When she went to the supermarket, with its bright lights and gloss of affluence, she felt constrained to pick up a basket and fill it with lots of items she did not want in order to disguise the one that she did. She was tempted to heave most of the contents of her shopping bags straight into the bin. Opening the door to her apartment, the smell hit her first. She usually got to the bathroom to vomit, but not last night.

'Fuck! You're disgusting,' she muttered. 'You don't have to live like a slut.'

Xanthe dumped the bags on the sofa and went to look at the sink. Bile rose again in the back of her throat. What had she eaten today? A banana and some chocolate from the vending machine. 'Right! It's time to take control!' and as she said it, Xanthe almost believed herself. A spattered pair of rubber gloves lay on the draining board beneath crusted monoliths of dishes. She extricated them and put them on, then remembered to take off her jacket.

Xanthe stood in the middle of the room, jacket trailing. There were drifts of grey silt at the edges of her white-tiled floor, which was sticky underfoot. She dropped the jacket and pushed a stiff towel and some wrinkled knickers back into the washing machine. The contents of the carrier bags shifted position. She grabbed the bottle of Old Lady's London Gin and plonked it on the table.

'You must learn to defer your pleasures,' she whispered, as if quoting someone. Xanthe looked at the bottle. The flat was stagnant. Unscrewing the cap made a crisp sound. The clean yet chemical whiff of gin was refreshing.

Xanthe took one swig, went to open the windows wide and fell to gazing at the cobbled courtyard two floors below. Her hand wandered automatically to the back of her neck, reaching down between the shoulder blades to that difficult-to-itch spot.

'Fucker,' she hissed.

'To show me how much you love me,' he had wheedled. 'It will be like having me with you always.'

Xanthe spat. A plane left its poisonous trail in the softly bruising sky. She turned back to the sink, doused the whole awful mess in washing-up liquid and blasted it with the hot tap.

Havoc demands as much willpower as harmony. Xanthe could clearly see what needed to be done – scrub vomit, wash clothes, clean floor – but after a few minutes she peeled off the rubber gloves, picked up the bottle and went to the nest of her bed.

'I love you . . . I love you . . . Why did I have to keep on proving it?' Her love had grown so strong, the seed sown on stony ground. All she had from the time before was a snapshot: her Papa in the park here, twirling her upside down by the ankles, her childself screaming with laughter before it all went black. Xanthe flinched as if she had been struck hard on the side of the face. She shook her head slowly to clear it after the blow, took another mouthful of gin. 'Why are you such a bastard?'

Because I can be, the silent voice replied. A firm hand seized her by the hair, ripping it from her scalp. The hand yanked her head backwards; another hand on her shoulder forced her onto her knees. Her green eyes filled with unshed tears. *That's it. You know how I like it. Go on. Sob your heart out. It will only make things worse. Or better. Depends on how you look at it.*

And something happened, a shift in perception, like a spotlight had found her. As Xanthe took him in her mouth she became not a subject, feeling pain, but an object, acting. And the tighter his grip, the more the spotlight burned. The toe of his shoe between her legs. His heel digging into her thigh. She became wet. She wallowed. She writhed. When he had finished, he kicked her away. Xanthe's hands slipped between her legs. *No.* Her hands were not her own. *Mine,* he said, *it's all mine. You wait until I tell you to.*

Defiantly Xanthe drained the bottle with a couple of Zopiclone that were in the bag close by. She shucked her clothes and was unconscious before they even touched the floor.

The first time Paul had sodomised her, she had lost control of her bowels. She thought the humiliation of it would last longer than any tattoo.

And after that, from poyson'd Bulk he cast his Venom fell,
For Grief and Pain whereof his Members all began to swell;

V

Yoshiko had walked past 109 a hundred times without noticing it, but today the door was open and the tattooist was watering his bamboo just inside. Yoshiko glimpsed the posters of the *irezumi* women, and scratched her arm through her shirt. Why not? She was heading for the cinema on Place de Clichy. A few of the people from class were meeting up to see *Brice de Nice*. It would be good for her French, but then again, so would talking to a tattooist. They probably wouldn't miss her anyway.

Yoshiko paused on the threshold. The sun shone black on her hair. She smoothed her short skirt over her thighs and took another step forward. This place was the antithesis of the studio she had been to in Shibuya. It looked old-fashioned. The only noise came from the street behind her.

'*Ohayo gozaimasu*,' said the tattooist. He was wearing combats and a black shirt with the sleeves rolled up. He appeared to have neither tattoos nor piercings, which was unusual and immediately gave Yoshiko to wonder, her eyes darting around his muscular frame.

'*Ohayo gozaimasu*,' she replied, inclining her head. He wasn't remotely Japanese but he did a passable impersonation. She was touched he knew enough to greet

33

her in her own language. 'You do that?' She gestured towards the intricately inked women in the posters.

Fabrice stared at the wall. You wait long enough and all your dreams come true. He quickly mastered his excitement. 'You want a full body suit?'

Yoshiko jumped. 'No. Not body. Arm.'

'Arm? Of course.' He was disappointed but still intrigued. She was trying so hard. 'You mean: one arm?'

'One arm. Yes.' Yoshiko touched her right elbow. 'Already have.'

A cover-up. Fabrice beamed. 'Well, you have undoubtedly selected the optimum establishment.' He talked swiftly and softly. Yoshiko stared at his face. 'I excel at this kind of work. In fact, it's a speciality.' The tone of his voice was gentle and, even if she did not understand every word, she felt she had come to the right place.

Fabrice turned his back on her to replace the metal watering can in the kitchen. Yoshiko took a few more steps into the room.

'You keep bad spirits away?' she asked, indicating the flourishing bamboo that guarded either side of the doorway.

He frowned but did not turn round to answer her. Instead, he said, 'I imagine that you will almost certainly have some delicate and revealing imagery in mind for your permanent body adornment?' Fabrice wheeled his stool to the front of the shop, where the morning light made the painted floor look dusty. He raised his eyebrows. Yoshiko realised he had asked a question.

He pointed to a chair and positioned himself in front of it. The stool was relatively low. He sat upright, staring into

Yoshiko's amber eyes. As she sat, her little pleated skirt rose to the tops of her legs. She was wearing black knee-high socks and sensible lace-up shoes. Yoshiko placed her hands demurely in her lap. She leaned forward as she spoke, struggling to shape the words with her tongue and full, pale lips.

'I'm sorry. I do not have much French. Can you repeat?'

'The design?'

'Oh!' Yoshiko smiled in relief. 'Pretty! Flower.' She scanned the posters for inspiration. 'Like her. But more colour.'

She had given it no thought whatsoever but it seemed right. Yoshiko believed in acting on instinct, despite the ugly warning currently despoiling her body. This man looked like an artist to her. He had an artist's hands. His feet were bare in simple Chinese slippers. She trusted him immediately.

'That is indeed an exquisite example of corporal decoration. But you will have to pay.'

'Pay. Yes.' Yoshiko grabbed the words she understood like shiny pebbles in a stream, and patted the bag slung diagonally across her chest.

'There are many ways to pay.' Fabrice continued to smile sagely. 'A design like that . . .' He wanted to be clear; it was important that she understood. 'It will take a long time, much pain. And yes, it will cost you a lot of money.'

Yoshiko nodded enthusiastically. Her long straight hair swung about her shoulders. She had money. Her father gave her a generous allowance. Happy anticipation fizzed and bubbled within her. She wanted to be the beautiful, proud woman in the picture. Maybe once her arm was covered up, she too, like that other young woman, would suffer her entire back and buttocks to be tattooed. That would make her special. 'When can we do?'

Fabrice let out a soft sigh and shook his shaven head. Yoshiko looked crestfallen. She did not want to return to the ordinary world of the Pathé Wepler and her botched spider web under long sleeves on a sunny day. Fabrice did not want to pass the time with a book. He stood up. She stood up too, ready to be dismissed.

'Let me see your arm.'

He was going to do it. Yoshiko was transfigured. She began to roll up her sleeve.

'No. Not that way. I have to see everything.'

Without a moment's hesitation she slipped off her shirt and stood naked from the waist up. Fabrice's eyebrows tilted at her insouciant exhibitionism. He placed his hands on her shoulders and turned her back to the window. Holding her right hand, he manipulated the arm to see what a truly amateurish job had been done.

'To work,' he declared, moving behind the counter and placing an angled drawing board on top of it.

'Today?' Yoshiko asked, following him with tiny steps.

'Today,' he confirmed.

Fabrice had the paper in place and had already sketched in the first convoluted lines when he glanced up. 'You can put your shirt back on.'

Yoshiko shrugged and giggled.

He had decided on a three-quarter sleeve of interlocking chrysanthemum heads. He would ask about colour, but knew it would have to be golden yellow for the heavy bloom that would cover her elbow. Yoshiko draped her shirt around her shoulders. Fabrice was oblivious to the twin buds of her breasts. He concentrated on the curving lines of his design. As he drew, Yoshiko soon became bored. She began to wander around the shop. She ran her hand over the head of the leather chair, like an old-fashioned dentist's one except that there were no arms and what seemed to be stirrups that folded out. She bent over and tapped the top of the plastic boxes that contained the bottles of ink. She studied again the posters of the tattooed women. She realised that some of them were old. Their hair was fixed in stiff blow-dried waves the way her mother's was at the back. Yoshiko moved to the bookshelf and touched each volume as she tried to decipher its title. They were all Greek to her.

'Sit down.' Her constant movement was beginning to annoy Fabrice, who was still at his board.

'Sorry.' Yoshiko placed herself on a folding chair and rebuttoned her blouse. She wished she had had lunch. There would be no big tub of popcorn for her this afternoon. Perhaps she could nip next door and get them both a bowl of instant noodles?

As Yoshiko stripped again and Fabrice transferred the design onto her skin with coloured body markers, she began to realise the enormity of the undertaking. She had been in and out of the Shibuya parlour in the time it had taken him to rough out the picture. He was holding her hand, tilting her arm this way and that to understand the way the smooth skin lay over her muscle and bone. The flowers were elegantly taking shape. It would be a masterful piece of work.

There was no clock in the studio and neither of them wore a watch. When he had finished the guidelines, Fabrice took Yoshiko to the full-length mirror near the back. She studied her brightly coloured arm. All trace of that horrible thing would be gone. In its place would be something she could show off. Yoshiko posed and grinned.

'Thank you,' she said, as if the job were done.

Fabrice wondered if she could really be that dense. Short attention span, from too many computer games and video clips. She was evidently proud of her body. Why would she have let some zero scrawl on it? Don't thank me, he thought, not yet.

'Now we really begin work,' he announced as he led her back to the chair. 'This is probably going to be the longest day you have ever put in in your life.' Fabrice smiled and murmured, his fingertips lightly guiding her. He could see that Yoshiko understood maybe one in ten of his words. He was utterly serene. She sat. The leather chair was cold against her bare back.

Fabrice began to assemble his equipment. He spread cling film over the top shelf of the chrome cabinet and selected bottles of ink from the tub below. He laid out six caps on the sterile field and fetched two spray bottles of the type used by gardeners. One contained antiseptic, the other a mix of soap and water. Yoshiko watched as he decanted colours into the little pots. Fabrice was methodical. His actions had a practised grace.

Yoshiko experienced a flicker of apprehension. 'It hurts,' she said.

'I see you live in the present, like an alchemist. So what

gold is it you are searching for?' Fabrice glanced across at Yoshiko's perplexed face. Gold. She understood the word and nodded. 'However, this perpetual present is more a result of your ignorance than of a deliberate quest, isn't it?' Yoshiko sensed that another nod was required. 'That's good,' Fabrice soothed. He had everything he needed.

He popped the needles out of their pack with his back to Yoshiko and selected two grips and tips. He slid the needles into position, a seven for outlining and a thirteen magnum for shading. Then he locked the seven liner onto the gun and attached the clip cord. He turned towards her. She seemed to be flinching. Fabrice took her arm and gently but firmly positioned it over the edge of the chair.

'Do I have your permission to begin?' This was important to him. It was important she understood. He had not asked her age, but she had to be over eighteen, right?

'Permission?' Yoshiko repeated.

'May I tattoo you now?'

Again Yoshiko looked confused. She stared down at her coloured arm, and then up at the confident and beautiful *irezumi* woman. 'Yes. Please.'

Perfect, Fabrice thought. He snapped on a fresh pair of latex gloves. It must have been about midday. He set the machine speed to six, depressed the foot switch and began to lay down a strong bold line on her upper arm. The moment the needle hit, Yoshiko gasped. He could feel her body tense. She was biting her lip. Her elbow contracted. Fabrice hummed over the sound of the machine. He would straighten her out in a minute. He glanced at her face. Yoshiko began to twitch. Her eyes filled with tears.

The uncontrollable spasms of her right arm shook loose a feeling of fear in Yoshiko. First of all, she saw her father's face. What had she done? He would be so disappointed. She knew he only wanted what was best for her. Work hard in school. Get good grades. Go to one of the top universities. Find a job with a reputable company. Beat the opposition. But there was no going back now. Yoshiko closed her eyes and clenched her jaw. Fabrice was going to cover up her past mistake. He was going to make her beautiful and special. She believed in him. She looked at his head bent to his task. He was entirely focused on her. She began to recover from the initial shock of the needle puncturing her skin, the sharp stinging sensation. After a few minutes she was almost relaxed. Fabrice was tenderly holding her hand, keeping her arm in the correct position as he expertly outlined the flowers. He worked in silence.

When Fabrice eventually stood up, his spine cracked. Yoshiko was unsure how much time had elapsed. Her arm was burning but the trembling had stopped. She wanted to see so she raised it over her chest. A few tiny drops of blood spattered her stomach. Fabrice noticed. He put down the gun and picked up the soap-water spray.

'May I?' He squirted and wiped her flat belly. Then he cleaned up the outline. When he was done, Yoshiko held her arm in front of her face. It was hers and not hers at the same time. She twisted the wrist and elbow to follow the patterns of petals. She could still see the web in parts.

'A full working day is eight hours for most people. We might have to put in some overtime.' Fabrice was pacing the width of the shop, looking at the floor.

'Eight hours?'

'Yes. We are going to spend the day together. Would you like some tea before I start the shading?'

'Tea. Yes. Please.' Yoshiko was unsure if she could remain immobile long enough to finish the job. But she had to. There was no choice.

As he placed sachets of sencha in twin mugs, Fabrice was delighted. He knew he was instigating a process that would transform this woman's life. She was lost in France. It was obvious. The end result was up to her, but she would be changed: no doubt about it. As he stirred her tea he felt again the weight of his responsibility. 109 rue Biot: *sang neuf*; new blood.

After drinking, Yoshiko almost dozed off in the chair. Fabrice put on a CD, a special mix he had for blessed days like these. Although her eyes were closed Yoshiko smiled when she recognised 'Sexual Healing', but it was a different version to the one she knew. A woman huskily breathed the words, backed up by a bass chorus of lusty men. Her arm hung at her side. He changed the grip, tip and needle. It was time to fill in the elbow.

'This is going to hurt,' he told her. He took her arm and bent it with her hand curled under her chin. 'Keep it like that.'

Yoshiko struggled up from under the warm blanket of sleepiness.

Fabrice was right, of course. The needles drilled ink into the thin layer of skin. It felt like he was paring the bone. Yoshiko yelped. Her arm began to twitch again. Sweat gathered in the dip of her back and trickled onto the chair. She ground her heels into the padded leather and concentrated on trying to keep her arm in the correct position.

'Listen to the song,' Fabrice instructed.

Yoshiko tried. A man was intoning in a deep, lugubrious voice. It was difficult for her to make out the words. Sometimes the English teacher would bring in lyrics for their lesson and they would have to sing along to the Beatles, which she found embarrassing on a number of counts.

'Who is?'

'Leonard Cohen.'

Yoshiko had never heard of him.

'I'm your man,' Fabrice whispered as he worked.

Every time he had to change colour, Fabrice stood up and gave them both a break. After completing the shading he moved through yellow, orange, green, scarlet and violet. Always the same order. It was comforting. He had a system. As he was cleaning the needle of orange ink, the door jangled.

'Oh, you're busy.'

Fabrice stood with the gun in his hand. He moved to one side so that Zairah could see Yoshiko, topless, sitting on his chair. Zairah's eyes lit on the other woman. She looked horrified. The three-quarter sleeve was almost complete. Yoshiko's arm was a vivid display of ink and blood. Her face was a mask. Fabrice said nothing, observing Zairah in the moted shaft of late afternoon light.

'Wow,' Zairah said, mainly to herself. At work all day

she had been feeling calm and confident about returning to Fabrice to get her tribal tattoo. Now she wavered. 'You're busy,' she repeated. 'I'll come back another time.'

'Good.' Fabrice nodded and smiled. He wondered fleetingly if she would, and turned his back before she was even out the door.

It was getting dark by the time Fabrice finished the scarlet petals on Yoshiko's forearm. He was tired. The music had long since come to a halt, and making conversation was tedious. When she was not dozing off the effects of the tea and endorphins, Yoshiko had kept her eyes mainly fixed on his posters, no doubt imagining herself miraculously transformed by his art. She had no way of expressing it, but it had dawned on Yoshiko that the day they had spent together was the most intimate and special of her life. She had never lain that long with another person; had never felt a man's touch on her skin like this. In fact, he had got under her skin. Fabrice was there, a part of her, and he would remain a part of her forever. Romantic, in a way.

When it was done, Fabrice pulled Yoshiko to her feet. She was unsteady, and giggled. He gave her one final spray with the soap solution, like polishing a broad-leaved plant, and cleaned up the arm with wads of kitchen paper. He took a step back, admiring her. Then he wrapped everything in a tight layer of cling film secured with microporous tape. He helped her into her blouse and chivalrously did up the buttons.

Yoshiko was numb. She fumbled with her purse, pulled out a thick wedge of Euros and laid them on the counter with a slight bow. On top of the money she placed a small pale pink card.

'My numbers,' she announced, hopefully.

Fabrice returned the bow. 'I am honoured,' and, for a moment, he almost believed it.

VI

Her phone was ringing. The alarm clock screeched. Xanthe sat up before she was even awake. With her eyes half closed she took the bottle that lay beside her on the pillow and staggered with it to the living room. She winced as she dropped it on top of the rest of the rubbish.

As the coffee dripped, Xanthe crawled into consciousness. She always dragged herself out of bed early because getting ready for work was such a laborious affair. She concentrated on the cool sensation of the tiles under her feet. Her feet were not hurting. Xanthe looked down, grateful. Her brain pan, however, was full of ball bearings, which rolled forward and created pressure behind her eyes when she tilted her head. The Nurofen were beside the filter. Just the thought of popping them from the pack and swallowing something solid made her gag. Xanthe rested her forehead against the kitchen cupboard. The machine began to gurgle. Xanthe rinsed a mug and poured steaming, strong Robusta.

The first sips of coffee were always painful. Her tongue was parched. Her stomach was scoured. The scalding liquid had no taste and she could feel it sliding inside her like swallowing a sword. Xanthe took the mug to the sofa and forced herself to drink. Outside, the light was dirty. There was a full hour before she had to go for the train. She ran her fingers through her hair, which was clumped together on one side and smelled vile.

After the first mug of coffee, Xanthe started to shake. Her fingers were trembling as she finally extracted four Nurofen and lifted them to her mouth. Mornings were only bearable because her pain kept her in the present.

Xanthe ran a bath. She lathered the aches and bruises. The irony of the situation did not escape her: no Paul, and yet still her body suffered. Why was that? It was too much to think about. She loved him; loved him as she had loved nothing else in life. And he had hurt her; tortured her in ways that defied explanation, continuing the gap-riddled story of her life. She shampooed her hair and sank back in the water, letting its warmth massage her aching head.

Standing in front of the mirror in her bedroom, Xanthe completed her regular magic trick. Her suit hung loosely from her shoulders and hips but it was passably clean. She dragged a brush through her damp hair and coiled it into a bun at the nape of her neck, which she secured with two children's paintbrushes. She dabbed concealer on the dark stains under her eyes and rubbed tinted moisturiser onto her face. A scrape of mascara and a couple of coats of dark red lipstick and she was ready to leave.

The train, as usual, was busy. Xanthe fought the nausea that threatened to engulf her. The body of the man sitting next to her spilled over onto her half of the seat. She could smell his newspaper and his breath every time he sighed and turned the page. Sweat gathered in the small of her back. Despite cleaning her teeth twice, Xanthe could still taste alcohol. She studied the advertisements. There was one for her school, showing a smiling young urban professional confidently picking up the phone and declaring, 'Yes! I speak English.'

Xanthe wanted to say 'Yes!', too. No one had listened when she said 'no'. Her head hung forward. The motion of the train was lulling her back to sleep. The man sitting next to her shifted his position so that their thighs touched. He coughed and rustled his paper, pressing harder against her. Xanthe let him. By the time they got to Nanterre the carriage was packed. Xanthe was jammed against the window. She had got used to the man's stale breath, which was gusting more rapidly now. He had stopped leafing through *Le Figaro* and was maintaining a steady pressure on the slim blonde beside him. He had crossed his legs and one suede brogue kept tapping Xanthe's calf. Every now and then Xanthe wriggled. They did not make eye contact.

Xanthe's stop was Auber, in the centre of Paris. As the train screamed into the station the man remained rigidly in his seat. Xanthe gathered her handbag and began to get up. In the press of bodies struggling for the doors, she lingered a moment above the stranger's lap. Xanthe brushed against his newspaper, now clutched as a flimsy shield. She shook her head to release the scent of her shampoo. She felt his knuckles under her buttocks, a fleeting furtive touch, and then she was gone.

Marthe on reception was surprised to see Xanthe smiling as she entered the school. She usually looked like death.

Xanthe had made a decision. She would start asking around for the name of a good tattooist.

VII

They were sitting just inside Café Jules on rue des Batignolles. You passed through a thick red velvet curtain at the entrance, which was promisingly baroque, but Fabrice found the place to be bourgeois and dull, like most of the 17th these days. It was Yoshiko's choice of venue. She often stopped off for a Coke on her way home from class, and felt comfortable here. Her jacket hung on the back of her chair. She was wearing an apple-green T-shirt over faded jeans and cowboy boots. Fabrice was admiring his work.

'You like?' Yoshiko held out her arm for his approval.

'Stand up.' Fabrice took her hand as gently as he had on the day he tattooed her. Without having to think, Yoshiko stood. In the cramped space between tables, Fabrice manipulated her into a variety of poses. He approved of her slender limbs and her tiny natural breasts. She enjoyed being looked at. He even turned her round to observe the back of the arm, easing her wrist level with her buttocks. The waitress frowned at them.

'You may sit down now.'

He had not said so, but Yoshiko knew he was pleased by what he saw. She blossomed in the glow of his regard.

They had arranged to meet at eight but he had texted at five-to to say he would be late. As she was waiting, Yoshiko had nervously downed two Mojitos, her eyes fixed on the patch of pavement in front of the café. She had not seen him come in, and had jumped when he laid a hand on her shoulder and kissed her cheeks in greeting. A flush had settled on her face then. She could feel it was not going away. She was so proud to be here with him, a genuine French artist.

'What are you drinking?' Fabrice's gaze flicked to the tumbler on the table.

Yoshiko glanced down. 'Mojito.'

'What's that?'

She looked perplexed. It was an expression Fabrice loved: her perfect eyebrows dipped towards the bridge of her nose, her lips pursed. She picked a stem of mint from her drink and held it up to him. 'Green stuff.'

'Mint leaves,' he supplied. 'Green stuff, like grass and moss and emeralds deep in delves. Green is definitely one of my favourite colours, Yoshiko, did you know that?'

She thought she had caught most of what he had said, and nodded and smiled.

'But,' Fabrice continued, apparently at random, 'you have changed your hair.'

Yoshiko's right hand went self-consciously to the back of her crown. Fabrice watched his tattoo in motion, the kaleidoscopic glory of it. Her hair was now feathered around her face with a short fringe and hung level with her shoulders. The whole was shot through with scarlet streaks. She had just had it done.

'I want red hair.'

Fabrice recalled the long smooth blue-black bolt that had

draped over his chair, and how he had touched the ends of it. He had already imagined the way it hung down her back as she stood naked before him. Could not help it. 'Why on earth would you want to do that? It was perfect the way it was, natural, harmonious.'

'Red hair like Anne. I try to explain. I want red hair like Anne. This not red like Anne, but I like. Good with tattoo.'

Fabrice tried to refashion her words so they made sense. 'Anne? Who's Anne?' The waitress came. Fabrice barely looked at her and ordered a San Pellegrino. 'Are you having another one of those?' he asked Yoshiko.

'Yes, please.' She did not drink at home but knew that things were different in Europe. She was feeling pleasantly light-headed, which she put down to the fact that Fabrice had come and was sitting so close to her that their knees were almost touching. 'Anne of Green Gables. I like Anne. Lots of Japanese like Anne. Is cult.'

Fabrice had never heard of her. 'Of Green Gables? What does she do, this Anne?'

Again, Yoshiko's face registered consternation. 'Do? Not do. Is. She is orphan. Come to live with Uncle Matthew and Aunt Marilla on farm. Good girl.'

They both smiled at that.

'So, Yoshiko, you're a good girl, are you?' His beautiful eyes were wide as he asked the question, boring into hers.

Yoshiko thought a moment and then her head drooped. She did not know what to say. Fabrice reached across the table for her hand. He raised the fingers to his cheek and laid them there, kissing the inside of her wrist. His lips softly brushed the purple petals. Yoshiko watched him in amazement. This man was nothing like all her other loser boyfriends, kids mainly, with spiky hair or chains dangling from their oversized jeans. He had a quiet confidence that overwhelmed her. Her arm hung limply across the table. Fabrice did not let go until the waitress brought their drinks.

'Good rebel girl,' she decided would be the best way of putting it.

'A rebel? What are you rebelling against?'

Yoshiko seized on the only element she could express clearly. 'My father.'

Fabrice took a sip of mineral water. He was studying Yoshiko's face. Coolly he asked, 'And what did your father do to you, little Yoshiko?' He lowered his voice, dropped his eyes to the table and muttered more quickly, 'Does he keep your soiled underthings in his briefcase to ecstatically sniff during empty moments at work? Does he take artistic photographs of you when you are slick and dripping from your ablutions? Does he get down on his knees and lick your sweet pussy like no boyfriend has ever done?'

He raised his eyes again. Had she heard? Had she understood? Yoshiko sucked up some more of her cocktail. She was beginning to feel somewhat drunk. She shook her head. The bright red hair danced. All the time Fabrice had been whispering, she had been working to get her words in order.

'He does not see me really. He thinks I am always his little girl. Work hard. Like him. I'm not. I'm me.' Yoshiko felt satisfied that she had communicated something important.

What Fabrice said next surprised her. 'I understand. My

father was exactly the same. He was always pushing me: do well in school; go to university; work hard, son.' Yoshiko noticed a sadness shadow Fabrice's lips. He was not looking at her, which gave his words an intimate, confessional quality. She put down her drink and reached across the table to pat his arm. He was still wearing the black shirt with the sleeves rolled up. Her mind flitted to another topic.

'You have tattoos?'

'So I was not incorrect when I hazarded that you have the attention span of a Sony-addled prepubescent?' Fabrice paused. Yoshiko did not respond. 'From father to tattoos? Well, I can see how you made the connection. Yes, my dear, I have tattoos.'

'Where?'

'You want to see?'

Yoshiko nodded.

'You are not the only one to throw some conversational curveballs. You will see my tattoos when the time is right.' He checked to see if she had understood. 'Later.' The penny dropped.

The café became more crowded as the evening progressed. Fabrice hated the middle-class, middle-aged clientele that tended to gather here, but he had wanted to see what sort of place Yoshiko would pick. He firmly believed in ladies' choice. Someone's elbow nudged him in the back of the neck. He shifted his chair so that he was sitting right beside Yoshiko. She was relieved; for the last half hour she had hardly picked up a word he had said. Perversely, the louder the voices around them, the more softly Fabrice spoke. She had been leaning so far forward in her chair to concentrate that her neck ached.

Fabrice drew something out of his shirt pocket and held it in his fist in front of them on the table. He opened the hand and a lighter lay on his upturned palm. A cheap Bic. Yoshiko glanced at it.

'You like to smoke?' she asked.

Fabrice did not reply. He looked at the lighter. She followed his gaze.

'A friend gave it to me,' he said.

Yoshiko recognised the design on the lighter as *hentai manga*. There was a bulbous-breasted female bent over. Her round bare buttocks echoed the shape of her tits. Beside her was a monster. The monster was probing her anus with the sharp tip of its tail. Yoshiko giggled and clapped a hand to her face. She read those types of books in secret. She liked the over-endowed *bakunyuu* women and the cute catgirls. She knew she was not supposed to.

Fabrice calibrated her response. It was a kind of test, but they did not know it was coming and so had no time to prepare.

Shortly after, he guided her from the café. They walked close together along rue des Batignolles towards the church and the dark, deserted park. Yoshiko kept peeking at the man beside her. She liked his shaven head and the way thick curls of hair protruded from the neck of his shirt. He was so clean, his fingernails scrubbed and perfectly shaped. She wanted to sleep with him but she was also scared. All her other boyfriends had been Japanese. Fabrice would be different. Would she be able to please him?

Fabrice said he would accompany her to her door. So they were going to stay at her place tonight, Yoshiko assumed. She slipped her hand into his as they skirted the tall railings overhung by trees. Her heart was racing. Her mouth was dry. Nearing the bottom of rue Truffaut, Fabrice observed the green skin of netting and scaffolding over her building. As she let go of his hand to enter her code she realised her fingers were shaking. The door buzzed and Yoshiko pushed it open. Their eyes met as she passed over the threshold. She did not press the button to bring on the hall lights.

Fabrice remained on the street. 'A lot of work to do,' he mused aloud, indicating the outside of the building with a jerk of his head.

He seemed suddenly distant. This was not what she had expected. 'Yes.'

They stood, suspended, the raised sill between them. Fabrice could see that she wanted to reach out for him, pull him into her web, but knew that she would not dare. He let the awkward silence spin . . .

'Goodnight, Yoshiko. I would like you to know that I had an excellent time this evening.'

Wounded pride squashed the edges of her smile. 'Me too. We meet again? I hope.' The words came out in an anxious gush.

Fabrice reached across the threshold and placed his hands firmly on Yoshiko's shoulders. He gazed into her eyes. 'We meet again,' he concurred.

And then he turned and walked away.

With drops of Poysoned sweat approaching thus his secret Den,
His Cave with blasts of fumous Air he all bewhited then:

VIII

Fabrice sat Buddah-wise, observing the patterns of light on the bamboo leaves. His soft hands lay on the rough fabric of his combat trousers. He was aware of the muscles in his back and legs holding him erect on the stool. Beyond the plants that guarded the entrance to his world, shadows slipped. Their movement was woven into the gauze of stench and noise that almost choked him some days.

He was thinking about the little rebel, Yoshiko. She had not been shocked by the idea of an alien arse-fucking, but perhaps it was cultural. After all, she had grown up with that kind of stuff on the supermarket shelves where she bought her sweets and cola.

Fabrice was intuitive with women. Growing up the way he had, his gift had developed as a survival skill. The black moods, his mother shrieking uncontrollably, drinking, screaming, hugging her to him then biting his heaving chest, his T-shirt still wet with her tears as she dumped him at her parents' house in the middle of the night. He had had to feel his way, listen, observe. It required patience. These days he considered himself unique among men. He was not after what they were after, a common coupling that comes to nought.

Fabrice sought something precious: a nugget of gold plucked from the shit of daily life.

He inhaled deeply, sadly, and went to wash his hands. As he was walking back to the bookshelf, he thought he recognised Zairah hurrying past outside. Zairah: the serious one. He already knew what he would say to her when their time came. (Her name on that generic tribal swirl guaranteed that she was going to return to him.) He wanted to be a painter too. He struggled with it. He painted during the holidays and long into the night sometimes. But he had to work, had to earn a living. Fabrice's eyebrows curved upwards at the centre as if appealing; his lips formed a rueful smile.

He looked down at his day uniform of black shirt and combat trousers. I never stop working, he thought. It was a vocation. And he sighed.

And from the which in space a Golden Humour did ensue,
Whose falling drops from high did stain the soyl with ruddy hue.

IX

The entry phone buzzed. Yoshiko jumped even though she had been expecting it for the past three-quarters of an hour. There was an unopened bottle of Johnny Walker on the table, two glasses, and a plate of *daifuku*. She had bought the little round rice cakes because they were lucky.

'*Konnichawa*. May I come up?'

'Hello. Of course.' Yoshiko pressed the button that unlocked the door. 'Across courtyard, middle stairs. I meet you.'

Unsure if Fabrice had been able to understand her directions, Yoshiko hurried onto the landing. The ground-floor door creaked open. She heard steady footsteps approach. Yoshiko's heart was pounding as she gripped the banister. From above, she saw how his hair was thinning slightly. Fabrice did not look up although he knew she was there. Yoshiko had skipped school to spend the day getting ready and studying pictures of tattoos on the internet. She had not seen a single design as beautiful as hers.

Fabrice reached the top step, where Yoshiko was waiting. Only then did he look at her. They smiled at each other. She was good, he had to admit. They had been texting after their first date. He had let her know that green suited her, although he was not sure about the scarlet highlights. Tonight

Yoshiko was dressed in a jade silk blouse with short puffed sleeves over a tight denim skirt and bare legs; the streaks in her hair had faded.

He kissed her on both cheeks in greeting. He could feel how frail she was, trembling like a baby bird. She was wearing perfume, which he had not noticed before. It made him want to sneeze to clear his nostrils.

Yoshiko indicated her front door with a small sweep of her graceful, coloured arm.

'May I come in?' Fabrice asked roguishly.

Yoshiko giggled. She had never done this. She was inviting Fabrice round for sex and they both knew it. 'Come in, please,' she answered.

Yoshiko's apartment was small and clean. The shutters were drawn and a number of tea lights had been dotted around. Fabrice commenced his study. Ultra-light Sony laptop, electronic dictionary and a neat pile of textbooks on the low glass coffee table. Futon folded up and covered with a grey throw. Polished parquet grooved with age. White walls. No posters, but a framed family portrait on top of the sparsely appointed bookshelf. White kitchen cupboards and two gas rings.

'This is a nice place,' he said, 'very simple. I like it.' The compliment brought a glow to her cheeks and forehead. Her eyes danced in the candlelight. Fabrice picked up the photograph. A stiff-looking man wearing a dark double-breasted suit sat in a heavy chair flanked by wife and daughter standing. Their eyes were joyless; the blossom in the background was fake.

'I can see you take after your father.'

Yoshiko glared at the photograph and took it from him. 'People say I have my mother's mouth. And my hands are like hers.'

'How are your studies going?' Fabrice sat down on the futon, crumpling the pristine cover. Yoshiko positioned herself beside him and gazed defeatedly at the textbooks.

'Going well,' she lied. She was finding it difficult to stay motivated and make progress. The lessons were not what she was used to: she had to play games with the wives and the waiters with their incomprehensible accents, rather than listen to the teacher and make notes. At the beginning of the week they had been made to eat cheese and discuss it together. The dried-up clumps of rancid fat had almost made her vomit. 'In summer I go to London to learn English properly.'

'I've never been to London,' Fabrice said, memories of a dingy flat in Tooting flashing behind his eyes, 'but I'd like to go one day.'

At this, Yoshiko saw a vision of them holding hands and leaping onto a red double-decker bus, discovering the city together. With that gift of his, Fabrice knew he had given her a glimpse of the future. It was like directing a film for him, in which real people – women – became actors in his drama.

'You like drink? I have whisky.'

'I don't drink alcohol,' Fabrice replied, 'but you go ahead.'

Yoshiko was taken aback. Obviously she had forgotten.

Fabrice stood and went to the table. He unscrewed the bottle and sniffed its contents, then poured a generous measure into one of the tumblers. 'Do you have any water in the fridge?' His hand was already on the door as he asked. He extracted a bottle of Evian. Yoshiko would have liked some ice but she did not say anything. Fabrice handed her the Red Label and chinked glasses as he stood over her.

'To us,' he proposed.

'To us,' she echoed.

He measured the passing of time by the bloody flush that crept up her neck as she drank. He guessed from the expression on her face that she did not usually take her whisky neat. Her eyes were becoming glassy. She shifted her position on the sofa so that her thigh touched his. Much of what she said was unintelligible, but Fabrice smiled and nodded and cultivated the growing intimacy between them as he would tend a plant.

Yoshiko's right arm drifted towards Fabrice's lap. He stroked the tattooed skin, tracing the patterns of petals.

'I love it. Thank you. I never see such beautiful work.' As the tattoo had settled, Yoshiko felt it changing her. She often touched it herself, unable to believe what she had become. The tattoo was her, and yet not her: familiar but strange. She was proud of it. Proud of herself.

Fabrice kissed the inside of Yoshiko's wrist, his cheek brushing the ball of her thumb. She was embarrassed but all the whisky had made her want to pee. She got up awkwardly, her hand still in his.

'Excuse me, please,' she said, and tottered off to the bathroom. She was gone for several minutes as she anxiously freshened her make-up.

When she returned, Fabrice had poured another whisky.

He took a small sip from her glass, made a sour face and handed it to her. Didn't she see? Without words he was trying to tell her that this drink was bad. How could she not understand what was right in front of her eyes? It was one of those everyday magic tricks that never failed to excite him. Yoshiko did not like to refuse.

'As you know, Yoshiko, I came straight from work. Would it be possible to take a shower? I'd like to get cleaned up.'

Yoshiko was surprised and immediately worried that she would seem dirty to him. 'Of course. I get you towel.'

She settled back down on the futon and listened to Fabrice in her bathroom. They seemed so intimate and relaxed that she was smiling as she sipped her drink. It was only when she tilted the glass and there was nothing left that Yoshiko realised he had been gone a long time.

Fabrice eventually emerged with the towel around his neck. His shirt was half buttoned and the dungarees were unhitched to his waist.

'Do you know what these are called?' he asked, flapping the bib.

Yoshiko shook her head. She did not think they were very stylish. They reminded her of the type of uniform given out to people who swept the floors in fast-food restaurants.

'Dungarees,' Fabrice enunciated, as if the lesson were an important one. 'Dungarees. Worn by plumbers.' He smiled and stood in front of her.

Yoshiko dutifully pronounced the word, looking up at him, admiring his muscled chest and shoulders. She was so desperate for approval that it almost broke his heart. He took her face tenderly in both hands. 'Yoshiko, you are beautiful.'

He heard it like the click of a lock tumbling. Despite relieving himself in the shower he was hard as he gazed into her unfocused eyes. He ran his thumbs along the line of her jaw. His fingers moved to the back of her neck. For a moment he wrapped his hands around her throat and he saw that nothing registered. He could strangle her now if he wished and she would not be able to resist. Poor lost girl. She was young. She would have to learn. It was lucky she had found the best of teachers.

'Take off your clothes,' Fabrice whispered.

Somewhere in the darkest distance Yoshiko experienced a shiver of apprehension. No one had ever had to tell her to take off her clothes before. Fabrice took a step back and folded his arms. Yoshiko stood up. She unzipped her skirt, wriggled out of it and kicked it to one side. Her top skimmed her narrow hips. She looked down as she undid the buttons. No underwear. The silk shirt slithered to the floor. Yoshiko stood, naked. Fabrice noticed how her eyes darted to the shuttered window and the tattooed arm curved modestly in front of her body.

'Put your arms by your sides.'

Unthinkingly, Yoshiko obeyed. Fabrice walked around her in a slow circle, bumping his leg against the coffee table. The mood was languorous. Yoshiko now felt a heavy calm. She had known Fabrice would be different. He saw how contented she was to rest under his gaze.

Fabrice ached. It was an ache, he thought, that came right from the soul. There was almost nothing he could do to assuage it, although God knows he tried: the countless experiments . . . He laid his hands on Yoshiko's shoulders and gently made her realise that he would like her on her knees. He took his time removing the dungarees, folding them, and laying them neatly in the corner. Yoshiko was aware of the rustling of the synthetic fabric. He removed his boxer shorts and came back to where she was still kneeling.

Yoshiko had entered a new world, intoxicated by her own femininity. She hesitated before touching his thighs. Fabrice took another step closer. Yoshiko's eyes were closed. She was kneeling up, her lithe body swaying. She took Fabrice in her mouth. A distant thought that he was so much bigger than her previous boyfriends flared and then died. With it, any uneasiness she might feel.

Fabrice ground into the willing face beneath him. She was all teeth. Her hands were brushing against his skin in such a way that he had to resist the urge to bat her off. He softly circled both her wrists and drew her arms away from his body. She remained latched on to his penis. Fabrice stepped back. She gawped up at him through that thick, now striped, fringe and sat back on her haunches.

'We have all night,' he whispered.

She looked solemn.

Without letting go of her hands, Fabrice manoeuvred her backwards on the floor towards the futon. Her head rested against the base with her hair fanned out. He switched his grip to her ankles and lifted her legs to rest against his shoulders. A new thought came to Yoshiko as if through deep snow: I have never done this before. But she felt secure under his hands, as she had done from the very first moment he touched her.

Fabrice liked the sense of resistance, the way her body folded beneath him. Her arms were splayed to the sides so she could not claw his back. He drove into her repeatedly. He could keep this up for hours. He trained. He exercised self-discipline. Yoshiko's eyes popped open with the thought that she must look so ungainly. Fabrice kept her legs pinned high over her head. Her fingertips gripped the rough wooden floor. The thought melted. She moved her head to engage him in a kiss.

With Fabrice's tongue in her mouth and the tip of his cock pounding deep within her, Yoshiko felt a gathering wave of pleasure. He seemed to sense it too. He alternated the steady long thrusts with swift, shallow passes that barely touched her slick and shaven lips. She tried to move against him, to take him further into her. He pulled back, pausing for a moment to look at her red face framed by her parted legs.

'We have all night,' he repeated.

Fabrice decided they would be more comfortable on the futon. While he went to the bathroom again, Yoshiko moved the coffee table, folded out the heavy mattress and fetched sheets and pillows from a cupboard. She felt dazed as she did so. Her entire body was beginning to seem transformed under Fabrice's expert touch, not just the arm. She slipped in under the covers.

When he came back into the room he chuckled at her false modesty and ripped the sheet away. She lay on her back at his feet, her hands raised slightly off the mattress, expectant. He knelt over her. First he kissed her right palm, his lips moving over the base of her thumb as his teeth nuzzled the fleshy mound there. He journeyed up the arm, paying homage to his own artistry, which glowed in the flickering candlelight. He paused to truffle around her armpit. She giggled and he bit her bronzed shoulder ever so tentatively so as not to leave a mark or even, hardly, a memory. Fabrice took each delicate breast in turn, teasing the nipples with his mobile tongue until they stood out like the sweet pips of a pomegranate. Yoshiko was beginning to thrash beneath him. Her groin was rising to meet his. Slowly Fabrice continued to map her body with his mouth. The artificially sweet smell of the perfume she had spritzed on her wrists and neck was fading; as he skimmed the silken plane of her stomach it was replaced by an earthier, muskier scent.

Fabrice ran his hands down Yoshiko's inner thighs. She tried to curl her legs around his back and draw him into her. He pressed her knees flat against the mattress and held her there with a dissector's precision. The pillows had been pushed away. Yoshiko was flat on her back and struggled to lift her heavy head to see what Fabrice was doing. She was dimly aware of her anxiety. The fear that her soft, wet, fragrant cunt would in some way be repellent to him was dulled as if by distance. Fabrice dipped his head between her legs, maintaining a firm grip on her knees. He brushed his lips against hers. Shaving made her more sensitive. He rubbed against the polished flesh of her labia. When the firm tip of his tongue probed the hood of her clit, Yoshiko could not help the gurgle of pleasure that escaped her. It surprised them both in the torpid night-time silence.

He glanced towards her face and considered saying something, but was aware his words would be wasted. Fabrice marvelled at how cheaply women sold themselves. Yoshiko was his as sure as the coursing of blood. How to explain that? It was impossible. Better to demonstrate. Fabrice bent back to work. He pressed the blade of his tongue flat against her swollen clit, the tip reaching towards her vulva. He licked. He licked assiduously, like a dog at a toothsome treat. The taste of her broke over his mouth. He burrowed towards her core. He danced wet circles around the heart of her.

And when he felt she was about to come, again, he stopped. A more experienced woman might have seen cruelty in him. A more confident woman might have uttered some sound of complaint. But Yoshiko was neither.

He pushed up towards the head of the bed and enfolded Yoshiko in his arms. He was still wearing the shirt. She snuggled into him and stroked his chest.

'Let's go to sleep,' he said, and she realised she felt very tired. Her limbs were like lead.

Yoshiko awoke incrementally. First, she noticed the room was dark. The last candle had gone out. Her shoulders were cold. Her body felt tense. Then she realised she was on her hands and knees, which hurt, as if she had been in this position for some time. Fabrice held her firmly by the hips, then plunged into her. No preamble. She bit her bottom lip. He ground against her. She felt him deep inside. As she was beginning to respond, he came.

Yoshiko did not see the tears that fell from his eyes.

X

He was saying something. Yoshiko struggled to pay attention. Five. It sounded like five. She buried her face in the pillow and tried to go back to sleep.

Fabrice locked his arm around the slumbering girl and pulled her across the futon towards him. She fitted neatly against his side. He placed her tattooed arm on top of the sheets, propped himself up on one elbow and admired what he had created.

'Perhaps a five-point-five.'

'Hmm?' Yoshiko rolled over. Her right hand went to his neck, where it lay hesitantly as she cranked her eyelids open. She did not want to wake up. She knew that when she did, reality – and a monstrous hangover – would hit. She pressed her face into his chest. She could feel hard slabs of muscle through the soft cotton top. Yoshiko reached under the covers to pull off Fabrice's shirt. He restrained her. He knew what she wanted. As if she could read his heart.

'See this?' he commanded, kicking one leg out on top of the bed.

Yoshiko sat up. She was surprised she had not noticed before: thick bands of ink encircled his thigh and calf. 'Who did it?'

'I did. To practise.' He had said this so many times it felt like the truth.

'Looks very good.' The repeating pattern of geometric shapes was blocked in solid black. It had cost Fabrice a small fortune to have his own half-arsed early attempts at tattooing covered up by an expert in Polynesian designs in Tahiti. 'You are true artist.'

He sprang out of bed and quickly re-hitched his dungarees as Yoshiko curled like a sick cat.

She let out what could have been a little mew. 'Come back to bed,' she pleaded.

Fabrice's face was stone. He began lacing his shoes.

She got up, wobbling slightly, and went to him. She was emanating need like a bad smell. For a moment she stood over Fabrice, her hand outstretched. She wanted to feel the back of his neck. A few fluffier strands of hair grew there, where the clippers had missed them. He straightened abruptly.

Need forced a perfect sentence out between her lips: 'We will meet again, won't we?' Need speaks of the future. Need pitches forwards. In the thin morning light, Yoshiko thought Fabrice's eyes seemed cold. She could not connect their present aspect with the passion of last night. She did not breathe in the time it took him to respond.

Fabrice placed a masterful hand on her shoulder. 'Do you really have to ask such a question?' And there it was: that puzzled expression he adored.

Yoshiko was unsure how to reply.

He let her twist in her uncertainty and then ran his hand down her arm. 'As if I could keep away. We are connected, you and I. I am disappointed that you don't feel it.'

Yoshiko's head jerked but she said nothing.

Fabrice continued, 'If you felt it, as I do, you wouldn't have to ask, would you? You would know that we will meet again.'

Yoshiko's looked at the floor.

'We are at the beginning of a great experiment, you and I. Allow me a linguistic digression. It will help you in your studies. *Expérimenté* in French means experienced in English, whereas an experiment in English is *une expérience* in French. Isn't that interesting?' He was looking at a spot somewhere beyond her right shoulder.

Yoshiko was lost, but smiling. She understood only that she would see him again. The flurry of incomprehensible words did not matter to her.

'And so, you will become more experienced through my great experiment,' Fabrice warmed to his subject. His brown eyes were alive with possibilities. He leaned back easily in the chair as she stood, naked and docile, in front of him. 'It's the kind of transformation young women like you can only dream of: the experience of a lifetime, while hardly growing a day older. For this to work, though, you have to remember the important thing is not to be a victim.' Hard luck if she did not have that vital noun in her vocabulary. He was not going to stop and explain it. Anyway: tell me and I will forget; show me and I may remember; involve me and I will understand.

Yoshiko said nothing but maintained her smile, even though an expression of bewilderment washed over her eyes.

Fabrice abruptly changed tack. 'Yoshiko – that's the name of a star.'

'It means daughter of Yoshi.'

'Ah! So that's the venerable Yoshi in the family photograph over there?'

Yoshiko nodded. 'Yoshi means excellent.'

'So, are you an excellent daughter or merely the daughter of His Excellency?' But Fabrice did not wait for a reply; he did not want to get sidetracked. 'You have star quality. I see it clearly.'

Yoshiko shifted her weight from one foot to the other and flicked back her hair.

'For a long time now I have been interested in making a film. I have studied. I go to the cinema and I see how other directors create scenes . . .' He was trying to grade his language to keep it as simple as possible. 'How they arrange the actors and sets. I want to do that. It is my ambition to make a film. But not an ordinary film. I want to make a pornographic film.'

He checked. Yes. She knew porn, as he suspected she would.

'I have this idea, an image: two women and one giant cock. The floor will be of black tiles. They will be kneeling.' He was afraid of going too far, but she was obviously fascinated. 'They will be sucking and, of course, the cock comes. It comes and it comes. It is a giant cock, so it will be like a volcano erupting. It will cover everything: the women, their faces, their breasts, white cum all over the black floor. Do you like that idea?'

He could see she had understood and was amused. She had taken an end of her hair and was twisting it around her index finger. She was grinning at him. She did not say anything.

Fabrice continued, 'I have been looking for the right woman for a long time. Somebody beautiful and brave and sexy.' He decided to spell out the implied compliment. 'I have been looking for many years for someone exactly like you, Yoshiko. Yoshiko, will you star in my film?'

Yoshiko was flattered and flustered in equal measure. She nodded her head but said, 'I have to think about it. Thank you.'

Fabrice stood up. Before she had the chance to say anything more, or touch him, he was out the door.

As he queued at the bakery for bread on his way home, his telephone buzzed. Fabrice flipped it open. The man standing behind him was much taller and peered over Fabrice's shoulder as he opened the photo file. Perfectly manicured fingers spread the glossy shaven lips of a woman's vagina. The hooded clit was pearled with moisture.

Fabrice pressed delete. The man behind him let out a yelp of disappointment.

And when his Corps the force of vital breath began to lack,
This dying Toad became forthwith like Coal for colour Black:

XI

'I'm sorry, I've been super busy.'

Fabrice stood and gestured Zairah towards the back of the shop. A serious woman requires a serious man. His eyebrows furrowed solicitously.

As he said nothing, she felt she had to continue. 'Work's been crazy. There's a big case coming up. I won't bore you with the details, and we're not really allowed to anyway, but suffice to say we've been putting in twelve-hour days. I go to work in the dark; I come home in the dark. Sometimes it feels like work is all I do.' She paused and looked around her. 'You've probably got the right idea here. Your life looks simple. Small-scale. I'd like that.'

Fabrice mimed a modest shrug. 'My life is simple,' he confirmed, 'but I work harder than you would imagine.'

Zairah was nervous. Her heart was racing and her breathing shallow. She was unaware that she might have given offence. Fabrice had her sit in the chair before she even said what she wanted. His fingers had rested lightly on the nape of her neck to guide her. She sank back and tried to relax.

'You remember me?'

'Of course.' Fabrice was a magician with words. In that simple response he conjured up an image of her beauty, a lasting impression of her unique loveliness.

Zairah crossed her ankles. Her slim feet, in what he took to be Tod's loafers, dangled off the edge of the chair. She was wearing a gathered skirt and peach-coloured cardigan that made her skin glow. The effect was wholesome yet sensual. Her short hair was oiled. Heavy gold hoops pierced her ears. He stood beside her. Her body twitched as he looked it over.

'It's time for Mickey to go,' Zairah announced, and pulled down the waistband of her skirt. They both examined her jutting hipbone. She had worn the skirt so that she would not have to strip entirely. Her thighs were huge today.

Fabrice fetched the design with her name on it from the drawer with several other similar pieces. He held it up for her approval.

'This is going to hurt, isn't it? I'm scared of pain – like everybody is. The first time, to tell the truth, I was a little drunk. We'd been having margaritas in some bar and then Eugenie said, "Hey! I know! Let's get tattoos!" She's a bit of a ring-leader, so of course we all followed her. We went to Lucky's, near the beach. I was more excited than scared. But the tattooist was very nice. Huge guy. Skulls and knives and such all down his forearms. Piercings everywhere. He even had a ring through his nose, here.' Her hand fluttered towards her septum. 'You wouldn't expect him to be gentle, but he was. Not to say that I didn't feel a thing, but it wasn't excruciating, you know? Eugenie had her back done.' Zairah squirmed around and indicated her lower back. 'She fainted.'

Zairah sounded exquisitely breathless to Fabrice. He could sense the air rushing through her narrow ribcage. He placed a hand on her shoulder and settled her back in the chair, which he then lowered. She strained her neck to keep her eyes on him.

'We said two-fifty, didn't we? Do you take cheques? No. Probably not. I've got cash as well. That's good. Should we settle up now, like I do with my manicurist? Although, it's not as if I'm going to be incapacitated afterwards, is it?' A shrill nervous laugh issued from between Zairah's teeth.

'As you like,' Fabrice said patiently. He was assembling his instruments. He had pulled the trolley forward and stood behind it, so that Zairah had a clear view of everything he did. He laid out the grips, tips and needles purposefully, like a pavement hustler setting up a three-card trick.

'It's all sterile, isn't it? These days, I mean, you can't be too careful. The guy in Miami had a certificate.' She scanned the walls where only tattooed Asian women were displayed. 'Everything guaranteed, one hundred per cent clean.'

Fabrice took a step back. 'I can go and fetch you a copy of my hygiene certificate, if you wish.'

Zairah realised she had been unreasonable.

'See these packs here? These are the needles I will use for your tattoo. They come in a sterile sachet. I break it open and assemble everything right in front of you. I always do that, to reassure the client. I destroy them afterwards. Obviously they are one-use only. These tips and grips,' he pointed out the stainless steel implements that slotted together into the gun, 'have been cleaned first in an ultrasonic bath, then in the autoclave. My autoclave is set at 134 degrees with two bar of pressure. I let the cycle run for thirty minutes, which is ten times what it needs to be. It's just this way . . .' His hand motioned towards the door at the back of the shop but his feet remained firmly planted. 'I can assure you, Zairah, I take your health and hygiene very seriously.'

'Sorry. Of course. I'm just nervous. That's all. I tend to chatter when I get nervous. It's a bad habit. You're the expert. I put myself in your capable hands.'

Fabrice nodded and pulled on his gloves. 'We are going to have to pull this down a bit further.' He looked meaningfully at her waistband. 'May I?'

Zairah's shoulders stiffened. 'Of course, go ahead.'

Fabrice hooked his gloved fingers under the elastic, gripping also her thong, and tugged everything down to her thigh on one side, noting the outside edge of thick pubic hair. He then tucked a piece of kitchen paper under the skirt. 'This will protect your clothing.'

'Thanks. I like this skirt. Got it from Bensimon last summer in the sales. They have some pretty things, and there's one just down the road from my flat. In fact, I probably spend too much money there. That bag's one of theirs as well.'

Fabrice did not glance at Zairah's handbag.

He took a wad of cotton wool and disinfected her hip. His tongue flicked his lips as he did so. He found her physically attractive: there was a spareness of limbs that approached his own.

'Feels cold,' said Zairah, wriggling in the chair to get a better look at what he was doing. 'That's a huge area you're covering. The new tattoo isn't going to be that big, is it? I don't want something giant; I just want to be rid of that dumb mouse. I don't want to look like a *racaille* when I get undressed.' Zairah clutched handfuls of her skirt as she spoke.

Fabrice knew he was going to have to do a lot of soothing: work, work, work. He crouched down by the chair so that their faces were level. His fist rested close to her head. 'Listen, Zairah. It's your choice. Everything is up to you. We have the perfect design. There's nothing common, or *racaille*, about it. Next, I am going to transfer it onto your skin. Then you can have a look in the mirror and see how you feel. If you don't like it, we can stop there. There's absolutely no pressure. But, as you said, this Mickey: he's not serious. You need to do something about him. Once we have transferred the design, and you're happy, then we will begin the tattoo. But you're in control. This is your body. It's important you like your body, Zairah.'

He had hazarded the last sentence, acting on instinct, and was rewarded as a subtle current passed between them. Lesser men would never notice. Fabrice, though, knew he was on to something. She was at war with herself. He was certain.

He left her lying with most of her groin exposed as he made a carbon of the tribal. Then he disinfected her hip again, leaving it damp so that the design would transfer onto her skin. He rubbed the sheet with the side of his hand, his fingertips straying towards her cunt, which he imagined to be tight and dry. She lay rigidly on the chair, crossing and uncrossing her ankles. He could hear the breath rattling in and out of her.

He peeled off the paper and took a moment to inspect

the design. The curves were clean and strong. Mickey would be obliterated.

'Beautiful,' he said, helping her up.

He knew she would need some convincing as she stood in front of the mirror. Zairah was peering critically at her reflection.

'See how it follows the lines of your body, here and here.' Fabrice's mobile fingers skimmed the outline. 'It looks beautiful. Your boyfriend will hardly be able to take his eyes off you.'

On cue and flushing, Zairah replied, 'I don't have a boyfriend. But if you're sure. It is better, I think.'

With a feather-light hand on her shoulder blade, Fabrice shepherded Zairah back to the chair.

'Get nice and comfortable,' he soothed. 'If your body is tense it affects the tattoo. Uncross your ankles. Kick your shoes off if you like. I'll put on some music. I find that often helps.'

Fabrice started the CD. The single serious violin seemed to have a negative effect on the young woman, or perhaps it was the sight of him picking up the gun and attaching the power cord. Zairah's hands curled into fists clamped against her thighs. Her face was clenched. Sweat was already beginning to puddle in her lower back.

'This is going to hurt, isn't it? Please. Work as quickly as you can.'

Fabrice set the machine speed higher than usual so that the needle would pound her soft skin. He depressed the foot switch, which unleashed the familiar whine. Vaughan Williams soared. 'Zairah,' he whispered, 'it is important to remember that this is what you asked for. No more childish Mickey Mouse games. You might feel a little discomfort at first, but that's nothing, I promise.'

She looked up, her pupils pools of fear in which he saw himself reflected. She was hardly breathing.

'Now I want you to take a deep breath.' Fabrice stood over her, smiling reassuringly, the gun-hand hanging loosely at his hip.

Zairah struggled to master her lungs.

'That's good. In . . . Out . . . A deep, deep breath to help you relax . . . And another one . . . It's important to remember that you're in control, Zairah. It is you who is paying me. You put your trust in me. You selected the design. Today is all about you. When you leave here tonight, that little Mickey Mouse girl will be just a memory. In her place will be something special and strong, something unique and beautiful. A fabulous woman. Now just relax. That's right.'

Zairah immersed herself in Fabrice's words. He had a very gentle voice. Warm. Soothing. She felt absolutely safe with him.

'Breathe . . . in . . . out . . . Beautiful. Are you ready now?'

Zairah nodded assent and her fingernails drove into her palms. Fabrice scooted the stool across the floor so he was close by her side.

'OK.' He was keeping up a softly insistent monologue. 'We're going to start now. Just keep your body relaxed, arms by your sides. There's no need to be afraid. Everything is going to be fine. That's beautiful.'

She jolted clean out of the chair when the needle first

hit. Firmly, Fabrice laid his hand on her stomach and waited for her to settle down.

'Sorry,' she said, her eyes welling with tears. 'I'm sorry. It's just . . .'

He could hear the terror in her rasping breath.

'I should have come with a friend, you know, someone to hold my hand.'

'It's all right.' The tattooist's face was a mask of patient concern. The violin was joined by others in the background. 'Do you know about endorphins?'

'Endorphins?'

'Yes. They are the brain's own morphine, produced when we feel pain. Zairah, if you would just submit in peace for a few minutes, let the needle play over your skin, your body's defences will come to your aid. It's a very simple, natural process. Let your endorphins be your friend. But you must allow me to do my work.'

She closed her eyes.

'Good girl,' he said, and watched the brittle little smile crack across her face.

As he laid down the outline, Fabrice could hear that she was struggling for breath. The chair was almost horizontal. Her ribcage began to heave.

Zairah stood it as long as she could, until her lungs felt like a punctured football. Her inhaler was in her bag. He was taking forever. She would have to make him stop.

Zairah began to struggle in the chair. She needed to sit up, to get oxygen into her body. She was light-headed. Fabrice had never seen anyone have an asthma attack before. He was fascinated. She was suffocating right there in front of him and he had hardly touched her. The wheezing had a mechanical quality. Eventually he lifted the needle away from her skin and pushed back his stool. She made a dive for her handbag and scrabbled around in it.

Zairah took three deep puffs of Ventolin. The tendons in her neck strained as she threw back her head and sucked on her medication.

'I'll be all right now,' she said groggily.

'Perhaps you would like some tea before we begin again? The outline is always the worst. It will soon be over. Although I understand that 'soon' is a relative term.'

She appeared to think about it. 'Yes, thank you, tea would be great.'

As he placed sachets in clean mugs, Fabrice could hear Zairah's voice piping away in the other room. The Ventolin had opened her airways.

'It always makes me a bit tipsy,' she chirruped as he returned with their drinks. 'I don't know whether it's meant to.'

Fabrice smiled indulgently as he handed her the mug. 'A short break and then back to work.'

She blew on her tea. 'This smells funny. What is it?'

Fabrice summarised the virtues of organic Japanese sencha: keeps you young and is good for the heart. 'Drink up. You'll feel better.'

Zairah was sceptical. The tea was bright green with a peculiar odour, but she did as he said and drained it. Voluntarily, she settled back down in the chair. The waistband of her skirt had slipped, and was stained with ink and blood.

Fabrice could tell from her eyes that she was feeling better.

The outline was hardly his best work: it jiggled and jumped as she had done. Mickey grinned, oblivious to his impending doom.

'Just relax,' he crooned. 'Beautiful. Fabulous.'

Zairah closed her eyes.

'I'm going to change needles.'

She heard him fiddling with his equipment. The CD had stopped a few minutes ago. She was relieved. It had annoyed her. All in all, she was feeling much better now. Zairah smiled and relaxed into the slick leather of the chair. She did not even realise that Fabrice was by her side before he eased her skirt back down over her hips.

'Remember, Zairah: let your friends the endorphins do their work.'

'Mmmm,' she mumbled. She was actually beginning to enjoy being here with him. He was such a gentle man. He tenderly laid his left hand on her stomach as his right drilled ink into her skin. Zairah felt the pain, but as if at a distance, and – as he had said – it soon faded.

'What happened to the music?'

'You want music? It didn't look as if you were enjoying my "Lark Ascending".'

Zairah felt ashamed of her poor taste. 'I don't listen to much classical. Dad's always complaining about it. Calls me his darling philistine.'

'I have some compilations. Let's see if you like those any better.'

Fabrice blocked in the tribal flash with deep indigo ink. He hardly had to think about what he was doing. He let the blood bubble up and coagulate on his gloves, her skin.

Smears of ink ran across her belly, down her thigh, near her crotch. It was a sloppy job.

Zairah kicked off her shoes. She even had an impeccable French manicure on her toenails. She abandoned herself to the pleasure of being remade. The tension of the working week slowly drained away. How many times had she dropped the ball, too famished to think straight as they stayed on into the night? It was not important now. Besides, there was always someone else on her team to spot her mistakes. She put in the hours; she looked the part. She was a completely different person to that green girl who had gone to Miami. Fabrice's tattoo would confirm it.

He was whispering along to the Leonard Cohen song, ready to do anything she asked him to.

Zairah smiled. I wish, she thought to herself, I wish.

XII

Fabrice correctly guessed that Zairah's mobile would be switched off during office hours. He left a brief message expressing his concern for her good health and politely asked her to call him when she had the time. Then he went back to his study of Antisthenes. The pattern of light on the floorboards shifted. The sounds of modern life on rue Biot battered against his shop front. Fabrice sat straight on his stool and gave the book his full attention. 'Virtue lies in action not theory.' When his mobile buzzed he knew who it would be: she had a break between lessons around this time and never failed to text him. Fabrice smirked at the message, replied instantly, and then went back to reading. 'The wise man is self-sufficient.'

The customer was leaning on the counter almost before he realised there was someone in the room with him.

'Looks interesting.' She nodded at the volume. 'What is it?'

Fabrice was caught off-balance. He answered the question, aware that he did not want to.

'Antisthenes the Cynic, eh? Why would anyone prefer madness to pleasure?' The woman smiled; her full red lips parted over straight white teeth. 'I want a tattoo, a new tattoo, to cover up an old one. Are you busy?'

Fabrice shrugged and gestured at the empty shop with upturned hands. She was dominating the conversation. He did not like it.

'Let me show you what needs to be done.' The woman placed her bag and jacket on one of the chairs. She was dressed in a simple black T-shirt, black cropped trousers one size too big and black baseball boots. 'Do you mind?' She gripped the hem of her top, as if to pull it off.

Fabrice shook his head. No, he did not mind.

Underneath, the woman was wearing a plain black bra. Her body glowed marble white. She turned towards the door, gathered up her golden hair and slipped the bra straps off her shoulders. 'See that? I want it gone.'

Fabrice stared at the name – Paul – blocked in great gothic script between her shoulder blades. The ink was a disgrace to her perfect skin. Another man had done this. She had let him. A lump rose in Fabrice's throat.

'I see,' he answered quietly. He wanted to touch her. She remained with her back to him.

'In his place I want a big black sun. The biggest, blackest sun of which you are capable.' Xanthe's eyes were half-focused on the sushi restaurant across the road. A couple were sitting in the window, pronging food to their mouths, talking and gesticulating with their empty chopsticks. She was minerally hard in her decision. 'I have a picture of the kind of sun I want.'

Fabrice felt the need to assert himself. 'Of course, I would be happy to do your sun–'

'Black sun,' she interrupted, as if it were important.

'Your black sun, but it's going to take some time. The

design is going to have to be big to cover your existing tattoo. It will take several hours.'

'I'm free today. How about you?'

Fabrice considered making a show of consulting the ledger he kept. Instead, he closed up his book and returned it to its place on the shelf. 'Let me see the picture you've brought.'

The woman left her T-shirt on the counter and went to her handbag. She produced a crumpled page. As she returned to stand beside him, Fabrice felt a chill of premonition.

His interest in the art of transformation had begun a long time ago. Shut in his room when he was not at school, he had tried to connect with the world beyond his miserable Marseille suburb through the radio dial. Late one night, curled under the blankets with the volume on low, Fabrice had listened to a programme about alchemy. Bony knees folded to narrow chest, shoulders hunched, fearing to touch and be touched, he learned that every human being is a *magnum miraculum*; that Divine wonders are latent in all of us. He ached to possess the glory of the brightness of the universe. There had to be more than his miserable vodka-sodden mother and teachers who told him he was '*nul*'. That which is above is like that which is below. It was just a question of harnessing his power, his passion to survive, and directing it out into the world.

And thus began Fabrice's practice of the transmutation of energy. From boy to man, he cherished his secret knowledge and from it his system had developed. He followed the precepts of Albertus Magnus: he was discreet and silent concerning his work; he resided in an isolated position; he exercised patience, diligence and perseverance; he performed according to fixed rules. His rewards were manifold.

'I'm Xanthe, by the way,' she said, as she flattened out the paper.

They both looked at the illustration, which was torn along one edge where she had ripped it from a book.

'Where did you get this?' Fabrice asked.

'Don't worry, it's not an original or anything.' Xanthe thought he might be a bit simple. Tattooists were not renowned for their towering intellect. The print did have an aged quality because she had been carrying it around for over a year, but it was obvious the paper was modern. She placed her finger firmly on the ornate sun that loured over a king and queen. 'I want that: a solid block of colour, with the rays coming out from the nape of my neck to the small of my back.'

'What is happening in the picture?' It was a scene of mutilation. Fabrice was transfixed.

'Isn't it obvious? The woman's lost her head. It's just blown apart. And she's reached into her own chest to pull out her heart to offer to him.'

'He doesn't look very interested,' Fabrice observed.

'He's sick.' Xanthe turned and smiled full in his face. 'So: do you want to do it? A friend of a friend said you did some really fine work on him – dragons, I think it was. It's Wednesday. I've got the afternoon off and there's the long weekend to recover. I really want this tattoo.'

She could have said, 'I really need this tattoo.' She did not ask the price. She had chosen her own design. She was making him say yes.

'I'll do it,' Fabrice consented, 'but while you are here, you will have to tell me about "Paul".'

'Paul?' Xanthe slipped into English as if quoting something – a pop song, perhaps. *'Hey Paul, let's have a ball,'* and her demeanour announced that there was nothing she wished to tell directly.

'Put your bag over on this side of the counter. We're going to be busy. Anyone could slip in and steal it.' Fabrice's calculating mind had started work already. The queen in the image cared for nothing. She possessed only her beating heart, which she was willing to sacrifice to her king.

Xanthe shrugged. She did not care if someone stole her bag: money, passport, keys. Like old bones she lugged these things around with her. Wordlessly Fabrice picked it up and deposited it under his bookshelf.

'Make yourself comfortable.' He stretched out a hand to invite her towards the chair, which he adjusted so that it was horizontal.

'I suppose I'd be more comfortable topless.' Xanthe hooked her thumbs into her bra straps.

'Perhaps not, but it's inevitable, I'm afraid.' Fabrice turned his back on her to retrieve the bottle of disinfectant and marker pens. He did not turn around again until he knew she was settled.

'Cold,' Xanthe said, in a tone that was more observation than complaint.

'Would you excuse me?' Fabrice went to the kitchen, where he washed his hands. When he came back she had bundled all her hair into a knot on top of her head, secured with one of his pens. She had her arms folded under her chin and watched him walking towards her. He stood over her and used both hands to gently wipe the disinfectant over her skin.

'It's almost a massage,' he said, as he kept swirling the wads of cotton wool from her shoulders to the dip at the base of her spine.

'Actually, I hate massage.' Xanthe was unused to such contact. There was a wet thud as Fabrice dumped the cotton wool in the bin. He was frowning. He pulled the stool close to her body and uncapped a red marker.

'I'm going to draw in the design now.'

She could feel his breath on her skin. 'Be my guest.'

Fabrice sketched in silence. Xanthe lay perfectly still. He found himself thinking about Paul. Xanthe, too, was pondering her ex. She had left Paul to save her life. How many times had he threatened to kill her? There was no one to miss her. No family, as far as he knew. She never spoke about her parents. No friends since they had started living together. Tightening the ligature until her world went black. No one who gave a shit. Tied to the bed, a bottle of whisky in his left hand, silence skewered only by the click of the lighter in his right. It was a mystery that, now Xanthe was free, she no longer wanted to live. She was tired. Terminally tired. Paul had been correct about one thing: she deserved to die. Xanthe intended to bask awhile in the rays of the black sun and then take a very long sleep. That was how she expressed it to herself. Nothing mattered. Except sleep.

Her breathing was deep and regular. Fabrice had noticed the shadows under her eyes. Too much partying? He would know from how she bled. She seemed to like being in control. He could play that game too. As he drew his nostrils flared. There was something in the scent of her that pleased him.

When he had finished she hardly glanced at herself in the mirror, asking instead, 'Is he gone?'

'He's gone,' Fabrice confirmed.

When the needle first pierced her skin, Xanthe did not flinch. Fabrice wiped away the drops of blood that gathered on the surface. From the way it flowed freely he could tell she had been drunk last night. Stained squares of tissue drifted to his feet. As the work progressed they both began to sweat. His hand described tight circles, blocking in the heart of the black sun. Tribal black. Blackest black. After an hour or so her body began to weep copious clear serous tears. It made the shading difficult.

'Where do you come from?' he asked. She spoke French perfectly, but there was a hint of an accent he could not place.

'All over,' she evaded. She had moved so many times as a child, it felt like the truth.

'A citizen of the world?'

'I suppose.'

'Me too. Xanthe: that sounds Greek.'

'Yes.'

'I have some Mediterranean blood.' He was trying to ensure a connection. It usually worked. 'Blonde hair and green eyes, though – that's pretty unusual.'

'Do I look like a natural blonde?'

Fabrice stared at the dark roots at the nape of her neck. 'I guess not.'

As the light began to fade, Fabrice suggested they take a break. Xanthe refused. She let the feeling drain from her arms. The needle kissed her skin but she found the noise annoying. Fabrice cued a CD and she laughed at his choice of music: 'Sexual Healing'- Anita Lane version. He wondered if she took drugs as well.

As he put the finishing touches to the slender rays that radiated from the main body of the sun, Fabrice was proud of his work. 'It looks good,' he said.

'Feels good,' she countered.

'I'm just going to wrap you up so you won't bleed on your shirt. Tomorrow morning, get some Bepanthen cream from the pharmacy and rub that into the tattoo.'

'That's going to be tricky.'

'I'm sure you've got a willing helper.'

'No.'

The word hung between them. Fabrice took a business card from a dish under the counter. It was a subtle shade of gold, with just the symbol from over the door printed on it. On the back he carefully wrote his name and mobile number and presented it to her as she slipped her arms into the sleeves of her jacket.

'Thank you.' She dropped the card into her bag. 'How much do I owe you?'

Fabrice shrugged. He had made enough from Yoshiko to last him all month and then some. 'Pay me what you think I'm worth.'

Xanthe smiled. She opened her wallet and emptied it of notes. 'Something like this is hard to put a price on,' she called over her shoulder.

As the door closed on the silence of his empty studio, Fabrice bent to begin cleaning up. He held her blood in his gloved hands. He wondered what her story was.

XIII

Yoshiko could not stop thinking about Fabrice. He was going to make her a star. She texted him dozens of times a day but was hesitant about popping in to the shop uninvited. She also lacked the confidence to call him. She was waiting for him to tell her when they would next meet. It always felt like it was going to be soon.

His telephone vibrated. Fabrice opened the message. She was pouting up at the camera, tugging on the neckline of her shirt.

'Very good but you know I want to see more.'

He pressed the send button and went back to his book. A few minutes later the phone vibrated again.

He could see the electric hand dryer behind her. She had gone into the ladies' room. The blouse was unbuttoned and she was caressing her right nipple, her lips parted.

Fabrice did not even have to bother keying in another message; he re-sent the same text. Her break lasted twenty minutes. They spent most mornings playing like this. He had a sense of tuning an instrument, like turning a peg to tighten a string that would work her up to the perfect pitch. Her next text came as no surprise.

'when start film?'
'When you are ready.'

'*ready now*'

And he grinned as he felt her heat. '*Show me . . .*'

There was a pause. Fabrice kept his eyes on the phone. What could she possibly have to reveal that he had not seen already?

It came. She had hitched her skirt above her waist and was bending over in front of the mirror. Her little red pants were pulled down to her thighs. One hand was spreading her trim buttocks. The tattooed arm was bent backwards to take the shot.

He sniggered as he pressed delete. It was almost time for her to go back to her desk. He imagined her straightening her clothes and padding with that quick catlike gait down a corridor towards a classroom. She would be holding the phone, awaiting his response.

He liked to make her wait. It was good for her.

Fabrice returned his attention to his book. When the door was pushed open he stood up and moved towards the front of the shop with his arm outstretched in welcome.

The men shook hands and then took a step back away from each other.

'So, what's going on?'

Fabrice shrugged modestly. 'You know – the usual – I've done a couple of tribals recently, nothing special. Still working on turning my little Japanese sleeve into a full body suit. Pity you weren't here a couple of minutes ago: you could have seen her.'

'Didn't notice anyone pass me on the street. What was she wearing?'

Fabrice nodded towards his phone and leered.

'Oh, I get it. She's dirty? Of course she's dirty if she's with you. Let's have a look.' The man thrust out his hand.

'Too late, my friend, too late.'

'You deleted it? What was she doing? Topless? What are her tits like? Does she have great tits?'

Fabrice just smiled. He had a toy that another boy wanted.

'Next time, forward it on to me. It might be worth a discount.'

And as if a timer had buzzed, the two moved spontaneously towards the kitchen. The man unhitched the sports bag that was slung diagonally across his chest. He was well built, wearing mint-condition tracksuit and trainers. He towered over Fabrice.

'To business,' he said, removing a number of thick brown envelopes from the bag. 'I'm assuming the usual? I don't suppose they call it a habit for nothing.' He often made this joke, but every time he did the words struck him as an original insight. He laid a fat plastic baggie of weed on the counter. 'I've gotta say, you've got style, man. No pissing about with small measures. It's all for you, right? You wouldn't be going behind my back? I bet you get all sorts in here.'

'It's all for me,' Fabrice confirmed. 'Enlightenment.'

This tattooist was a weird fucker. There was something in his manner: he was always polite, paid up straight, but the dealer did not like Fabrice. 'Funny. I don't see any dreadlocks. And these . . .' He placed a strip of tablets next to the Eyes.

Fabrice inspected the pack.

'Japanese,' the dealer explained, 'two milligrams, like you're used to.'

Fabrice sounded out the katakana. 'Ro-hi-pu-no.'

Warning: takes effect within 20 to 30 minutes and lasts up to 8 hours. Acts as a sedative by inducing amnesia, relaxing the muscles and slowing down psycho-motor response. Can also cause decreased blood pressure, drowsiness, visual disturbances, dizziness, confusion and urinary retention. Tolerance likely with repeated use.

'Ro-hi-pu-no.'

They both laughed.

Fabrice slid a sizeable fold of notes across the counter and dropped the drugs into a drawer. 'See you next month.' He opened the door. The man's bike was leaning, unlocked, against the shop window.

The dealer did not bother to reply as he pedalled away.

That evening, in his dark and tiny bedroom, Fabrice stretched out on his mattress and lit a joint. His limbs were throbbing from the weights and asanas he had sweated through for the allotted number of minutes.

'Repeat and repeat,' he muttered to himself. 'The Artist must wait for the fruit with Patience.'

He let his thoughts drift with the smoke towards Xanthe. His nostrils twitched. He could still remember the smell of her. Something acrid and sweet: despair. He let the joint smoulder in the ashtray and rested his hands on his thighs. He remembered how she had felt, smooth and still underneath him.

Another man had had his name tattooed on her skin. Not 'Paul' in modest cursive, enclosed in a heart or a scroll to decorate an underdeveloped bicep: this was 'PAUL' in block gothic letters eight centimetres tall, like a shadow over everything she did. Fabrice felt a tinge of envy. He had never signed any of his work. Then he let it go. With an emerald scuttle and scratch of claws on bare boards, ego was dismissed. He did not need to put a name on them to know they were his.

Fabrice commenced his meditation. He started with the hair, her long blonde hair. His fingers twitched as he grabbed it in handfuls to direct her head. He circled her, observing her from all angles, her narrow shoulders, the tilt of her breasts, the long bones of her legs. The black sun on her back: the sun that shone over the king and queen in the sacred texts. How had she found it? How had she found him? The same way that they all found him: their need for transformation.

And Fabrice felt his power.

He began to massage his leaden cock. His balls ached. It had been eight days since he last allowed himself some release with Yoshiko. He ran his fingertips lightly up and down his fraenum – tightening a chord to achieve perfect pitch – and alternated caressing his head in the warm palm of his hand with firm strokes down the length of his shaft. He noted when his breathing changed from deep and restful inhalations to shallower gasps. He noted tension and pleasure rising from his groin. He noted the first spasm, and abruptly grabbed two handfuls of duvet and clenched his anal sphincter. He would not come.

Fabrice's face was a rictus. His eyes were screwed shut. His tongue became welded to the roof of his mouth. His chest rose dramatically and his nostrils flared as he took a profound and cleansing breath. He fought his instinct for a moment and then floated back down to the bed.

The joint hissed and crackled as he took a puff. He picked up a book from the nightstand, settled under the covers and began to read himself to sleep.

It is important to have control.

XIV

A pure white wad of gauze showed over the waistband of her jeans.

'I'd just like you to have a look. I'm a bit worried. I don't think it's healing properly.'

Fabrice knitted his eyebrows in a show of serious concern and guided Zairah to the chair. He knew what he was going to see and wondered if this was a ruse on her part. He could tell she was curious about him: a bit of rough, but not too rough, for her smooth middle-class existence. He peeled back the adhesive tape and removed the spotless dressing.

'There, see,' said Zairah, craning her head and resting a perfectly manicured index fingertip close to the tattoo. 'That black scab. Is it OK? It's not infected or something? God, I hope it isn't infected.'

Fabrice smiled and rested the back of his fingers against the design. 'Doesn't feel hot. No pus. Have you been using the Bepanthen?'

Zairah twitched guiltily. 'Yes, of course, just like you said. Twice a day, morning and evening.' Her tone was plaintive. She was not telling the truth. She had applied the antiseptic cream every hour or so, obsessively rubbing it into her skin.

'Then there's no need to worry, is there?'

Fabrice looked into her eyes. It felt as if he really saw her and Zairah, for a moment, was unable to catch her breath. What he noticed, she realised, was not that she was foolish or timid but that she was interested in him.

'I'm sorry. I'm wasting your time.' She was already swinging her lovely lean legs over the side of the chair.

'My time is yours,' Fabrice offered gallantly.

She paused.

'Would you like me to put the dressing back on?' The gauze was on top of the inkstand.

'Perhaps I should have a fresh one?'

'It doesn't really need to stay covered up any more anyway.'

'I know. I just feel like I want to protect it.'

Fabrice's groin ached for her vulnerability, the clean lines of her limbs. He pulled up the stool and sat on it beside her, patient as a milady's page.

'Do you always wear the same thing?' The question popped out of Zairah's mouth. 'I mean, I don't mean to be rude.'

She cared about what he thought of her. Fabrice looked down at himself. 'Like you, I have different clothes for different occasions. You have only seen me here at work in the studio. These trousers are cheap and practical. I get them from an army surplus stall at the Marché de Saint-Ouen. As for the shirts, black is the only colour: you can imagine the mess of ink.' In reality there was very little mess. The ink was squeezed straight from the bottle into the cap and anything left over got bundled up in cling film and thrown out at the end of the job. It was the client who got dirty. 'I don't like to spend too much money on my clothes.'

Fabrice observed his words smack straight into the target.

He was merely picking up on her comment last time about Bensimon. For Zairah, though, he had penetrated right to the heart of her; that petty place she did well to keep from others.

'I should be more like you,' she observed ruefully.

'I don't think this would quite fit in your office.'

'No, you're right.' She brightened. It felt like he had given her permission to spend most of her income on pretty clothes so that her father had to cover her rent.

There was a lull in the conversation. Zairah became aware that she was stretched almost horizontal on the chair with the top button of her jeans still undone. Fabrice's face was close to hers, calm and attentive.

'I suppose I'd better be going. It's Saturday. You're bound to be busy.'

'I am busy with you now.'

Her hands rested over her lap.

Fabrice was waiting.

Zairah could tell he was attracted to her. The air between them was electric. She undid her fly again and revealed the whole of her new tattoo. 'I love it. I really do. It makes such a difference.' She was remembering that he had called her 'fierce' – or was it the design? – and wanted to live up to his expectation.

He was enjoying watching her steel herself.

'I was wondering, would you? Well, what I mean to say is, would you like to meet me for a drink one evening so that I can say 'thank you' properly for what you've done? Just for a drink,' she added lamely.

It was the first time in her life she had asked a man out.

Fabrice seemed to mull it over as Zairah did up her jeans and belt again. He reached out a hand, shakily, and rested it against hers.

'It would be a pleasure. Thank you for asking.'

He must be shy, she thought. It was true, what he had said. She really had changed with the tattoo. She stood up: daring and fierce. Fabrice stood too. He said nothing but his eyebrows appeared to be asking a question.

'Oh! Yes! Of course.' Zairah realised she had been silly. 'I almost forgot. When, then?'

Fabrice looked at a loss. He wanted her to decide.

'Tonight? I don't suppose you're free tonight?' In fact, she was so flustered Zairah had temporarily forgotten she had already made arrangements with friends who would not look kindly on a hoodlum tattooist joining them for cocktails.

Fabrice seemed about to acquiesce.

'No, sorry, I can't tonight,' she continued. 'How about tomorrow? Sunday supper? I know a great place not far from here. Fuxia, near the Parc de Batignolles.'

Fabrice knew it too. It was hard not to notice the herds of *bobos* that gathered there for overpriced pasta. 'Perfect.' He nodded.

Before leaving, she reached out to touch his hand. He had smooth, small hands. Her fingers brushed his palm. He did nothing to return the gesture and as she adjusted the bag on her shoulder she felt embarrassed. He was shy around women. She had been too forward.

'Goodbye, Zairah,' Fabrice said formally, opening the door for her.

'Eight o'clock?' She wondered now if he would be there. 'Fuxia at eight. Yes. See you tomorrow.'

Zairah felt thrilled as she walked along rue Biot towards the Metro. It was a full spring day. The sky was dazzling blue and made even the tawdry Place de Clichy look exciting, with its big old-fashioned restaurants, baskets of oysters heaped outside, ozone fresh in a grey sea of traffic fumes. Zairah had never met a man whom she felt could understand her. Fabrice, though, was different. He listened. He was sensitive. He had such beautiful eyes. She was smiling and humming an old Leonard Cohen song as she descended the steps to the station.

XV

Zairah clutched the menu and gnawed her lower lip. Her knuckles were as white as the blouse she had on. Fabrice approved. He had said that white was the perfect colour for her.

'I don't know what to choose,' she complained. They had already sent the waiter away once. 'Everything looks so good.'

Zairah had not eaten all day. Since arranging to meet with Fabrice she had consumed one apple (peeled and diced), one orange (with all pith and pips surgically removed) and a plain, no-fat live yoghurt. She had seen him looking at and liking her body. She did not want to feel like a bloated heifer sitting at the table with him tonight. But now she was hungry, painfully hungry.

'What are you having?' she asked.

Fabrice smiled. Why were women so unoriginal? 'The rocket salad.'

'I love the cannelloni here. What about that?'

'Not for me.' Fabrice did not elaborate, but the thought of all that fat and red meat repulsed him.

Zairah glanced around at the neighbouring tables. Other women were giving themselves permission to eat pasta with their boyfriend on a Sunday night. The aroma of baked cheese and tomatoes and herbs was causing her to salivate. Fabrice observed her scowling at the menu and sat with one arm draped over the back of his chair. He signalled for the waiter.

Zairah was still not ready to order but Fabrice had called the guy over again and begun to speak in Italian. She was taken by surprise and, feeling harried, named a dish at random and a glass of Ramitello.

'Or shall we get a bottle?'

'A bottle, if you wish.'

'A bottle, then,' she said to the waiter.

'And some San Pellegrino,' Fabrice added.

There was a pause as they both watched their waiter disappear behind the counter. The pause lengthened and Zairah became uncomfortable, as she always did in silence. 'So, how have you been?' Her head bobbed brightly. She was wearing the huge gold earrings, which bounced against her slender neck.

'Since yesterday?' He was not going to make this easy for her.

'Well, since yesterday . . . always . . . I don't know. I don't know you, do I?' She almost added, 'I'm only trying to make conversation.' Her hunger was making her tetchy.

Fabrice spread his hands out on the table. They both watched. 'I am always fine,' he said evenly.

Zairah wondered if she had made a mistake. Maybe he was a bit strange. And he had come to dinner dressed in what looked like workman's dungarees over a black shirt with battered brogues. The effect was disconcerting, but she had noticed the label on his jacket was Yves Saint Laurent.

She had made an effort. Her blouse was new, from Anne Fontaine. The crisp collar and cuffs were irritating in the heat of the restaurant.

'How about you?' Fabrice enquired, in the certain knowledge that she would find this question captivating.

'Oh, I'm fine too. Pretty good. You know how it is.' She sounded less sure of her initial statement with every subsequent addition.

'No,' charmed Fabrice, 'I don't know how it is with you, Zairah, and I would very much like to. Why don't you tell me: how are you, really?'

All the background noise – the clatter of cutlery, a dozen trivial conversations – faded to nothing as Zairah took a breath. He had such sympathetic eyes, the colour of dark chocolate. In some ways he reminded her of her father.

'Well, work's hard, for one . . .'

Thus the litany commenced. Fabrice was now leaning forward in his chair. He occasionally offered a brief question; sometimes a nod and a perceptive comment. Zairah had polished off her first glass of wine in three nervous gulps. It was only when she was halfway through the second that she realised.

'You're not drinking.'

Fabrice topped up his fizzy water. The bubbles squabbled and fought their way to the surface. 'No. I don't.'

Zairah's cheekbones burned. 'You could have told me! A whole bottle to myself! I'll be under the table!' She was not an excessive drinker but she suddenly felt like one in his sober company.

'Surely not. Besides, I won't let anything happen to you.'

You only have to ask, Fabrice thought, as his cock hardened under the table.

Zairah raised her glass. Despite the way he dressed, she knew he was a gentleman. The wine had seared straight through her empty stomach. Her frustration had evaporated. In its place she felt giddy.

Fabrice raised his mineral water and they chinked glasses.

He muttered something in a low voice. 'A genuine alchemist should only use vessels of glass.'

Zairah did not quite hear, so she chose to ignore him and continue with what she was saying. When their food came she emitted a heavy sigh.

'What? You don't like the look of your rigatoni?' Fabrice picked a pine nut off the top of his salad and popped it into his mouth.

'Oh no, it's not that. It looks divine.'

Fabrice smirked at her choice of adjective. 'What, then? Is it me?'

Her head snapped up. She had hurt his feelings. 'No, no, of course not.' She reached across the table but his hands were busy with his cutlery and she let her arm droop to the side of his plate without touching him. 'It's just . . .'

Fabrice nodded at the great steaming bowl of pasta. 'Would you like pepper? Oil? Parmesan?'

'Why does it have to be so difficult?' she whined, ignoring him. Zairah felt that in Fabrice she had a confidant. She was certain he would understand.

'What?' he asked, pushing salad leaves into his mouth. He knew exactly what was coming. He could almost smell the anorexics and bulimics.

'Food,' Zairah answered simply. 'I love food. But ever since I can remember it's been impossible for me to enjoy it. I should be enjoying this.' Her voice rose. 'An excellent restaurant, excellent company. But I'm not. It's hell.' Her eyes were brilliant with tears. He could see flecks of mascara clinging to her lashes. Self-pity. It disgusted him.

Fabrice placed his napkin on the table and laid his knife and fork on top of it. Then he looked into Zairah's strained features. She was trying to smile but her eyes were threatening to flood. He stretched across and held her face tenderly in both hands. His thumb brushed her lower lip, which was sticky with gloss and beginning to tremble. For what felt like a long time he said nothing. She became still. She looked into his face and saw such patient concern that she was awed.

Finally he whispered, 'Zairah, you must give yourself permission: permission to enjoy all that life has to offer you.'

She could not answer immediately. He excused himself and went to wash his hands in the bathroom.

When he returned Zairah said, 'You're right. Fuck it. Life's too short,' and she dug into the heart of the congealing dish.

'Bravo.' Fabrice raised his glass. He was surprised to hear her swear, but then, she was two-thirds of the way through that bottle of wine.

He watched her eat with an expression of benign indulgence plastered across his features. When she ordered the tiramisu he knew he would be putting her into a taxi alone later that night. He could see her hooking her slim fingers down her lovely throat and hear the violent torrent of undigested food hitting the pan. He did not need to be there.

'I don't touch refined sugar,' he explained as she urged him to order dessert too.

Zairah showed little curiosity but he felt the need to elaborate. 'I was brought up by my grandma. She was Italian. Always feeding me. Her *gnocchi di ricotta* would put this place to shame. And her *tortiglione* . . . She always made them into little snakes, with a red tongue of candied fruit.' Fabrice looked wistful. He was building to a point. 'Obviously, I was a fat kid. She just wanted to show me how much she loved me to make up for, well, other things. But there I was: the chubby little immigrant . . .' He let the words drift between them. He wondered himself how much of it were true. He was talking shit and she was lapping it up.

Zairah's face lit with recognition. His intuition had been correct: she was really the overweight interloper.

Zairah was beginning to suspect they had a lot in common, despite their diverse lives. 'My mum missed home so much. She was always cooking. When she fried *acras* the smell used to float out into the hallway. I'm sure our neighbours didn't like it. Pork and pineapple; stuffed crab; yams; sweet potatoes; breadfruit *migan*. I started secretly making myself sick when I was about thirteen. It just got to be a sort of habit.'

Once she had finished her dessert, scraping the spoon around the sides of the dish, Fabrice took out his cigarettes and lighter.

'Look at this,' he commanded, holding up the cheap Bic for her inspection.

Zairah took it from him. Her hand-eye coordination was slightly skewed. 'What is it?' she asked stupidly.

Fabrice said nothing.

Zairah peered at the lighter, which seemed perfectly ordinary to her. She turned it over in her hand. There was a design on it. At first she could not make it out. There was a kind of monster, with a tail. And then she realised.

Zairah dropped the lighter and gave a shiver of disgust. The girl's bottom was spread – you could see her puckered anus – and the creature was about to enter her.

'That's disgusting,' she said vehemently.

Smoothly Fabrice replied, 'Yes. Isn't it? A friend gave it to me last week. I wanted to know what you'd think.'

And now he did.

She leaned against him as they left the restaurant. Fortuitously, there was a taxi waiting around the side of the church. Fabrice opened the door for Zairah and helped her in. He kept hold of her hand as she arranged herself on the back seat. When he had her full attention he kissed the smooth skin just above the ridge of her knuckles.

'Goodnight,' he whispered, 'and Zairah, remember this: the important thing is not to be a victim.' He looked straight into her eyes as he said it.

'Goodnight, Fabrice,' she whispered back. 'I'm sorry. Thank you.'

Orange streetlights flared and faded as the car sped along boulevard de Courcelles. Zairah rested her head against the black vinyl. Her right hand found the special place on her hip. With Fabrice she was no longer the silly Mickey Mouse girl. He was teaching her to be a woman. She would try to keep the food down, which currently lay like lead in her stomach. She did not have to be a victim. It was true what he said. She was no longer helpless at her mother's table.

XVI

The owner of the restaurant across the road was unloading sacks of rice from the back of his Mercedes. His team of waiters conveyed the delivery from kerb to kitchen with Japanese efficiency. Fabrice stood between the bamboo, which was flourishing, as bamboo always will, and took deep breaths of morning air. He raised a hand in greeting to his neighbour, who nodded curtly in return. As an experiment Fabrice had forgone his usual joints last night. Perhaps he smoked too much. But he did not need anyone else to tell him. His head felt as clear and untroubled as the strip of sky between the buildings of rue Biot.

Fabrice reached into the map pocket of his combats and switched on his phone. It began to buzz immediately. Too early for Yoshiko. He had wished Zairah a chaste goodnight around eleven and knew he would not hear from her again until she finished work later that day. He opened the first message.

'*hello . . . is anybody there?*' It had been sent just after three o'clock that morning. Fabrice had been asleep. He did not recognise the sender's number.

He clicked on the next message.

'*your black sun is shining on me and i cant sleep*'

The black sun: it had to be that raddled blonde – Xanthe.

She had taken his card a couple of weeks ago, just before the first May bank holiday. Her tattoo would have peeled and healed by now. He wondered how she managed to take care of it. Did she find someone to smooth on the antiseptic cream? Fabrice experienced a spasm of envy.

There were two more messages. She had composed four texts within twenty minutes of each other in the middle of the night. Fabrice's nostrils flared: the scent of a lonely woman.

The third text read: *'you know im Dirty.'* He wondered at the capital D but his grin showed his eye teeth. Yes, he knew. Fabrice leaned against the front window of his establishment and let out a sigh. Above his door the ancient alchemical symbol for gold was openly concealed. Nobody noticed. Nobody saw him really.

'Hello, Dirty,' Fabrice whispered. There was a slight tremor in his hand as he opened the final message.

'FUCKMEFUCKYOU'

He frowned. Such crude language. And she was shouting. Why? He went back inside to consider his response.

Fabrice sat on his stool, spine straight, Motorola in hand. This one might be more of a challenge: surely less innocent, and therefore more of a risk. He saw again the man's name – 'PAUL' – in blood and ink across her back, and his own work, obliterating her former lover. She had remained still and calm as the pain swept over her. She had borne the needle silently. He read the ratty hair and shadows under her eyes as proof that she was, as she wrote, dirty.

Fabrice composed the message in his mind first and then

his thumb jumped over the keypad. In gravelly, accented English he sang. He could wear a mask for her.

In her claustrophobic classroom, Xanthe was swallowing a couple of Nurofen. She sucked on a litre bottle of Volvic. She had crashed out pretty much the moment she got back last night, and woken around midnight feeling desperate and lonely. She had drunk cheap gin and listened to music, then cooked up a couple of jellies for a treat. She had no recollection of texting Fabrice.

Her telephone beeped and she dug it out of her bag.

'Miss X, I was asleep last night and dreaming of you . . .'

Xanthe frowned. She became aware of the thud of her heart echoing in the empty room. She was shaking, but she always shook in the mornings. Sometimes she could barely get a legible phrase up on the whiteboard.

She had to know. She replied instantly: *'who is this?'* Fear had joined her in the classroom.

As she waited for the response she drained the bottle of water. A cool trail dripped from her chin onto the front of her shirt. She was aware of this, even as her mind and body were increasingly consumed with absolute terrorpanic. PAUL. **PAUL.** Her new number. He had got her new number. If someone had given him her new number, they had probably given him her new address as well. She would have to move. If she wanted to see out her year – the year of freedom she had promised herself – she would have to change everything again and she was tired, too tired and sick to do it all again; doing it once, escaping once, had almost killed her with the effort, and she wanted to live, paradoxically, as she also planned to die.

Starved of oxygen, Xanthe's torturing brain began to run. When the message alert sounded she dropped the phone.

'Fuck,' Xanthe moaned as she stabbed at the button to reveal the incoming message.

She had to read it twice, three times, before she could be sure.

Fabrice. The tattooist with the mournful face, who had given her his card. Had she told him her number? He reminded her of a monk with his plain clothes and shaven head, the green calm of his studio.

Fragments of the night before floated like bubbles to the surface of Xanthe's recollection. She accessed the phone's message editor and reread the last text she had composed. '*FUCKMEFUCKYOU*' in English, the words all jumbled together. It hardly made sense. Xanthe shook her headache slowly from side to side. The door swung open and a couple of students strode in. They were in the middle of an animated conversation.

'I'll be with you in just a tick,' Xanthe announced.

The young men nodded at her and continued chatting.

She bent over her phone and considered what to say. Sorry? No. Sorry, I was drunk?

'*I'll call you later. At work now.*' She pressed send.

On receiving the message, Fabrice replied instantly, '*I am working too.*'

Squashed into the RER on her return to Saint Germain en Laye, Xanthe looked at her phone. He had been on her mind all day, lurking at the back of the classroom or behind her desk, the thought of him so intense it had almost a physical presence. True, Xanthe was lonely. She remembered the warmth of his gloved hands to her back; the gentle way he had wiped the blood from her suffering skin. But there was something . . . Something about Fabrice that she realised instinctively . . . Something disconnected . . . A hidden darkness . . . Xanthe sighed to herself in exasperation. Her hand reached around, jogging her neighbour's elbow, as she stroked the upper rays of her tattoo. The darkness was not in Fabrice: it was in her. It was in Paul. Paul had made her suspicious. Paul had terrorised her. Not every man was Paul.

Yes, Xanthe thought. Yes! I will.

But what to say to Fabrice now? How was your day? Banal. How are you? In truth, she did not really care. Who are you? Xanthe smiled. She wanted to know, but that was too cryptic. She was still pondering as she went into the supermarket, picked up wine instead of gin, then headed automatically towards her backstreet.

She stripped off all her clothes at the door. The suit was a dry old skin she had to shed as swiftly as possible. Her bare feet slapped against the tiles as she went to open the windows. None of the neighbours could see directly into her flat, except perhaps from the top-floor of that bigger building across the courtyard. Xanthe leaned on the lower half of the frame and gazed at the faded sky. Her shoulders were aching from the weight she was carrying. A rat dodged across the mossed cobbles and disappeared down a drain.

'A year,' she murmured. 'One fucking year. That's all I

want.' Coming back to where she had begun, as a girl in the park with Papa. 'One last year. Here.' The fixed idea that helped her through her days. It would soon be summer. The winter months had been dark indeed. Should she count the year from the day Fabrice had covered up his name? 'That's cheating.' Xanthe was talking to herself.

Although the evening spread around her, all balmy and birdsong, Xanthe shivered. She could not remember now how the black sun had come to evolve. It was associated in her mind with waste and pain and perversion. But these were only words. They seemed the right words – decadence was too weak – however, when she sought their origin, it was like watching a film three-bottles drunk. Scenes flashed past. The sets changed. Saint Germain en Laye. Tokyo. Rome. New York. Papa's job. Papa needed his little girl, toted with him like a suitcase, unpacked brutally in the dark of a hundred strange bedrooms, in the cold white absence of his wife. Scripts faded in and out in a multitude of languages. Flash forward. Flashback. Never escaping the black sun, which shone through her. It had been there before Paul. It helped explain why she had found him, and then stayed with him. Xanthe hugged herself, her fingertips touching the steady rays emanating from that hole where once her love had been.

Then she poured a glass of wine and took it, with her phone, to the bathroom. The sides of the tub were sticky and grey. She lit a candle instead of switching on the light and closed the door so that the small room became a kind of cave.

Lying in the bath was another one of her simple pleasures.

Memories of Paul. She would never be free of the memories unless she lost her mind entirely.

Xanthe eased her body into the warm, foamy depths, and even as she luxuriated in its tenderness she remembered the needles when he turned the freezing shower on her and made her stand – *you know how pussies hate the water* – and laughed like a drain at her misery. *This'll warm you up.* The unbearable heat and obscene sound as he pissed against her.

Xanthe screwed her eyes tight shut and gulped the wine in one. She opened the last message from Fabrice. She still did not know what to say. It was like a game she wanted to play, but without knowing the rules yet.

Xanthe wrapped herself in a towel, went to fetch the bottle of Bordeaux and took it to bed. She propped herself on the stained pillows and began to drink steadily. She dropped off, as she always did, before daylight had entirely abandoned her room. When she awoke it was dark and the cold towel clung damply to her stomach.

Her thumb composed a message. She hardly knew what; she was so stupid with pain and weariness. She groped around for her baggie of mixed downers. She kept everything jumbled together to persuade herself they were dolly mixtures, with their different colours and shapes. Depakote, Diazepam, Halcion, Nitrazepam, Prozac, Risperidone, Rohypnol, Temazepam, Zopiclone. She had not even had time to extract the cork from the second bottle in the living room when her phone beeped.

'You seem to me to be extremely tired . . . Is everything ok?'

Xanthe blinked in disbelief. She responded immediately. *'im a stranger so how come you know me?'*

There was a pause. Xanthe remained staring at her phone. *'Never forget: I see a lot . . .'*

Pensively she extracted the cork, poured another glass, left the bottle on the table and went back to bed. She took her pills, curled up under the covers and cradled the phone close to her face. *'you see me?'*

As she waited for him to reply, she kidded herself that they were lying together having an intimate conversation.

'I see everything . . .'

The pills did their work. Xanthe plummeted into unconsciousness.

Perhaps he had gone too far? Fabrice was frowning as he waited for Xanthe's text. His bedroom windows were open, allowing in the savoury smells of other people's meals. He turned his attention to how to get her back. An English teacher would probably like poetry, right?

On the RER next morning, Xanthe reread the message that had been waiting for her when she woke up.

'On the emerald moss
Three drops of blood
Face leaning over'

The words had a kind of Zen calm. Perhaps he is a rogue monk, Xanthe thought. On the opposite side of the carriage somebody caught her eye. She looked so happy. He thought she was smiling at him.

XVII

Fabrice hitched the straps over his shoulders and tucked a small foil square into the breast pocket of his dungarees. The phone by his bed told him that he was already almost an hour late. He plopped down on the corner of the mattress and composed a brief text. She answered immediately: *'no problem get here when you can.'*

He would see how far he could push it. They had arranged to meet at eight. Fabrice picked up a book and determined to aim for ten. He had read an entire chapter on *mens rea* and mistakes about consent in rape – the subject was deadly but he kept on stopping to test his recall of key facts – when his phone began to vibrate. He smiled as he opened the message.

'where are you? I'm getting hungry and lonely.'

'on my way . . . you may commence the feast without me . . .' Fabrice wanted to give her permission to gorge herself, to run her beautiful fingers over her slick tight pussy in readiness for him.

And the thought of that set him on his feet. As he left his apartment he tapped the pocket to reassure himself he had everything he needed.

Zairah, meanwhile, was pacing the length of her living room. She had opened the bottle of Chablis a couple of minutes before she expected him to arrive. That was over two hours ago. She had had a mouthful to taste. It was crisp and delicious. She had laid out costly *petits-fours* from Dalloyau. He was still at work. She did not doubt that for a moment: a tattooist would have to keep unsociable hours; it was not like being employed in an office. She imagined he had to take jobs whenever they presented themselves. It did not strike her as a secure way to earn a living. Zairah glanced around her home. What would he think? The moulded ceilings, the old-fashioned mirrors, the building itself?

Fabrice stood at the gates of Zairah's address on rue Palatine in the so-swanky 6th. He took in the overblown architecture and allowed a sense of righteous indignation to bloom a moment in his heart. He entered the code she had given him and leaned on the heavy portal. Inside, white gravel crunched under his feet. The gate whispered shut behind him, discreetly doing its business of keeping undesirables out.

Feeling like a criminal, Fabrice crossed the courtyard. She was in the east wing. He found her name on the second computer entry panel and she buzzed to let him up. The main hall was tiled in black and white marble. Wide stone steps were carpeted in red. A carved balustrade curved majestically upward. The higher Fabrice climbed, though, the narrower the staircase became. Stone was replaced with wood. Zairah lived on the sixth floor.

'Where were you?' Zairah immediately sensed something from the expression on his face. She did not mean what his look implied. 'I was waiting at the lift. You took the stairs?'

Fabrice said nothing but stepped forward and kissed her lightly on both cheeks. She was, as he had anticipated, wearing white: a tight white vest that showed her ribs and nipples, and billowing white silk trousers. A few narrow gold bangles jingled on her wrist as she raised her arms to his shoulders, returning the greeting.

He paused at the door to her apartment.

'May I?' he asked.

'Of course. Come in.' She stood to one side and allowed him to precede her into the hallway.

He inhaled delicately: wealth and –

'It's incense. From l'Occitane. Don't you like it?'

Fabrice gave a nod. He liked it very much. A place like this must cost, what? Two thousand? Three thousand Euros a month?

Several doors opened off the main hall. Zairah led them to the far end. They stepped down into a large living room dominated by an arched window that gave onto a narrow stone balcony. An easel was set close to the light, a cloth draped over the canvas. The walls were painted pale yellow. There was a cream corner sofa unit and a small round table with two chairs set with glasses and snacks. The overall effect was minimal and elegant.

Zairah watched Fabrice, trying to decipher his feelings. She thought he approved.

'You have a beautiful home,' he said, and watched his compliment flower.

'Some people think it's sterile – my mother, for instance – but I have to keep it like this. If it isn't neat it aggravates my asthma.'

Fabrice's hands grew sticky and hot; he almost shook them and held them out in front of him, such was the need.

'Let me take your jacket,' Zairah offered, stepping forward.

She was reassured by the YSL label, even though he was wearing those awful dungarees again.

'The bathroom?' Fabrice demanded.

'Oh! Second door to your right.'

He went to wash his hands. The bathroom was perfect: pure white, very clean. When he came back, Zairah had poured two glasses of wine. She held one up to him.

'I don't drink alcohol.' Fabrice was disappointed. Had he made that scant an impression?

'Sorry. Of course you don't. I remember now. That's why I was so . . .' Their eyes met. She felt dizzy. His appeal was magnetic, such that her body was drawn towards him. Zairah dropped her gaze. '. . . so emotional the last time we met.' It seemed an apt euphemism.

Fabrice saw an opportunity to move on. 'You said, I remember, the first time we met,' actually, it was the second time, but that did not have the same poetic ring, 'that you wanted to live a simple life. It would appear, Zairah, that your home is a model of simplicity.'

Warmth spread from Zairah's heart. Fabrice really listened; he really cared about what she said. She often felt like she spent all her days talking and talking but that no one ever truly heard her.

'Thank you.' She was at a loss for how else to respond.

'May I have some mineral water?' Fabrice raised an

eyebrow. He had caught her out: she had already taken a sip of her wine: bad hostess.

'Yes, yes, of course. Sit down, won't you? I'll go and get some. I've only got still, I'm afraid. Is that OK?'

Fabrice wondered what she would do if he said no. 'That's fine,' he answered, settling on one side of the sofa.

When she came back into the room carrying his drink, Zairah's breath was short. They were at the beginning of something important. There was a definite mutual attraction but she was already wondering how she should present him to her parents. What would her father think? A tattooist!

Fabrice noticed the slight shake of her head as she handed him the glass. 'No to what?' he enquired.

'What?' Zairah was startled. It was as if he could read her mind. 'Oh! I do that sometimes – you know, have conversations in my head.'

'Me too. What was it about?'

'My father.' Zairah sounded resigned.

Fabrice took a sip of water. Ice cubes clinked. The thick walls of the apartment isolated them from any of her neighbours' noise. A woman could be screaming her head off and no one would hear.

'Fathers.' Fabrice sighed knowingly.

'It's all right for you,' she expostulated, 'you're not a girl! Not an only daughter. I love my father so much but I'm constantly terrified of letting him down.'

Zairah sat cross-legged on the giant sofa cushion opposite Fabrice. Unexpectedly, he reached into his trousers pocket and extracted his mobile. He read the message as she plucked at her waistband, allowing an indigo tongue of flame to peep out. She caught Fabrice glancing at it. She was aware of her thighs open in his direction.

'Do you mind if I answer this?' It was Xanthe.

'Not at all.'

How does one pass from being unknown to being known? By opening your lips . . .' Fabrice's tongue bucked behind his clenched teeth as he pressed send and closed his mobile. Xanthe he was unsure about, but with Zairah he knew the price he would have to pay: one monologue. He would have to be patient, as always, but it would be worth it.

She watched him switch off his phone and then continued undeterred with what she was saying. Eventually he interrupted her.

'Zairah, I came straight from work and I am feeling a little tired. Would it be possible to take a quick shower to freshen up?'

The Chablis bottle was on the floor at Zairah's feet. He had fetched it for her. She had almost emptied it.

'What a great idea,' she concurred sleepily. 'I might join you.'

Fabrice was horrified at the thought. Purification happened alone.

'You look like you need a little nap.' He drew the cashmere throw from the back of the sofa, tucked it around her bare shoulders and plumped a cushion for her to lie on.

'Maybe forty winks.'

It was late. Zairah was docile as she was usually sound

asleep by now. Fabrice brushed her cheek with the back of his hand. Her eyelashes fluttered. He noticed for the first time a light scattering of freckles across her cheekbones.

On his way to the bathroom he switched off the living-room light. He was feeling unusually tender.

Fabrice got under the shower and adjusted the jets so that they pummelled his body. He let the water cleanse him. Thinking of Zairah prone next door he grew hard. With one hand raised, throttling the showerhead, and one hand expertly massaging his burgeoning cock, Fabrice continued the ritual. He came powerfully – it had been ten days – and let that peaceful feeling radiate from his core. Then he switched the shower to cold and stood in all humility, head bowed, for a sixty-second count.

As he stepped onto the fluffy white rug, Fabrice's skin was tingling. His heart was pounding like a navvy in the empty stone cellar of his chest. He dried himself and replaced the towel on the chrome rail. Then he began to look through Zairah's things. She used Clarins skincare; there were a number of different perfume bottles, including Ralph Lauren's *Romance*; in the cupboard under the sink were several boxes of Super Plus Tampax and pads and a medicine tin. Opening the tin he learned she had bought two tubes of Bepanthen, suffered from cystitis and – no surprise – period pain. Nothing out of the ordinary.

Fabrice began to get dressed. He pulled the dungarees up to his waist and considered his bare upper body in the mirror. The muscles were well-defined; the tattooed band around his bicep expertly executed. A mat of dark hair descended in a line past his belly. Fabrice's hand rose to his crown, where he was sure his scalp was becoming increasingly exposed. Time . . . Time was passing . . . But the true alchemist can manipulate time. Fabrice smiled at the thought of all that lost time women spent with him. He fingered the pocket of his dungarees: the powdered Rohypnol was still there; his elixir of youth. On bare feet he padded back down the hall towards Zairah.

She was not asleep, she told herself; she was waiting languorously for Fabrice to return to her after his shower. When she heard the bathroom door open, her stomach lurched, her cunt clenched in anticipation. She stretched like a cat on the sofa.

He sat down and regarded her a while. She was not so drunk that she was likely to vomit. She looked sleepy and relaxed. Was there really any need?

No, Fabrice decided, not with this one, not tonight. No drugs for the naïve and starving lawyer.

He took her foot between both his hands and began to massage her instep. She sighed and shifted. Lovingly he worked on the foot, inducing in her a deep peace. When he took the other foot she let her perfectly painted toes rest lightly in his lap. As he applied pressure to each little joint in turn, Zairah's other foot curled in pleasure against his hardening cock. She felt his response and began to play with him.

Fabrice bent to his massage. Zairah stretched her beautiful long legs and moved her feet in his lap. Eventually he let out a sigh.

Saying nothing, he stood up and drew her body against

his. He pressed his face to her neck, inhaled the scent of her hair oil and face powder, and resisted the temptation to tell her to wash.

'What do you want?' he whispered.

She was silent. In answer, she kissed him on the mouth. Not good enough. She had to say it.

Fabrice broke the kiss and repeated his question.

Although wet and hot and hungry, Zairah was seized with anxiety. She had never had to say anything like that before. I want you? I want to make love? I want to have sex with you? Wasn't it obvious?

'Say it, Zairah,' Fabrice urged, his deep low voice resonating close to her ear.

'I,' she faltered, the word barely more than a breath.

Fabrice was coaching her now. They had to acknowledge what it was they wanted; what they lacked; what he was prepared to give. She had to say this. 'What do you want, Zairah?' His tone was soothing, sweet, but she felt perhaps he was taunting her.

A sliver of ice formed between them. Fabrice regretted his decision not to spike her drink, but there was still time.

'I want you,' Zairah announced levelly, much to her own surprise, looking him in the eye. Her hand had dropped from his shoulder and was resting on her hipbone. Fierce, she thought to herself; I can be fierce.

She led the way to her bedroom. Her brass bed was made up with old-fashioned ivory linens and stacked with pillows and cushions. On a wing chair beside it sat a host of goggle-eyed dolls. A cheval glass was placed near the door. Fabrice considered it speculatively. He would move it later.

'May I?' he asked, hesitating on the threshold.

'Ever the gentleman,' Zairah replied, laughing and pulling him in by the waistband of his preposterous dungarees.

XVIII

It was the last bank holiday in May. Zairah was with her parents. She thought that maybe Fabrice had wanted to come too – they were driving up to Deauville for a picnic – but she had not felt able to tell them about him yet. Watching him leave her apartment after their magical night together, she was scared. No man had ever been so assiduous in his pursuit of her pleasure. She was afraid that it had all been some wonderful dream, or a game on his part. She was terrified to call him in case he was brusque, brushed her off, dismissed her as the spoilt little daddy's girl she suspected herself to be. But he had phoned her the moment he got back to his studio. He had been whispering intimately – she had not caught it all – something about six, over and over, and that he was impatient for their next meeting.

'Daddys driving too fast.' Fabrice glanced at the message and decided that it could remain unanswered.

'It's nothing,' Fabrice responded to Yoshiko's questioning gaze. 'Work.' He replaced the phone in the map pocket of his combats and trained all of his attention on her.

'Seems long time,' she said, expertly conveying salmon sashimi to her over-painted mouth.

'Ay me, sad hours seem long.'

'*Romeo and Juliet*,' she shot back straightaway, which surprised him.

'You read Shakespeare?'

Yoshiko briefly considered telling a lie. 'Leonardo de Caprio not Shakespeare.'

They both laughed.

The afternoon was going well. He had suggested they meet in front of the gilded roofs of the Opéra. They had wandered hand in hand around the *quartier* – she was wearing high-heeled clogs, and her clacking gait coupled with the incessant traffic and crowds had abraded his good humour – but now they were in the Passage Choiseul and he was feeling calm once more. The Passage probably had not changed much in the hundred years since it was built. Light filtered through its glass roof had an underwater quality. The disparate small businesses thrived, inexplicably to Fabrice as they did not seem to sell anything people would want – cheap and shiny Chinese clothes, expensive old American jeans, poorly researched picture books on foreign countries. There were several noodle bars, and at the rue des Petits Champs end a decent sushi restaurant.

A couple of carrier bags rested on the stool beside Yoshiko. He reached across and removed a magazine from one.

'Japanese *Vogue*. I like very much. Do not know you can buy here.'

Fabrice flipped the pages. They had happened across a huge Japanese bookstore on rue Saint Augustin. Her eyes had lit up like Christmas in Ginza. Never discount the power of coincidence.

He left the magazine open at a photograph of a woman

wearing enormous sunglasses, posing in a field of snowy white goats. Her legs too had a caprine quality, soaring from polished heel to sleek and muscular thigh.

'Too tall for Japanese.' Yoshiko bobbed her head dismissively. 'Japanese men small.'

Fabrice smiled, his heart hardening. And did she dare to think that he was a small man too? 'To work,' he announced, as much to himself as to her. 'Our film.'

She beamed back at him. He thought she sat straighter in her chair, pointing her tiny breasts in his direction. She took a strand of hair and began to twirl it around her index finger.

'First I want to thank you, Yoshiko. You have given me so many ideas, so much inspiration.' It was true. She had been bombarding him with images for the past month. 'I told you that you had to be patient.' She dipped her head. Patience was not one of her strong points. 'And your patience will be rewarded.'

Fabrice paused to push the scraps of *oshinko maki* around his plate. 'What do you think of the food here?'

Yoshiko shrugged. As usual, she was finding it hard to follow the logic of his conversation. She thought they had been talking about her. 'OK,' she mumbled, but every time she tried sushi or sashimi in France it just made her more homesick. Not even the rice tasted the same.

'Patience, you see: it is important to wait . . .' Fabrice let the words float into silence between them.

Yoshiko finished her lunch, her chopsticks clicking angrily. She was very aware of time passing.

'So: film: when?' She was due to go to London at the end of June.

'You are absolutely sure that you want to do this for me?'

Yoshiko nodded vehemently. She knew that she would never have another opportunity like this. Fabrice was an artist, and he wanted to make a film with her as the star. It was going to be a great film; she had faith in him. He had talked about light and camera angles and props and a whole load of other things she barely understood. That was why they had to wait. He had spotted her talent and was going to develop it. No one else had ever done that.

'You want to be in my film?' Fabrice repeated.

Perhaps he thought she had not understood. Yoshiko nodded again.

'Talk to me, Yoshiko. Do you want to be in my film?'

Then she realised what he wanted. 'Yes,' she replied, 'I want to be in your film,' her assent accompanied by a confident flick of the head.

He reached across the table and held her hand, then raised it to his mouth. His lips grazed her knuckles. Her fingers smelled of soy sauce. 'Good girl,' he whispered, knowing she would take it as a compliment.

'And so, my dear, there is one final piece of business that we must conclude before shooting may commence: the matter of your certification.'

Yoshiko's eyebrows knit.

'You did not know? Oh yes, that's right: I remember now. You are but an *ingénue* in the pornographic industry. All the best actors and actresses need a clean bill of health.'

She continued to stare quizzically at his lips.

'I am talking about AIDS, Yoshiko.' He emphasised the key word, perhaps a little too harshly as an older gentleman eating alone at the next table stopped to stare at him.

'AIDS?' Her eyes widened.

'An AIDS certificate, yes. You must go to a doctor, before we start filming, and ask to have an AIDS test.'

'AIDS test,' Yoshiko repeated. Things were feeling suddenly real.

'Yes, an AIDS test. The doctor will give you a form to take to the laboratory, where they will test your blood. Do you have a doctor here?'

Yoshiko nodded. Buds of tension unfurled in her gut.

'Then it is all very simple: get your blood test, get your certificate, bring it to me, and we start the film.'

He could sense she was unsure.

'Yoshiko, I cannot tell you how much I am looking forward to working with you. Those pictures you have sent me . . .' He looked away, over her shoulder, his unlined features a rapturous mask. 'Mmmm . . . It is going to be so beautiful, this work of art that we create. It is going to be something completely new, Yoshiko. Nobody has ever made a film like this before. Aren't you excited?'

She edged forward in her seat so that their knees touched. He reached across under the table and placed his hand between her thighs. Yoshiko's eyes shone.

'I'm exciting,' she answered, her groin pushing against his fingers.

'I am excited,' he corrected, popping the button fly of her jeans.

Yoshiko began to grind in her seat. Fabrice delicately

hooked his fingers around her slippery clit. He kept his eyes on her face, teasing her under the table.

She was going to come really quickly.

Fabrice withdrew his hand, playfully pinching her hip before settling back on his stool. With the same hand he brushed the hair from her face. Yoshiko grabbed it and kissed his fingers.

'Time to go,' he said, standing up.

She became flustered. She had to adjust her clothing, see to the bill and then meekly follow him out.

Thus drowned in his proper veins of poisoned flood;
For term of Eighty days and Four he rotting stood.

XIX

Xanthe had had the most peculiar weekend. She had spent the entire time indoors. Waking up late on Saturday morning, she had known what had to be done. The carrier bag with all the cleaning stuff in it was still by the door. Dressed in an old Neil Young T-shirt, she began by taking out the rubbish. Three clanking sacks of it.

Then she decided to wash all her dishes. She hated washing dishes. She was not chained to the kitchen sink here. Sometimes she bought new, just to avoid washing up. As the soapy pile on the draining board grew to precarious dimensions, Xanthe resolved to clean out the cupboards before drying and putting everything away.

Xanthe opened the windows and turned on the radio. The cleaning was absorbing. By late afternoon she realised she was hungry, and sober. She spooned Nutella from the jar and ate a pot of yoghurt that had lingered a long time at the back of the fridge but tasted fine.

The fridge.

She removed the gin. The ice cube tray was welded in place. Green hunks of lemon and cheese went straight in the bin as she set the dial to defrost.

After dark on Saturday night, Xanthe sniffed the bed linen she had hung from the windows to dry. She gathered great damp armfuls to her chest. The sheets smelled clean. Xanthe could not remember the last time she had had clean sheets. It made her want to cry. But she did not cry. That was what he wanted, Paul: a snivelling victim. Her arms and chest ached as she fell asleep on her bare bed.

She awoke slowly on Sunday. Bright sunlight was filtering through the curtains. Xanthe listened to her neighbours moving about upstairs. She watched her chest rise and fall. Her mind was blank, scrubbed, rinsed, cleansed.

While the coffee dripped she switched on her phone. Three messages. She had missed a party last night; the other two were from Fabrice.

Firstly: *'It must be sweet to curl up in bed in bourgeois st germain en laye. In the quiet tranquillity of satisfaction, to let your fingers roam deep inside yourself. An animal parade before the most beautiful torture . . .'*

And: *'There is also sleep, which relaxes . . . A prelude to the dawn . . . Have a peaceful night Xanthe . . .'*

She smiled at her phone. Peace. Beyond all other things, Xanthe needed peace. She took her coffee back to bed, selected a couple of Halcion from her pharmaceutical pick-and-mix, and slept long into the day.

Fabrice wanted to meet. He wanted to come to her place. When Xanthe had left Paul in Montrouge at Christmas, she had moved to the other side of the city, both geographically and socially. She was going back to where she had started, in the chateau gardens with Papa, snapshot of an ordinary girl upside down and laughing, eyes closed. She had not risked having a landline installed in her new flat. There were three locking doors between her and the street. She had taken only what could be fitted in her handbag or shopping bag, her heart hammering every time she changed from the Metro to Line A in case he was behind her, watching. She had transferred schools. Everyone knew from her taut pale face that it had been a messy break-up. Marthe had tried to enquire. Her colleague, John, had offered to help. She had rebuffed them all, her dark secret a seemingly impenetrable barrier between herself and others. It would have been more logical just to leave France, but Xanthe no longer had the energy for those international dislocations that had characterised her youth.

'Break-up!' Xanthe snorted. 'Breakout, more like.' Although she spent her days manipulating language, being clear and precise, she often felt that words – like people – let her down.

There was something about Fabrice that intrigued her: his eyes, his hands, his way of communicating. When she awoke in the middle of the night and texted him, he was always there. She had been bumming around after dropping out of university when she met Paul, who was thirteen years older than her. Back then he had seemed like a proper grown-up, focused and direct. She had wanted to buy some dope from him but he gave it to her for free. With nothing better to do, she had moved into his tiny flat when he asked her six weeks later.

'Eight years,' Xanthe mourned, 'eight fucking years.' She had loved him. It was the only explanation. He had clapped a collar on her. It was used and smelled of sweet leather and old dog. At least she had belonged somewhere. After her father had died and her mother slammed the door in her face, she was blind to the alternatives.

Xanthe decided to see Fabrice on Wednesday, which would be the first of June; she would soon be halfway through her year. She sent the text on Sunday evening. On Monday morning when she woke up, her cheek was stuck to the pillow. She had had a nosebleed.

'That's fucking ironic,' she muttered as she slid soiled pillow and pillowcase into a bin bag.

Xanthe finished work on Wednesday lunch time, as usual, and was smiling as she left the sunlit streets and let the escalator carry her down into the glossy scarlet bowels of Auber station. When the train screeched out of the tunnel after Nanterre Préfecture, the sky had never seemed so blue. Xanthe knew she was taking a risk, letting a man into her sanctuary, but Fabrice was not Paul. What were the odds of meeting another Paul? And even if he were another Paul, she would not love him as she had loved Paul. There was no danger of that happening again. Not now. Not with the black sun at the heart of her. Tattooed on her skin. Forever.

She opened the door to her spotless fridge: gin, beer, water, wine, lemons, a bag of salad and some olives. Xanthe wanted a drink. She was thirsty. It was hot. She prised the cap off a Gold and glugged it standing by the window.

'That's enough.' She tried to convince herself. She did not want to be drunk when he arrived.

Xanthe tried to remember Fabrice's face. She could still feel the touch of his fingers on her back . . . Brown eyes, she thought, dark . . . Paul's blue eyes had been her sea and sky: her world.

Xanthe took the empty beer bottle straight down to one

of the bins in the courtyard. She ran a bath and wallowed in the cooling water.

She had told Fabrice any time after eight. The light was now turning the colour of old wounds, and Xanthe began to get restless. She poured a glass of wine and tried to sip it. When the phone went, her arm leaped, slopping retsina all over her dress and the sofa.

She read the message: *'the little orange lights have betrayed me . . .'* which she guessed was Fabrice's way of saying he had got on the wrong train.

Xanthe dabbed at her damp dress with a towel. It would be dry by the time he arrived, for which she was thankful. Without thinking much about it she tapped out a reply.

'if u r 2 late ill have drunk all the wine'

She riffled through her CDs. What would he like? What was suitable? She thought she remembered 'I'm Your Man' from her time at the studio and put that on, but Leonard sounded too mournful this evening.

'He can choose,' Xanthe whispered, sitting back down.

Her phone beeped again. Two messages. One had come in when she was at the stereo. She opened the first: *'if you do . . .'*

'If you do what?' she asked, puzzled.

Then she clicked on the second. *'. . . you will be punished . . .'*

Xanthe stared at the screen. Her stomach lurched. **PAUL.** Paul's coming. Paul was going to punish her for thinking she deserved better. She struggled for air. She ran to the door, checked it was locked; leaned out into the courtyard, saw that the door to her building was shut, locked; the street door always clicked closed automatically, you needed the code to open it.

'Breathe . . . Just breathe . . .' Xanthe told herself. Her face was wet. She thought perhaps she had been crying without realising. She swiped a hand across her nose and mouth. It came away dirty red.

'Fuck!'

Xanthe went to the bathroom and hung her head over the sink. She watched the drops of blood splatter onto the porcelain.

Blood blooms like flowers in the garden of true love.

Gathering up her hair, Xanthe confronted her reflection. Her skin was shining, her green eyes ringed with the kohl of terror, her mouth glossed with dried blood.

Clarity coagulated.

Even if he was Paul, what did it matter? She did not love Fabrice. They would spend perhaps eight hours together, not eight years.

Xanthe rinsed her face and reapplied her make-up.

'I'm waiting, man. Bring it on.'

She deleted the messages without rereading them, drank a glass of water and did not even flinch when her phone went off again.

'*I am at the door.*'

Strangely excited, she did not reply but jogged downstairs to open it.

Fabrice's first words were, 'It would have been easier if you had just given me the code,' and they kissed perfunctorily in greeting.

She was wearing a black short-sleeved tunic dress with

a mandarin collar over the same cropped trousers she had on last time he saw her.

Fabrice followed as she picked her way in bare feet back across the cobbles of her courtyard.

'I'm on the second floor,' Xanthe said, quoting some half-remembered song. Sometimes her brain felt too full of lyrics or fragments of poems and books.

Fabrice remained silent but nodded when she glanced over her shoulder.

'Mind your head,' she advised, unnecessarily, as they entered the narrow stairwell.

Fabrice was looking at the paintwork in amazement. The walls, bowed with age, were a moss green colour; the thin banister was red. As Xanthe preceded him up the worn wooden stairs, he knew he had to be on the right track with her. The alchemical texts that he created were formed of living female flesh: green is the colour of commencement; the goal of the Greater Work is red.

'Interesting colour scheme,' he commented as she stopped outside her flat.

'Is it? My grandma always used to say red and green should never be seen.' Xanthe reflected a moment. 'Or was it yellow and green?'

She pushed open the door for him to enter.

Fabrice would have felt more secure if she was on the other side of the threshold verbally inviting him in, but there was nothing he could do about it without seeming odd.

He stepped into a pristine white and echoing box.

Xanthe watched him taking in his surroundings. She

laughed hollowly. 'Yeah, I know. I've still got to move in the rest of my stuff.'

Fabrice saw a cheap but new sofa; a cheap but new folding table with two matching chairs; a stereo balanced on its packing box and next to it a large collection of CDs; a small pile of books and an ashtray beside a floor cushion in front of the window. It was not that the flat was sparsely furnished; rather that it had a temporary feel.

'How long have you been here?'

When Xanthe answered, 'Not long,' she had no idea if it was the truth. Since she had left Paul the days were blurred. She always managed to turn up for work punctually, but the only time that mattered was the one year of freedom she had allotted herself. Fixing on this, no matter how perverse, was her way of guaranteeing that she had a future. Her time was evaporating like fluid over a philosopher's fire.

'What would you like to drink?' She stood in front of the fridge.

'Mineral water, please, if you have some.'

There was something about Fabrice that did not fit. His manners were charming, his voice low and relaxed, but his eyes were skimming over her belongings like he was casing the place for a burglary.

Xanthe poured two glasses of Perrier, handed one to Fabrice, who stood with his back to the window, feet shoulder-width apart, and sat down on the sofa with her legs curled beneath her.

They watched each other. Neither attempted to break the silence. A crow landed on the roof opposite and they listened to its great claws ticking on the corrugated iron. Fabrice toed the pile of books: some English, some French. A name leaped out at him.

'What is this *Anne of Green Gables*? Somebody else was talking to me about her recently.'

'It's a children's classic. American. Very innocent. It's my comfort reading.'

Fabrice nodded. 'So you like to read in English?' She was no adolescent innocent. She read to escape.

It was Xanthe's turn to nod. She thought he was going to question her again about where she came from, and she had prepared a plausible answer. But Fabrice moved on. He picked up *Blue of Noon* and examined the back cover.

'It's my favourite book. He lived just down the road from here – Georges Bataille. He thought the world turned with the energy of men and women making love on it.'

Fabrice placed the volume back on top of the pile. 'I will have to make a note to read it.' The blurb mentioned sex as a subversive force; 'a holocaust of words'.

Although she stank of alcohol, Xanthe seemed more sober than he had expected. She was wary, he could tell. She did not even trust him with the code to her building. A pilot light of anger burned in Fabrice's gut. Egotistical bitch. Who did she think she was? At the far end of the main room was a kitchenette. He went to what he assumed was the food cupboard above the stainless steel sink. Xanthe observed, amused, as he took inventory of one pack of spaghetti, Nutella, and various types of coffee.

'Are you hungry?' His voice was gentle, almost a whisper.

In his experience, all women as skinny as Xanthe were hungry. 'Don't tell me you don't eat pizza. Let's order a take-out,' and he removed his phone from the bib pocket of his dungarees.

Xanthe stood up to fetch menus. She had never used any of them. Fabrice picked a leaflet at random and made his selection. Xanthe offered to phone.

'No, no. I'll do it,' Fabrice offered. He had already dialled. He greeted the person on the other end with cheerful civility.

Xanthe had gone to the fridge and was topping up her empty glass with retsina.

'Remind me of your address.' Fabrice turned in her direction. She duly supplied the required information. 'And the code to the door?'

Xanthe stood still, glass half raised to her lips. 'Two, four, six, eight,' she replied.

'We're on the second floor,' Fabrice said into the receiver, and then to Xanthe, 'Twenty minutes. Can you wait?'

Xanthe nodded and smiled. Of course she could wait. She knew she had been finessed.

Later, when they were sitting at the table around the greasy pizza box, she had no compunction about lying to him when he asked again where she came from. In her account Xanthe was educated at the nearby Lycée International, the only daughter of successful, globe-trotting professional parents who adored each other: French father, American mother; senior school here for stability; university in England with a year abroad in Quebec; a few years of travel, Asia and South America mainly; then back home teaching English to businesspeople while she made up her mind what she really wanted to be.

Fabrice listened intently. The story was bourgeois and commonplace. It did not admit of the black sun and they both knew it.

Xanthe was pacing her alcohol consumption. The second glass stood in front of her almost untouched.

'Would you get me a pen?' he asked.

She rose to go and fetch one. Fabrice watched, satisfied, as she instinctively obeyed him.

He wrote carefully on the lid of the pizza box.

Xanthe noticed the letters first – an idiosyncratic mix of upper and lower case, much like her own. 'You mean decadence?'

'Everything in excess is opposed to nature.' Fabrice read back what was in front of them. 'Do I mean decadence? What is decadence?'

Xanthe took a sip of her wine. 'Decadence?' She looked him straight in the eye. She liked his eyes; they seemed to see clearly. But the word hung between them like a whiff of shit. 'For me, I suppose, it's linked to decay, a falling away . . .'

He waited for her to say more. When he realised she had become mute on the subject he commenced his lecture. 'Not decay: dec: ten.'

She wanted to interrupt – decadence has nothing to do with the number ten – but he continued in an urgent whisper. When he was done she got up to go to the loo.

Fabrice was humming to himself as he listened to her urinate. He deftly unfolded the foil wrap and emptied the contents into her drink. In every house I enter only for the good of the patient, he thought; my intentions are wholly benign. The glass was still in his hand when she came back out. He swirled it, as if to release the aroma, and took a sip.

Xanthe saw his pained expression and laughed. 'It's retsina. Greek. That's pine resin dancing on your delicate palette.'

'Well, then, this is for you.' Fabrice stood and handed her back the spiked drink with a slight bow. He had to shower.

XX

The tiles were cold to her bare knees. He had closed the windows and pulled the curtains and was now circling her.

'You see: I am standing, you are on the floor; I am clothed and you are naked. That means I dominate you.'

Xanthe hung her head.

Fabrice moved one of the chairs and settled down in front of her to smoke a joint. He had not been able to give up for long.

'Fetch my lighter.'

She stood.

'You can crawl if you like.'

Xanthe looked at Fabrice sprawled on her chair, his clean dungarees and black shirt with the sleeves rolled up. For Paul she would have crawled. But not straightaway.

'You can try.' There was laughter in her voice as she walked slowly to the sofa, aware of his eyes on her arse.

Fabrice snatched the lighter and held it up for her to look at. Some tentacled alien was about to sodomise a pneumatically breasted woman.

'Cute,' Xanthe offered, and sank back to her knees

She felt at peace as she listened to him smoke over her. She observed his bare feet, the tendrils of dark hair that showed at the ankles, his neat toenails. Her stash was hidden in the pocket of her winter coat. She was sure she had not taken anything and yet a familiar lassitude was leadening her limbs.

No matter. No matter even if he took the sharp new knife they had used to divide the pizza and sliced open her throat. Paul had threatened that, and worse. Xanthe breathed deeply and calmly.

When Fabrice was done he carefully stubbed out the cigarette and sighed as he stood up.

'Do you know what these are called?' he enquired mildly as he undid his shoulder straps.

'Dungarees?' Xanthe modulated her voice to his.

'Dungarees. Yes. As worn by plumbers.'

Xanthe was looking at the floor. Her brow creased. Her plumber wore jeans.

'They remind me that I am a working man,' Fabrice continued. He stepped out of his trousers and underwear, unbuttoned his shirt, and placed everything neatly on a chair.

He planted himself in front of her and laid a hand on her head. Xanthe wondered if he was going to grab fistfuls of her hair. Paul had loved that, yanking her neck back so violently that her eyes bulged and she could hardly catch her breath. This felt more like a papal blessing.

Fabrice guided her towards his swollen cock. Xanthe closed her eyes and took the entire length of him in her mouth. She measured his girth with her moist lips. Slowly she withdrew, warmly massaging his length. Her hands hung at her sides. She wanted to cup his balls. She wanted to give him pleasure. Paul had hated her touching him there.

She had done it once, a long time ago when she was young, and he had secured her arms behind her back with a belt so forcefully she had pulled a muscle in her shoulder.

Xanthe's hand crept to Fabrice's thigh. With her tongue she plucked his fraenum. He eased the tip of his cock against the back of her throat. They kept a steady loving rhythm and when she began to work on his head, he withdrew.

Xanthe looked up, surprised.

'I think the bedroom would be more comfortable.' He took her hand and helped her to her feet. 'Lead the way.'

They stood, two naked dishonest people, as the black sun of midnight made their soft skin shimmer. Unable to resist the impulse, Xanthe laid her head on his shoulder. Her hair fell across his back. He let her rest there, temporarily havened. She stroked the ink that patterned his bicep. He traced the rays of his tattoo from her nape to the base of her spine.

The Greater Work. He had never had a ten, but he lived in hope. Fabrice had never looked into the eyes of a woman he had destroyed so utterly that she could no longer summon the word 'I'.

'To bed,' Xanthe murmured. He followed her. They were holding hands. She opened the door of her bedroom and he was surprised by what he saw. This room was the antithesis of the white box next door. The whole had a womb-like quality. It was small and furnished in shades of red – vermilion curtains, scarlet bed linen, pink rugs on the floor. An orange lamp cast a bloody glow. One piece of furniture took up most of the space. 'I like my bed,' Xanthe said, to herself.

Fabrice had stopped on the threshold.

'You can come in,' she offered without needing to be asked.

She sat on the edge of the mattress. He pushed her backwards and stood over her. She gazed up at him with tranquil, dilated pupils. Roughly he pulled one of her legs over his shoulder, hoisted her towards his mouth and began to bite her cunt. He was surprised to find she was so wet. He worked her with his tongue, probing and teasing and never releasing his iron grip on her ankle. She flung her arms backwards and crossed them at the wrist.

Fabrice's jaw began to ache. He seized her other leg and grappled her towards the bottom of the bed. The top of her head was jammed against the pine frame. Getting onto the mattress, he folded her over and splayed her feet his arms-width apart so that her arse and cunt were raised and open to him.

Sometimes they protested against the indignity of this position: too proud. Well, he taught them. Fabrice looked down at her.

'You would let me enter you without a condom?'

Xanthe did not respond. She thought she was dreaming. She was keen to see what would happen next.

Fabrice let out a hiss of irritation, released his hold and padded out to fetch condoms from his wallet. When he returned she was curled like a foetus, still at the bottom of the bed.

Harshly he returned her to her former position and began to pile into her. She was silent. Her eyes were closed. Fabrice began to grunt. He could feel the taut muscles of her thighs as he kept a firm grasp on her ankles. Pounding her like this was tiring, so he alternated deep hard thrusts with smaller movements, playing the tip of his cock against her inflamed lips.

'Stop. Stop, please.'

Fabrice halted a moment and searched for her face in its scraggy mess of hair.

But it was not what he thought.

His smell, his cock, the way he held her: it was all so different from Paul. Xanthe was about to come and she was not alone and she was terrified.

Fabrice released her legs. They stretched out next to each other. He groped for her cunt and began to circle her clitoris with his fingertips. Xanthe twisted her head so that her face was hidden from him. He wanted to enter her again. He pulled her onto her side, guided her upper leg over his hip and thrust into her.

Xanthe gasped. He knew she was about to come.

'I want to give you pleasure,' he whispered in her ear. 'I want to give you more pleasure than you have ever experienced in your life before.'

Xanthe was shaking her head desperately.

'Pleasure, Xanthe,' Fabrice wheedled. 'We have all night. For your pleasure.' Very slowly he moved inside of her, his right hand lying softly on her breast.

'No,' Xanthe murmured. No. No. No. Nobody listened. Nobody saw.

Fabrice was perplexed. She was saying no to her own orgasm. Not many did that. As requested he withdrew and thoughtfully took her nipple in his mouth. They lay awhile and dozed.

Must be like a well-trained dog, he concluded. Accordingly, he coaxed her onto all fours next to the lamp and wandered off to the bathroom. She waited in that position. He examined her buttocks, the backs of her thighs. No scars, as far as he could see. He stood over her and grabbed a handful of her hair, yanking her head back. She remained impassive. Paul's obedient little bitch. Mine now, Fabrice gloated.

Finally he switched off the light, but he kept on waking, hungry for the taste of her. He placed a pillow under her hips, raising her sweet cunt to his avid mouth. He was conscious of the stubble bristling on his chin, which he rubbed against the tender skin of her inner thighs until he thought he tasted blood. She moaned sleepily, squirmed a bit, aware of his tongue lapping her to pleasure.

But now he knew. She had given him a weapon to use against her, a weapon more effective than the Sabatier on the table next door. She was so alone it was killing her. Several times he sensed her body stiffen on the brink of a volcanic orgasm and he would stop and listen to the sound of their breathing return to normal in the cold dawn. He wanted to hold her tight, folded her to him as they tried to rest, each tense with the other's desire. As soon as she saw he was asleep, Xanthe slipped away to the sofa.

Birds began to chitter outside.

'I'm sorry. I couldn't sleep,' she apologised when he appeared above her.

Wordlessly, although he knew he was taking a risk, Fabrice got Xanthe back onto her hands and knees. The tiles were bitter and uncomfortable to his own joints as he entered her from behind.

He let himself come in a flash.

Blood dripped from her nostrils and fell in sunbursts on the clean white floor.

XXI

Fabrice stood by the door. He pressed his palms together, brought his fingertips towards his forehead and made a shallow bow.

Xanthe was sitting on the sofa with a mug of coffee, enjoying watching him go.

'*Namaste*,' she replied, surprised. He had been talking about making a porn film and she was glad that the last word out of her mouth was something other than, 'No.'

Once he had gone she got up and turned the key. She dumped the pizza box in the bin and went into her bedroom. She could smell him, a blend of smoke and metal, but not unpleasant. The sheets were a palimpsest of where he had lain. Xanthe shoved everything into the washing machine, along with the towel he had used to wipe up her blood. When the drum ratcheted into its rinse cycle, she realised she must have been standing there for almost an hour.

'Getting my head clean,' she stated, and it seemed to make perfect sense.

She was late for work.

The further the RER took her away from the scenes of last night, the less real they became. Fabrice was transformed into the dark monk of a modern gothic story. Xanthe was certain she would never hear from him again. She could not tell how she felt about this. There was a black hole at the heart of her; emotions were lost in its echoing void. But the sex had been good. Fabrice had pissed over Paul. She could have come ten times over. And there was not a mark on her body.

Xanthe had her earphones in but the shriek of the train killed all other sounds. She was mouthing the words of a song, God and seven, repeatedly. The line got stuck in her head. She did not understand why until she was making the return journey at six o'clock, staring calmly out the window at the familiar blocks of flats.

In the early morning, between fucking in bed and fucking on her living-room floor, Fabrice had stood beside her and whispered, 'Seven. Seven. Seven,' over and over again. It was as if he had materialised out of her dreams. Xanthe had wanted to scream but no noise emerged. He had smoothed her brow and stroked her temples, crouched next to the sofa. He had not been Paul ripping her brutally from fitful rest. Fabrice had whispered, she remembered, and she was glad.

Looking at the other people wilting in the heat of the busy carriage, Xanthe realised what she had always known: the important thing is not to be a victim. She had chosen to stay with Paul, just as she had chosen to leave him. She had never talked about it to anyone. It would have been inexplicable. Why would any woman stay with such a brute? To answer that would mean studying the blank film of her past. She had chosen to invite Fabrice into her house, even knowing what vampires men can be. The black sun that shone on her adult life: she had chosen that too. She had willed it. Xanthe sat straighter in her seat, rubbing the back of her neck and shoulders against its graffitied upholstery. She thought she owned this black sun – the waste and pain – it did not own her.

She stopped off for gin, wine, limes, and a bag of ice. Even before she unscrewed the cap she felt intoxicated. She felt like singing. Leonard Cohen was still on the stereo from last night.

She belted out the words to 'I'm Your Man', and they seemed apt. No ego. Just a psychopathic lack at heart.

Xanthe was soon exhausted. The sheets were in a tangled wet wad on the floor in front of the windows. She stumbled into bed and woke at three with a very clear thought in her head and the phone already in her hand. She texted Fabrice: *'Decadence is not a question of number for me.'*

He took less than a minute to respond. *'The number is important for good chemistry and decadence is only a different form of restriction . . . as I would like to help you understand . . .'*

Xanthe frowned at her phone. *'Help me understand.'* She wondered whether to add a question mark but decided against it.

She drank the melted ice from the glass beside her bed.

The answer came: *'The basis of the great alchemical principle . . . Dissolve the ego like melting lead . . . and gold will appear . . .'*

Fabrice, in his plumber's dungarees, worked with the dark matter of the feminine psyche. He stripped them as efficiently as crumbling pipes are ripped from a building. Like the workman, he did not stop and feel pride over what he had done; he moved on to the next job.

XXII

A fat black fly was hurling itself repeatedly at the dusty window. Fabrice used his copy of *Le Monde diplomatique* to shoo it out the door and felt compelled to wash his hands.

He leaned on the nozzle of the soap dispenser with one elbow and the viscous white ejaculate spurted over his left palm. He thought about his film, and Yoshiko, and Xanthe, who had said bluntly, 'No.' Her refusal served only to strengthen his resolve, just as he knew where he was heading with Zairah. Her reaction to the lighter test had been precious. Fabrice grinned. He realised he would have to be patient, careful, sedulous, but that was all part of the deal. They did not know how lucky they were. He would help them understand.

With a spasm of annoyance he worked the soap into his hands. His sleeves were rolled. Methodically, as if scrubbing up for surgery, Fabrice lathered his forearms. The little hairs became claggy. He turned on the tap, leaving his sticky mark on it. Cupping his soapy hands under the jet of water he first erased the trail of filth he was leaving and next rinsed his skin. He let the cold tap run until his fingers were tingling, then he splashed his cheeks.

Fabrice tilted his head in the mirror. His face was smooth

– he lived a healthy life – but he was aware of Old Father Time, that bastard, plucking hairs from his scalp. Yoshiko was the youngest, at nineteen more than half his age. Zairah too refreshed him, her cunt the elixir of youth. He had told her he was thirty-six, thirteen years her senior. Xanthe was the oldest. Judging only by her face, he was surprised to learn that she was over thirty. He confirmed the fact to his satisfaction later, during his assessment of her body. She had said she was not worried about getting old but he knew she had to be lying. They always tried to lie to him. He could see the skin of her belly and thighs losing its elasticity, could sense her inexorable descent into middle-class middle-age. Being with him would make her feel young. Fabrice was prepared to offer her that dizzying reckless sensation like a nugget of gold. She would have to face up to her total nothingness and start all over again once he was finished with her.

Fabrice checked the ultrasonic bath, which was running as usual. This was his secret Den, his Cave. The studio reflected the workings of his mind, and he was the studio. It was not that he did not feel for them, he told himself: he did. Many times he cried as he drove into their all-too-willing flesh. They were dull as lead, that was all, and he had to work to reveal their inner shine. They were ignorant of the process – they had to be – but they could not deny its results.

In all humility Fabrice bowed his head and repeated the words of Bernard Trevisan, who had turned to alchemy when he was a teenager over five hundred years ago. Trevisan used blood in his quest for the Philosopher's Stone. He travelled the known world and yet acknowledged that the artist must expect to be in Prison a long time.

'The artist must expect to be in Prison a long time.'

As he spoke the words aloud, Fabrice looked anxiously about at his circumscribed universe – at the steel and ink, the sheets of hand-drawn designs curling at the edges – and for a moment, he was afraid. What if this was not the Prison? Fabrice accepted it as such; he embraced the monastic lifestyle, the simplicity and purity and dedication to a higher purpose. But what if? No. He was careful. He went only where he was invited. There was no point trying to force the experiment: no point in shouting when you can whisper.

The air was hot and close. Fabrice could feel the prickle of sweat on the back of his neck. He stood at the door, between the pots of bamboo that he nurtured for a long and lucky life. He inhaled the odours of the street – the car fumes and savoury smells, the pungent vapour trail of cheap perfume left behind by a couple of teenage girls walking arm in arm – and almost gagged.

He locked the door. In his bedroom, with the shutters closed, Fabrice stripped off his clothes and performed the asanas he had learned many years ago in India. He had been young then. Always searching. Sweat rolled down his back. He picked up the weights and counted under his breath as the muscles in his arms bulged and popped. Memories of his time in America, the Fake Bake tans and blinding teeth. He had not liked it there. His breath came in aggressive gusts. Salt stung his eyes and trickled over his lips. He completed the series of exercises and then started again. Repetition and purification, over and over. Sulphur, salt and mercury. Spirit, body and soul. Trinity. Unity. This was Fabrice's mantra. Eventually he dropped to the floor and lay there throbbing with the heat of his own humanity.

After showering thoroughly he lay on the bed and picked up his phone.

XXIII

Yoshiko stumbled coming out of her building. She was wearing strappy wedge-heeled sandals and had to grab at one of the scaffolding poles to prevent herself from crashing onto her knees. Good start.

She was nervous. Now they were ready to begin filming, he had agreed. She just needed to take her medical certificate round to the studio and Fabrice would talk about their shooting schedule. They did not have much time but he had hinted he would be willing to follow her to England. He was angry when she told him she had hired some pornographic DVDs from Stereorama. She did not need to prepare, not in that way, he had informed her by text.

Their relationship had become almost professional of late. They had not slept together since that one night in Yoshiko's apartment, and yet Fabrice often promised her the most incredible pleasures. Her vocabulary notebook was singularly loaded with sexual swearwords. She had never uttered them out loud but she knew about fisting and rimming and sodomy. He was inviting her into a new and exciting adult world. She spent her evenings deciphering his messages rather than revising tenses. She usually replied in pictures rather than words.

Yoshiko worked her way uphill towards rue Biot. On

virtually every street a building was being remodelled. The air was thick with dust and painful with noise. In her guidebook she had ticked off all the places she had seen. Fabrice had said he would take her to the new Cinémathèque française, where they had the robot from *Metropolis*, but she was not sure when. She had enjoyed walking with him near the Opéra Garnier but had had to take a bus tour to learn about its phantom and the lake beneath.

At the corner of rue Biot, Yoshiko stopped to buy a *pain au chocolat*, which she ate gazing at the great mural painted on the end wall of the street. It looked like it could have been an advertisement for something, but was not. Four stunted trees stretched up from the concrete, planted where another building once had been. Brushing crumbs from the front of her shirt, she walked the last few metres with her heart hammering. The shop door was closed but she could see him sitting behind the counter, immersed in a book. He was always reading or working. She did not know how he found the patience.

Yoshiko went in. Fabrice stood to greet her. She had dyed her hair back to its original colour. It hung in lustrous panes to her shoulders. She tottered towards him with her arms outstretched.

Coming out from behind the counter, Fabrice took her hands in his and used them to position her squarely in front of him. Slowly and deliberately he looked over her body. Without realising she was doing it, Yoshiko held her breath. Fabrice dropped her left hand and clasped her right in both of his. He angled the tattooed skin this way and that, admiring the sinuous perfection of his art.

'Still there,' he pronounced with a satisfied smile. It was what he always said in such circumstances.

Fabrice indicated one of the folding chairs, shifting it so that her back was to the door. He set himself directly opposite, so close that she could feel the rough fabric of his combat trousers brushing her bare knee. It was, whether or not she understood, a warning: this was war.

'You have brought something for me?' he enquired, raising one thick dark eyebrow.

Yoshiko was shaking as she unzipped her bag and dug around inside. She retrieved the sheet of paper and opened it out.

'You see?' Her voice trembled. 'No problem. HIV negative.' There was a pause. 'Ready for film. I am excited.' Then she thought of a better word. 'Hot.'

'Hot,' Fabrice repeated, looking at her feet rather than the lab report. 'In those shoes you are triple hot.'

Yoshiko relaxed and took a breath at the compliment. He saw her little toes wiggle in their leather confinement.

Fabrice's head was buzzing with ideas. In many ways, the younger the better. He was looking at an average adolescent rebellious streak that he could convert into something precious. Sexually he had next to no interest in her – she was awkward and lacked passion – but he could definitely use her. He sat back with a sigh.

'You know, Yoshiko, that this is going to be hard work?'

She nodded.

She had yet to experience a proper day's work. 'And you know that I expect you to cooperate with another friend of mine, a lady, a professional actress?'

Her face fell. Of course she had forgotten, although he had told her clearly. Once. That morning in her flat. She had thought she was going to be alone in the glory of the spotlight of his attention. Not so. Never so. Mercury, sulphur, salt. Three.

'What she look like?'

'Oh,' Fabrice waved a hand vaguely, 'a bit older than you. Pretty. Nice. You'll like her, I promise.'

Again Yoshiko nodded. She would do whatever it took to make this film. She wanted to be Fabrice's star more than she had ever wanted anything in her life. She thought of the workman outside her window – she had not seen him in ages – he would be stunned by her performance. Maybe he would even ask for her autograph. 'I have already found the location. An apartment. One hundred metres square. The bathroom – you'll love it. There's a huge round bath there. It's all decorated in yellow.' Fabrice was gazing past Yoshiko's shoulder. His mind was on Ripley: commit her to the 'gentle Fire' and what next? Actually make the film? Sell the film? Fools' gold. Better to watch her watch herself being totally humiliated. Fabrice smirked and stroked Yoshiko's knee, his middle fingertip curling behind the joint and exploring the hot tight space there.

She was still holding the laboratory report. Fabrice stopped caressing the plump crease at the back of her leg and took it from her. He looked at the heading. She had gone to a place on rue des Batignolles. He had noticed it before. He read the immunology results. Both tests for HIV had been returned negative, as she had said. There was also a record of viral hepatitis markers. All negative. Except . . .

'Yoshiko.' Fabrice spoke very slowly. His heart seemed suddenly large in his chest. It beat so forcefully he could feel it in his throat.

'What?' Her voice was sharp.

'You tested positive for hepatitis C.' HEP C, he wanted to scream, HEP FUCKING C, YOU DISEASED FUCKING CUNT.

Yoshiko nodded.

'It's a disease,' Fabrice continued, willing himself to be calm, 'a viral disease of the blood. Highly infectious.'

Yoshiko nodded again.

'Hepatitis C can cause fatigue, abdominal pain and loss of appetite. As the condition worsens you might experience muscle and joint pain, fevers and insomnia. When your liver begins to pack up you will go yellow with jaundice. Then there's the depression, headaches, and mood swings. Am I making myself clear?' Fabrice's words had an obsidian edge. 'Ultimately, hepatitis C leads to cirrhosis and liver failure. To death. Do you understand?'

She shrugged. Fabrice's hands were curled into fists, pressing the canvas of his trousers. He leaned forward so that their noses almost touched. He wanted to hit her, pound her, mash her glib stupid face and kick her out the door. But the thought of her blood on his hands . . .

'You, Yoshiko, are carrying an infectious disease,' he enunciated in a low tone, 'within you, in your body.' His mind was racing. What risks had he taken? She seemed now all teeth and nails. Repeat and repeat. Repetition. Purification. That was the way. He would have to get a test done. Straightaway. A real test.

She could see that he was annoyed. Colour had rushed to his face, settling on his cheekbones like peony petals.

'I know,' she replied. 'My mother has. Uncle also. Lots of people in Japan has hepatitis. No problem. Take drugs for a while. But I am healthy now. No problem,' she repeated, 'just hepatitis. Not AIDS.' She gazed at him.

Fabrice's expression was stony. 'Yes problem. I cannot work with you.' He stood up and moved towards the door.

'No film?' Yoshiko raised her voice. It was her turn to feel the scaly wingbeats of panic. She remained seated, twisting around in the chair so that her legs were parted. Fabrice glanced down at her inner thighs. 'No film? But you say we make great film together. I send you photos. Lots photos.'

Yoshiko reviewed the time since she had got her tattoo. Her digital camera was packed with snaps of the Eiffel Tower, Notre Dame, pavement cafés and plane trees. But the images that were burned on her memory she would never be able to show to anyone. What on earth had induced her to behave in such a stupid, undignified way? She had never done anything like that before, but she knew some of her friends did. They even made pocket money from salarymen the same age as her father. Yoshiko's eyes began to flit around the studio.

Fabrice was standing beside a pot of bamboo with his hand on the door, which remained shut because he could see the storm brewing. He bowed his head.

Yoshiko sifted frantically through the sand of the past few weeks. 'Want my photos back.' She was glaring at him, daring him to look at her. 'Want my fucking photos back, Fabrice.' It was the first time she had called him by name.

With his eyes still on the floor, which needed vacuuming, Fabrice shook his head.

'What?' She was shrill. She stood up.

'That is impossible, I'm afraid, Yoshiko,' and he showed her his empty palms.

Yoshiko saw how calm he was and it infuriated her. Her frustration ignited. She opened her mouth and Fabrice stood fast as he was blasted with a searing flow of Japanese invective. Certain words he recognised and plucked from the rest, examining them as she continued unabated. Her hands were flashing close to his face. He noticed the way the light shone on her hair, making it seem blue at the roots. She was not wearing a bra. Her nipples jiggled with her agitation.

It took several attempts. He was whispering. Eventually Yoshiko heard her name. Fabrice motioned her to come closer. She thought about it for a moment, took two steps towards him and subsided into tears.

As he stepped around her to fetch the box of Kleenex that he kept next to the chair, her tears amplified. The tissue sat like a white dove on his palm. She accepted it and commenced sniffling and honking. They both sat down again as if weary.

'No film,' she sputtered, 'but but you still see me yes? Hepatitis. Lots people has hepatitis. No problem. You use condom. No problem,' and her tiny fingers scuttled crab-like towards his lap. Fabrice was the only friend she had made in France. He was an artist. She had never known a real artist before. She did not want to be left alone again.

He should have stopped to consider his answer, but the demon of self-preservation spat out the words before Fabrice had time to censor them. 'No, Yoshiko, I think it best if we do not see each other any more. In any case, you are going to London soon. It is you who are leaving me.'

'You say you come with me. You say lots of things. You lie.'

'Yoshiko, we all lie. That is what men and women do.'

She had no answer to that. She had not lied. She had shown him a part of herself that nobody else had ever seen. It had not been easy. She remembered being sick after sending that first photo of her pussy still sweet with the memory of him in her bed. Afterwards she just wanted to give him more and more, more of what he wanted, snapshots of her secret places immortalised forever.

And he had rejected her. She was not good enough for him either.

Yoshiko shook her head.

Fabrice began to breathe more deeply. It would soon be over.

'You,' she said very firmly, staring right into his face. He was taken by surprise and had to maintain the eye contact. 'You use me.'

Fabrice leaned back in the chair. He could not get control of the grin that stretched his lips.

Yoshiko saw it. 'Yes, you use me. I pay you too much for tattoo. I know. Teacher tell me. You steal.' Indignation flipped her stilted sentences once more into a hot flood of Japanese.

When she was done, Fabrice shrugged.

She hated him then and he saw it in her eyes. She had never been treated this way before; Yoshi's perfect little tattooed princess. She was learning something about men and, Fabrice hoped, about herself.

The next word she uttered was so perfectly pronounced that it shocked them both. 'Rapist.'

'I beg your pardon?' Fabrice became very aware of his face, its features now a mask turned towards his accuser. 'You have to be careful, Yoshiko, here in France, about using words like that. Rape is a very serious crime. Accusations of rape are also a serious crime. It's called slander. You can go to prison for it.'

She was not listening to him. She had found the grain of truth and was fighting hard to keep hold of it.

'I do things with you I never do. You do things to me I not like.'

As if for the first time she saw herself clearly, her legs hoisted above her head and Fabrice fucking her like in one of those porn films. Yoshiko was ashamed. She had not asked for that.

'You get me drunk, make me do things.' In the heat of her humiliation she was casting around for someone to blame.

'I get you drunk? Yoshiko, do you mean to tell me you have been drinking alcohol every day since we met, and that you were under its influence every time you turned that cameraphone upon your body?' Fabrice mimicked shock.

'No, no.' She was confused, that was not what she meant. 'Drink at my flat. Drink. I drink but not so much. You rape me. Say no.'

'Let me see that I have understood this correctly.' Fabrice assumed a professorial tone. 'You are claiming that, at your apartment that night – our one special night together – I deliberately got you drunk and initiated sex with you to which you did not consent?'

There it was: that quizzical look. He wished he had a photograph of that.

Fabrice sighed. Yoshiko saw how sad and hurt he appeared and for a moment regretted her words. It was not the whole truth of the matter, and she knew it.

'Yoshiko, did you, or did you not, invite me into your home in the expectation that our time together would lead to sex?'

She remained mute.

'Did you?' he pressed. 'Did you ask me round to have sex with you?'

She answered in a small voice. 'Yes.'

'And did you, or did you not, carry on drinking on your own while I was in the shower?'

Yoshiko had forgotten that, but now he mentioned it she remembered: yes, he had been gone for quite a long time. She had been drinking on her own.

He could see it happening: her ego like lead melting. Without it she was defenceless. He could make her believe that night was day and black was white, if he so chose. Fabrice changed position in his chair. He leaned forwards, hands on his knees. He was getting a hard-on.

'I am older than you, Yoshiko, therefore I have more experience. It stands to reason, does it not, that I might introduce you to new sexual positions?'

Hesitantly, she nodded.

'And those sexual positions: were they pleasurable for you?'

Her eyes were rat-red with self-pity. She pictured herself moaning beneath him.

This was the moment he treasured: when they saw themselves as they truly were: nothing.

Even the street outside seemed silenced.

'Accusations of rape are a very serious offence, Yoshiko. I am prepared to overlook this because you are young and because you are unused to powerful emotions. But be warned.' He flipped the hem of her tiny skirt. 'Not all men are like me.'

The bamboo shivered the length of its cruel stalks as she slammed the door.

By Tryal then this Venom to expel I did desire;
For which I did commit his Carkass to a gentle Fire:

XXIV

In the emerald afternoon light of her apartment, Yoshiko kicked off her uncomfortable shoes and howled. There were no words for what she was feeling. She ripped off her shirt and flailed herself with her skinny arms. She hurled her textbooks and verb tables at the wall, breaking their backs. She ran to the bathroom and pulled down her skirt, almost incontinent with rage. Facing herself in the mirror above the sink she spat up a dense jade web of phlegm and turned away in disgust. She wrestled her futon onto the floor – where they had had sex – and collapsed onto it. Yoshiko's cries eventually modulated into coughing. The coughing subsided into hiccups. Then she reached for her phone.

'im at work but id rather be playing with you'
Xanthe eyed her class, heads bent to their exercise books and the present perfect tense. ('The fireman has rescued the cat. The lady has written a book. She has forgiven him.') Surreptitiously she pressed send.

Fabrice had switched off his mobile. He knew that Yoshiko would eventually exhaust herself. He washed his hands, which seemed drier than usual, and settled down with a new book on Neuro-Linguistic Programming. It had been all the rage with the used-car traders and telesales twats he

used to share a house with in California. He always suspected
they did not understand its true potential. Every now and
then he glanced at one of his *irezumi* women. Yoshiko had
been an unworthy vessel. That particular experiment was
over. His mind scuttled to Xanthe.

Late afternoon and she would be on her way home from
work. She seemed to Fabrice to be unreasonable. She
obviously drank too much. Sometimes her texts made no
sense at all. Without reason to guide her conduct, she deserved
to be led like a beast on a leash. Cynicism suited them both.

Fabrice switched on his phone. His inbox was full. He
deleted Yoshiko's messages without opening them. Having
assuaged his paranoia about contracting her disease, he
resumed a teacherly attitude. He hoped she had learned a
valuable lesson. To Xanthe he wrote, *'I have been busy all
afternoon but now my mind is on you, languid Miss X,
body covered in sweat, stomach on fire . . .'*

Jammed into the RER carriage, hair damp around her
flushed face and shirt sticking to her back, Xanthe could
not help but smile. *'i am so hot right now . . .'*

*'HOT! If you have your pretty passport ready for
debauchery then I will let myself be guided by the forces
of evil . . . you are going to love it . . .'* He wondered about
'forces of evil'. Too strong?

The train was just cresting the slope into Saint Germain,
where there was no signal. Xanthe slid her phone back into
her bag and exited the station, an automaton keeping step
with all the other automatons. Time slipped. When she
awoke it was dark. She read his latest message and laughed.

'Amateur!' She addressed the empty space beside her in

the bed. An evil man does not announce his intentions like that. An evil man, Xanthe knew, makes you love him. Then he steps back covered in your blood and reminds you that you brought all the pain and humiliation on yourself. Then he makes you thank him.

'my true face is nothing like my passport photo'

Fabrice opened the message. He was eating a late supper alone. Due to the hiatus in their exchange, her comment lacked context. It seemed to him as if she were confessing something in the dark. He pictured Xanthe sprawled loose-limbed on her red sheets. He licked his lips. She had tasted good.

'Where are you?'

Each in their separate universe, they breathed in unison.

'in bed'

'What are you doing?'

'thinking of u . . .'

'And what do you think of me?'

The rhythm was broken. Xanthe lay on her back with the phone raised in front of her face. Squinting into its hard blue eye she whispered, 'I'm thinking I neither like nor trust you but I want to fuck you right now, fabricator.'

Fabrice watched his phone, which lay beside his empty plate. Eventually a message came: '. . .' She was trying to keep him in suspense. He had been feeling calm. The anger when it flashed sometimes even took him by surprise.

'I want to come back to st germain . . .'

'i want u to fuck me under the arches near the marketplace'

He smiled then. *'I will raise your black dress to cover your face and turn you to the wall . . .'*

'the old stones will be cold to my pale bare skin . . .'
'You will feel me entering you like a rod of fire . . .'
'and i will sigh . . .'
'We will fuck and howl like dirty dogs . . .'

The phone slipped from Xanthe's fingers. Barely conscious, she conjured up her orgasm from the smooth glass phallus that slept beside her every night.

She did not read his final text until the following morning.

'Dear Xanthe, I would very much like you to take an HIV/hepatitis test . . . I will do the same, because I have the sweet intention of licking you greedily, fucking you at length and deeply from behind . . . to begin with . . . and fucking with condoms is like eating without taste . . .'

XXV

Zairah and Fabrice chose a table to the right of the bar as they walked in, with their backs to the rest of the room. The front of 3 Pièces Cuisine opened directly onto rue des Dames, in the 17th. Its faded flock wallpaper was torn in parts, exposing bare plaster. Dusty track lighting illuminated bad paintings for sale. The crazed tile floor and mismatched chairs and tables added to its mysterious air of hipness. A bossa nova version of 'Heart of Glass' was playing. Fastidiously Fabrice wiped the spotted Formica and laid an envelope in front of them.

'I've never had it done before.' Zairah leaned forward as she spoke. She did not want anyone else to hear their conversation.

'Are you scared?' Fabrice laid his hand on hers and leaned forward too, mirroring her behaviour. She was wearing a pale yellow cotton dress, which looked good against her skin. Her gold hoop earrings jerked as she shook her head.

'A little,' she acknowledged.

'It's very important these days to be sure.' Fabrice was now gently stroking her palm, his expert fingers massaging the ball of her thumb. The gentle but steady pressure, the fact that they were sitting so close . . . despite herself Zairah wanted him. She sat back.

Fabrice shook a sheaf of papers onto the table. 'Look,' he directed her.

She looked. He held up the top sheet. It resembled a page from a prescription pad, with the doctor's name and address at the top. It was dated three months ago.

'You've had a lot of tests.'

'It is necessary in my line of work.' Fabrice held the sheet steadily for her inspection.

Zairah frowned. She knew what her parents would say: what kind of man needs an AIDS test for work? Then she smiled.

'What?' he asked, following her interior monologue.

'Nothing.' Zairah had imagined Fabrice as a porn star. It fitted somehow. 'So you got this test because of work?'

Fabrice shrugged. He knew she would ask too many questions.

'What's the matter? You look sad.' She bent forward again.

'It was . . .' Fabrice kept his voice low. She leaned even closer. He could smell her Diet Coke breath. 'A situation like this, at the beginning of something that I thought was going to be great, something that could have changed our lives forever.' His eyes bored into her. Zairah maintained his gaze but shifted in her chair. 'She was . . .' And a tear formed.

'I'm sorry,' she said, grabbing his hands in hers. It was obvious he had been hurt badly in the past. She ignored the pangs of jealousy that stung like ice crystals in her lap. 'Would you like to talk about it – her?'

Nobly Fabrice shook his head. 'No. It's over. She's gone.'

He let silence reassure Zairah of that fact. He thumbed through the papers in front of them. Each sheet was identical: same headed prescription paper, same typed results. HIV negative. Hepatitis C negative. He made sure she could see; watched her eyes flick from left to right continually, taking in the message that he was tested and clean.

'I've never had an HIV test,' she repeated. 'Where should I go?'

'That's up to you,' he offered, with the impression that this was something she could decide. (Always give the mark the illusion of choice.)

'Perhaps I should see your doctor?'

Fabrice shook his head. Bad idea. The doddery old sod probably died years ago. 'He's up near the *periph*. It's not so pleasant, especially if you don't know where you're going.'

'What about my gynaecologist?'

What about him? Fabrice thought.

'Maybe I should go to her?'

He nodded. To stop the incessant questioning he lifted her hand to his face and nuzzled the fold of tender skin between thumb and forefinger.

The flicker of his tongue on her body rekindled memories of their night together.

'Are you hungry?' Fabrice had noted the way she fished the ice cubes out of her drink to gnaw on.

'Not really,' Zairah lied.

He continued to caress her captive hand. 'Of course, there is more than one kind of hunger.' His other hand snaked under the table. Zairah looked away as his fingers travelled up her thigh. She should have been embarrassed. What would people think, say, if they saw? But she let him anyway. She was starving. Every day was a battle. Only Fabrice could satisfy her: her boyfriend, the gentleman tattooist.

He whispered something. She was not sure if she had heard correctly, and could not ask him to repeat, but the blood flushed from her heart. She could feel his skin on her skin, his breath on her body. The people around them receded; the music was turned down. His confidence, his experience, the intensity of his regard and the pleasure she felt when she was with him. Fabrice was so charming. Disarming.

'Are you hungry, Zairah?' he enquired again. He had undone some of the buttons at the front of her dress. His fingertips were tracing the bony contours of her hip. He watched her fighting, hard at the heart, and knew she would lose. Like bitches on heat. It was that easy.

A great wave flooded the cave of Zairah's stomach. She was assailed. She wanted to eat, wanted to make love with Fabrice, which was even better than food. He was touching the place where the tattoo was.

'Yes,' she replied, with such ferocity that she surprised herself. 'I'm hungry. Let's eat. Where shall we go? Pizza?'

Abruptly Fabrice sat back in his chair. He enjoyed telling her that he needed to return to his flat, his expression a perfect mask of tender regret.

As he laid coins on the table to cover the bill, he added, 'Of course, for me sex with a condom is like food without taste.'

With saliva pooling at the back of her mouth, he knew she would understand.

'In a weird way, it's like a modern kind of marriage licence, isn't it?'

Fabrice nodded. The message had been passed.

XXVI

Zairah's gynaecologist frowned.

'Like dotting the *i*s and crossing the *t*s?'

Zairah nodded. It was Fabrice's phrase. He was right, of course. She had to do this before they could reach the next stage in their relationship. It sometimes felt like he was giving her little tasks to complete in order to understand her better, or to test her devotion. It was courtly, in a way. They were taking their time to get to know each other.

'And you will be needing a prescription for the contraceptive pill?' The doctor peered at the well-dressed young woman, who was clearly suffering agonies of embarrassment.

Zairah started. He had not said. 'Yes, of course.' She looked at the floor. Why hadn't they thought of that? She chastised herself for being so foolish. This whole experience was humiliating. She had even gone to a laboratory miles away in the 8th, which she had noticed recently when shopping for shoes, because no one there would know her.

The results arrived three days later. Zairah stood in her living room beside the unfinished canvas, letter in hand. She wanted to phone Fabrice but he was away all week climbing the Monte Rosa. No reception. He had said he needed to breathe pure fresh air. Apparently he often went climbing. It was how he kept in shape.

Zairah's parents had reacted coolly when she told them about her new boyfriend. They were gathered around the big glass table as usual on a Sunday night. She had described Fabrice as thirty-six years old, self-employed and an artist. Her father had started firing questions at her, fork halfway to his mouth, fragments of chicken flying all over the place. Disgusting. She could hardly bear their weekly get-togethers any more. She did not even have to try to make herself sick afterwards; her stomach was so knotted with tension. Spooning golden mounds of buttered yam onto her plate, her mother had said Fabrice sounded 'nice' – and it was a creative name – but to 'be careful'. They were both concerned about the age difference. Any man in his thirties was bound to have a past. Was that what she wanted? The ghosts of old girlfriends haunting their relationship? Zairah remembered the tear in his eye at the café. She shook her head, the food she had swallowed lying like lead weight in her gut. 'No. No ghosts.' Perhaps he could spend some of August with them down at the summer house? Perhaps.

With her blood results in her hand and the morning sun slanting through the window, Zairah wanted nothing more than to see Fabrice. She had never known a man like him. A good listener. A good lover. He was a world away from the type of guys she used to date, in their Ralph Lauren polo shirts and Gucci loafers. Zairah's skin tingled. Just thinking about Fabrice was exciting. He had seen the fire in her, the fierce determination to get what she wanted. Right now she wanted him. Her face split into a huge grin.

The letter fluttered to the floor. Zairah laid her long slim fingers against her hipbone, loving the part of herself that he had touched forever. She undid the ribbon tie of her pyjama trousers and looked down at her body. Her knees were fat. Her ankles were fat. But her stomach was perfectly empty. The indigo flames licked her skin. She remembered Fabrice's tongue, warm and probing. She had tried to wriggle away from him but he had stopped her, stilled her, reached up and stroked her breast as he teased the orgasm from her. Then he had kissed her mouth and she had hated it at first, to smell herself on him, but in his acceptance of her body Zairah too would learn to accept, learn to love. It was a gift he was giving: the gift of knowing herself.

One perfectly manicured fingertip was poised on the recently waxed apex of her pubic mound. Zairah wondered what it would feel like to masturbate in front of her open window – something else she had never done before. She became aware of the slight breeze on her naked skin. She slipped the finger between the neat folds of her flesh. She closed her eyes and grabbed the easel with her left hand. She thought of Fabrice.

They had been seeing each other for over six weeks but had only slept together once. Doubt then beset her like a blow to the back of the legs. She felt weak, tearful. Fabrice did not love her body; he hated it. Of course he did. Who could love this? Zairah looked down at herself in disgust. He thought she was carrying a deadly disease, thought she was sick. What would a man like Fabrice possibly be doing with a woman like her? He was so wise, so romantic; she was a fool. It was absurd. They were too different. And she hardly knew him. He did not talk much and sometimes when he did she had no idea what he was muttering about. He did mutter, too. That low sensual voice.

Zairah pulled up her trousers and collapsed onto the sofa. She wanted to see Fabrice, wanted to talk to him, and then everything would be all right. She needed reassurance. She needed his gentle hands on her belly. She needed him whispering close to her ear.

Even though she knew it was pointless, Zairah dialled his number. She would just leave a message. He would get it as soon as he came off the mountain. As the line switched into voicemail, her throat tightened. She looked at the blood test results lying face up on the parquet and did not know what to say.

His phone buzzed. Fabrice glanced at it on his way to water the bamboo. He saw Zairah's name displayed and smiled.

She would have to wait.

Waiting is an important part of the process.

XXVII

Xanthe allowed herself to float on the current of strangers. It was only when she washed up on the same platform as usual that she looked around and realised she was in the wrong place. She had arranged to go to Fabrice's straight after work. He had said Line 3 was easiest from Auber. She could not be bothered to change platforms and so squeezed onto the RER as far as Charles de Gaulle, where she took Line 2 instead. Place de Clichy was closest to rue Biot anyway. She wondered why he had lied. Or had he simply made a mistake?

She was conscious of a sheer veil of perspiration covering her face as she pushed against the door to the studio. Her black shirt clung damply to her tattooed back. Normally she would be in her flat by now. Clink of ice cubes in a glass. Cold bottle of beer in hand. Xanthe licked her lips. Fabrice did not drink. No booze waiting for her in his fridge.

He was with a client. Xanthe was surprised.

'Shall I come back?' There was a café on the corner. She could enjoy a chilled glass of wine while she waited for him.

'No. Sit down.' Fabrice nodded towards the hard chairs. Xanthe sat.

The customer was stretched out flat on his back. His toecaps bounced as the needle buzzed and Fabrice bent over his ribcage. Xanthe looked around her. Her eyes settled on the floorboards. She observed the gloss of the paint, the individual brush strokes, the grey drifts of dust in the joins. She noted nails, counted them, and tried to read the pattern of old scars scored in the wood. She felt for the scars; there was something poignant about them, the way they endured even under their black disguise. Her breathing came slow and regular. Her world became just black and breath.

'Black and breath,' she said out loud. The men did not hear her over the sound of the needle.

When Fabrice laid his hand on the back of her neck she jolted in her seat. His fingers dug deep into her hair, loosening the golden knot in which she had secured it for work. She looked up.

'Hello.'

'Hello, Xanthe.'

A current passed between them. Oblivious, the customer buttoned his shirt and came to the counter, where he lit a cigarette. He offered the pack to Fabrice, who took one and let it smoulder in Xanthe's face. He liked smoking other people's cigarettes the most, like Antisthenes's attitude to wine. She felt she had to say something.

'What did you have done?'

'It's not finished yet,' the man grunted, and gazed out the window.

Above her Fabrice took a long drag. He caressed the top of her head. Good dog. My bitch.

'Guy, I owe you.' The customer was reaching for his wallet. Fabrice moved so that he stood directly in front of Xanthe, blocking her view of the exchange. A wafer of notes was laid on the counter. Fabrice scooped them up and pocketed them without counting. 'Catch you again next month?'

Fabrice nodded.

Once the door had closed Fabrice said, 'He wants a great deal of work but he cannot afford to pay.'

'You do tattoos on instalment?' Xanthe laughed.

'For him, yes.'

'Who is he?'

Fabrice shrugged and turned away. The subject was no longer of interest.

As Fabrice went to make tea, Xanthe settled in the leather chair, which was still warm from the previous occupant. The steel bin nearby was full of stained tissue. She thought she could smell blood.

Xanthe closed her eyes. Sometimes, when she realised the burden on her back, it was overwhelming. This much pain was impossible to carry forever.

'Wake up,' Fabrice ordered, laying the mugs on the floor and returning Xanthe to an upright position. He was aware of the irony but today was a time for talking.

'I'm not asleep.'

He sighed to himself. She liked arguing too much. 'You have something to show me.'

It was a statement, not a question. Xanthe looked at her hands. She spread the fingers, observing the lilac ropery of

202

veins, and then turned them palm up: nothing. She had nothing to show.

Fabrice sighed again, loud enough for her to hear this time, and reached behind him. He extracted a manila envelope from among the papers on the counter and stood over her, holding it out.

Xanthe knew what was inside. He said he had already taken the test. It would be his results.

'I know, but I want to go together.'

'You are afraid. It's natural. But I can't go with you. Why don't you ask a friend?'

Xanthe snorted. There were people she worked with, people she talked to, and people she partied with, but since Paul there had been no friends. He had seen to that. He had broken that in her.

Fabrice again probed the back of her neck, that hot tender spot where the skull joins the spine. He knew. He knew she had no friends. That was one of the many things that made her perfect.

'I can't.' Xanthe's voice was hushed. She hung her head, submitting to his touch like a diffident pet.

The envelope rested in her lap. They both looked at it as Fabrice continued massaging her scalp. She began to twist in the chair. His steady touch was making her wet.

'Just take a look,' Fabrice whispered, eventually untangling his hands. He pulled up the stool, sat down and sipped his tea.

Xanthe was trembling as she undid the flap of the envelope. He helped her pull out the results.

'HIV negative, hepatitis C negative,' Xanthe read aloud

from the top sheet. It was typewritten, which struck her as odd. She thumbed through the rest of the letters. They were almost duplicates. Not carbons, but – except for the date – each report exactly resembled the one before. Who used a typewriter these days?

She nodded.

'It is normal to be scared. You have taken risks in your life – terrible risks, I imagine, and I do not blame you for it – but with me I want there to be no risk.' Of course, what Fabrice meant was: for me I want there to be no risk. Fucking the same dirty hole more than once was a source of stress that could send him into paroxysms of anxious cleansing.

Xanthe looked into his eyes. She wanted to believe him. She wanted a drink.

'OK. I'll do it as it means so much to you.' Xanthe stood. She wanted to go. The papers fell to the floor. 'But for all I know, your certificates could be fake. You could have typed them yourself, although I have no idea why.'

She was shaking so much she had to stop at the Café Wepler before taking the train to Saint Germain en Laye. She drank two glasses of wine and mindlessly chewed the olives the waiter placed in front of her.

It was a game they were playing. She was certain of that. But whatever Fabrice was, he was not Paul, and she did not have another eight years to give. In fact, Xanthe had nothing.

It was dark by the time she got back. Xanthe smoked a cigarette at the window and got into bed. She was tired.

She was asleep even as she raised the pill to her lips. Outside on the wall where she had stood was a black mark. She had taken to stubbing her cigarettes out in the sign of a cross, believing that hers was a plague house.

XXVIII

Zairah looked at Fabrice standing at her door, and something inside her flipped, probably her heart.

'You're wearing the dungarees again,' she commented.

He smiled and spread his arms. 'You look perfect,' he replied, resting his hands on her narrow waist as he kissed her on both cheeks. 'New?'

She grinned guiltily, her head hanging to one side. 'Of course.' She was wearing a white *broderie anglaise* skirt with a wide yellow belt and matching espadrilles. 'I went shopping this afternoon when you were probably hard at work.'

'Ah!' Fabrice pantomimed a sigh. 'Men like me: we are always working. May I come in?'

'Of course. You don't have to ask.' She hesitated to say so, as it was early days, but Zairah had even thought of giving him a key. She liked the idea that he could come to her whenever he wished.

There was a bottle of Evian and a bowl of ice studded with mint leaves on the table in the lounge. He let her fix him a drink.

'No wine?' he enquired, studying his glass.

'Oh, yes, of course, if you want some. There's an open bottle of Bourgogne Aligoté in the fridge, which is quite decent. And I've got champagne.'

They looked at each other. He could almost see the need-heated force field that surrounded her. 'Perhaps champagne, later. I may be persuaded to indulge with you.'

Zairah bowed her head as if accepting a compliment, which was exactly the effect that Fabrice had been aiming for. He ambled towards the easel. He wondered if it was the same canvas under the cloth.

'It's not very good.'

'You said that last time.' It was true: she had, and she had placed her hand in front of the picture so that he would not look at it. 'I want to see.'

Zairah hung back. She was afraid Fabrice would ridicule her. 'My mother is the artist in the family. She's had shows and everything. I'm just a dauber. Everyone agrees.'

Fabrice flipped back the cloth. It was the same painting – he had had a good look while checking out the flat the last time he was here – she had just added a bit more shading. 'You always work from a photograph?' He picked up the glossy print.

'I don't have much time, or rather, I'm a slow painter. Any still-life arrangement would have turned to dust before I got to finish it.'

'Some of the old masters managed to capture that decay and make it beautiful.'

'I know. I'm not an old master.'

'And you don't like decay?'

'Why would anyone like decay?'

'That's a good question. I don't know the answer.' His hand brushed the bib pocket of his trousers, where his phone was stashed. He was thinking of Xanthe.

Zairah came and stood beside her picture. It was not good, it was not bad, she knew, but she wanted him to say something about it.

'When I paint, I always have this feeling that what I leave behind on the canvas does not do justice to the image I have in my head,' Fabrice said.

'I know!' Zairah became animated. 'Isn't it weird? Like something gets lost in translation. I get that all the time. Sometimes it makes me despair, and I throw away all my paints, my brushes, and then a few months later I'll get the urge and have to buy everything all over again.'

Fabrice assumed a solemn air. 'Never give up, Zairah. Never give up trying.'

Her full lips parted but for a moment she was unable to speak. When the words 'thank you' escaped her, she sounded choked.

Hope is the most corrosive emotion of all; it drags you naked into the future. That Zairah would have to learn. Fabrice was more than willing to teach her.

'The painting is fine,' he muttered dismissively as he went to sit in the angle of the sofa. She failed to hear him. He leaned back against the upholstery, kicked off his shoes and crossed his legs. 'Come here.'

She did.

'Tell me about your week,' Fabrice whispered in her ear. He nibbled the plump flesh of her lobe, tasting gold.

Zairah wriggled against his lap. Her skirt spread over them both. His thumbs were pressing into the muscles at the base of her neck. It was painful, but in a pleasurable way.

She talked as he massaged her shoulders. All the petty details of her work life, her spoilt stupid friends, Sunday dinner with her parents. The words left her in a scalding gush. She felt better – lighter – to be rid of them.

Fabrice smiled. He did not need to listen. Occasionally he murmured something into the warm crook of her neck and she would repeat one random detail like he was interested. Eventually he untucked her little white shirt from the wide leather belt and his fingers found her willing skin.

'Do you mind if I smoke?'

Zairah opened her eyes. The massage had been so relaxing she was almost asleep. She leaned backwards and kissed him on the cheek. 'Of course not, but can you use the balcony?'

The balcony. Banished outside like a dog. Who did she think she was? His master? Fabrice dug a clear plastic bag and a packet of papers out of his dungarees.

'Is that what I think it is?' She was watching him keenly.

'That depends on what you think it is. Do you want some?'

Zairah shook her head. 'Can't. Because of the asthma.'

'Then perhaps I should pour you a glass of wine?'

Zairah was worrying about the smell of marijuana circulating over the courtyard as Fabrice went to the fridge. 'You stay there,' he ordered. She remained seated.

In the kitchen he removed the cork from the champagne bottle, tipped the powdered Rohypnol into the bottom of a crystal flute and shook the cocktail. He returned to her.

'What are we celebrating?' She had heard the pop.

Fabrice shrugged and began to roll a cigarette.

'How about us?'

He nodded, licking the paper to make the final seal. 'Us.' The lighter scraped. She saw he was still using that obscene one with the naked woman on. He noted her expression of disgust and could barely keep from giggling. So much ego . . . It was laughable.

She did not follow him outside when he went to smoke his joint. She did not – could not – approve of taking illegal drugs. Zairah sipped her champagne and said nothing. Fabrice was here with her and she could only feel glad. Eventually he came back in. Without realising, she had drained her glass.

'Did you enjoy that?' Her voice was high and tight.

Fabrice said nothing. He advanced. Standing over her, he unbuttoned her blouse and removed it. Fumbling with the buckle, he also took off her belt and threw it to one side. It landed with a clatter on the polished wooden floor. 'Take off your skirt.'

He seemed so serious. Zairah's hands were trembling as she unzipped the skirt. She stood up but he did not move to give her more space, so she had to bend awkwardly to slip it off. He took it from her – the fabric was warm – rolled it carelessly into a ball and lobbed it over the back of the sofa.

'The underwear, too.'

It was La Perla. She had thought it would please him but he hardly noticed. The inelegant tribal tattoo flashed out from behind a taut scrap of ivory silk. They were standing so close their breath mingled. He smelled like deep water. He was trying not to inhale. Her perfume was nerve gas, a toxic cloud with which she tried to disguise and protect herself.

Zairah reached behind her back and unhooked the bra. As she did so her chest pushed forward. Fabrice ignored it. His eyes were drilling into her face, scrutinising her every expression. He could see how much she had changed already. There were no murmured complaints or deferments. She was revealing her body to him as he had asked. She was making progress. They both were, therefore. She dropped her bra on the cushions behind her and ducked to pull down her thong. Their feet remained a few centimetres apart.

She stood. Waiting.

Fabrice laid his hands on her head. Her hair was so short, too short; it did not offer him the sensation he was craving. He pressed against her skull. He imagined her brain like eggs cracked into a pan. His fingertips travelled the ridges and contours that protected her personality, her memories, her sense of self. He pictured his increasingly impassioned touch scrambling the soft mess within. His thumbs followed her hairline down behind her ears; they found the delicious hollow at the base of her throat.

Zairah's eyes were closed and she was swaying. Fabrice bent his face to hers, not touching, but so close that he could feel her warmth. His hands circled her delicate neck. She remained slack in his grasp. He applied light but definite pressure. It was as if she were made out of wax. He increased the pressure. Her lashes batted against her lightly freckled cheekbones but her slender arms hung loosely at her sides. He could strangle her now and she was too stupid to put up a fight. Fabrice marvelled at his self-control. How they tested him. All he suffered for their benefit.

'Zairah, you are now ready for magic and liberation,' he breathed. More distinctly he said, 'We need to take a shower,' and pushed her towards her pristine bathroom with a firm hand on her nape.

The sound of water running woke Zairah up a bit. She stood where he had told her to and watched him undress, carefully laying his clothes on a chair. She reached out to touch the tattoo on his bicep. Fabrice looked down at her hand on him, smiled, and lifted her fingers to his mouth to kiss.

'Clean in body and mind,' he stated as he stepped under the jets.

Zairah gazed, fascinated, as the pure water trickled down his golden skin. She was light compared to other Martinicans; her mother showed more in her hair and eyes. She and Fabrice were almost the same colour. He squeezed gel into his hands and began to soap his armpits and chest. He had a powerful chest. She liked his body. He took more soap. The bathroom was beginning to smell like crushed mangoes. Watching Zairah watching him, Fabrice began to lather his genitals. The tip of her tongue flicked her upper lip. She took a small step forward.

'Your turn.' Fabrice pulled her into the shower. Water was pouring all over the floor.

He positioned her with her back to him, facing the showerhead. He began by soaping her shoulders then running his hands in firm, fluid strokes the length of her spine. He brushed her sides from hip to armpit. When he reached around to caress her breasts she moaned and leaned against him. When his fingers found the wet slit of her cunt she ground her buttocks into his groin.

Zairah was twisting her head. She wanted to turn around and kiss him. His hardened cock was nuzzling against the small of her back. She wanted him inside of her. It would be all right, since the trip to the gynaecologist. She turned her face the other way, water running into her eyes.

Fabrice wrapped his arms around her waist. He pressed his lips to the side of her neck and they stood there, new baptised. Craning around her, he reached for the shower gel again and poured some into his right hand. With his left arm still clamping her body in place, Fabrice slipped his soapy fingers between her legs from behind. He played with the swollen bud of her clitoris, his thumb resting as if by accident on the tight kiss of her anus.

Zairah was overcome. Fabrice had the power to entrance her. She had never made love in her shower before. She would never have dared, and neither would her former partners. She clasped her hands behind her neck and stretched her body against his. In this moment she loved herself, every imperfect fold and curve, because he so obviously loved her. If not, why would he give her so much pleasure?

They both sensed her climax coming. Water thundered against the porcelain tray. With one hand she gripped the hairy arm about her waist; her other hand flapped uselessly against his muscled thigh. Her knees weakened. He was supporting more of her bony weight.

He felt her vulva contract like a bloody anemone he had once poked his finger into on the beach as a kid. Deftly, swiftly, he applied pressure with his thumb. It slipped, obscenely thick, inside of her.

Zairah's eyes popped open. Her muscles stiffened. She let out a sound. It could have been outrage. It could have been joy. He was doing something filthy. To her. And she was having the most powerful orgasm of her life.

Fabrice did not let her go. His slippery fingers explored her arse, which pulsed and dilated at his touch. One finger. Two. She hung slackly in front of him. Three? She was a dead weight. He whispered feverishly against her neck. Perhaps he was praying, repeating ritualistic words over and over in the hope of salvation.

The water began to turn cold.

He wrapped her in a bath towel, pinning her arms to her sides, and drove her towards the bedroom. She was stumbling. She fell asleep instantly, her lips parted, her breath coming in sweet, deep gusts. Fabrice looked at her fondly. Then he pottered about her flat for a bit, letting her rest. He found the spare set of keys in the kitchen drawer and tried the weight of them in his clean, clean hands. He rifled through the cupboards and arranged various snacks in lacquer bowls. The open bottle of Piper-Heidsieck was still in the fridge. He sniffed it disdainfully.

'In honour of our special night I have decided to take a chance,' he announced as he returned to the bedroom carrying a loaded tray. He had poured two glasses of champagne. A caramel smear of lipstick was visible on the rim of one.

Zairah shifted under the covers.

'Wake up sleepyhead,' he commanded.

In a voice that seemed to travel over a great distance she

replied, 'I am awake,' and sat up. He passed Zairah her glass. The lamps were still lit outside, illuminating the four corners of the courtyard. The silent bedroom looked moon-silvered.

'To new experiences,' he toasted.

'New experiences,' she echoed, although the words were empty. Her eyes were unable to focus. The glass swayed but did not approach her lips.

'Eat something,' Fabrice said, holding a bowl of tiny, Roquefort-stuffed crackers under her nose. Her cupboards were full of unopened items like this: high salt, high fat, overpriced junk in foil sachets created by NASA rather than people who actually cared about food.

Zairah's stomach was hollow hungry. She snatched a savoury bite. And another. And another. Fabrice watched, grinning broadly. All the empty snack packets would get her in the morning, even if the arse-fucking didn't. She emptied out the bowl. The salt had made her thirsty so she drained her champagne.

'Well done.' He placed the dishes on the floor, clasped both her hands and let his lips graze her knuckles. 'May I stay the night?'

Even in her addled state Zairah thought this was a stupid question. 'Of course. Please.'

He fixed her with his serious brown eyes. 'It's just that . . .' He let his voice trail into the darkness. Her arms hung limply where he held her hands level with his heart. 'Zairah, as you can appreciate, I am not yet fully satisfied. I want you. I want you very much. You are my queen. May I stay? Do you give your permission?'

She nodded. 'Yes,' she said, and peeled back the sheet for him to slip into bed beside her.

'I will just take these things back to the kitchen.'

Zairah smiled to herself. He was such a tidy person. Just like her. She rolled onto her side and was asleep again before he returned.

XXIX

It was three o'clock in the morning. Fabrice had poured away his untouched glass of flat champagne and smoked a joint instead, stubbing it out in one of the pretty lacquer bowls.

He was freeing her. Fuck the diet. Fuck being a good daughter. Fuck being a nice girl. He was fucking freeing her and she should thank him for it. The magic was that he cared so much.

Fabrice got into bed. He could see the bones of her shoulder hunched against him. She did not stir even as the tube of lubricant made a farting sound as he globbed some onto his fingers.

He yanked the sheet off them both and insinuated his hand between her buttocks. He worked the lube around the rosy bud, which he found so fascinating. She began to kick against him, rather in pleasure or play than resistance. Fabrice massaged more lube onto his colossal erection. He rolled her onto her stomach and lay on top of her, taking some of his weight on his arms. She turned her face into his bicep, appeared to kiss the tattoo straining there.

'No.'

Her voice was infinitesimally small. Hesitant.

'No,' Fabrice whispered close to her ear. 'You know you don't mean no, don't you?' He pulled away from her, running the tip of his cock up and down the dip of her lower back. 'Mmmmm,' he coaxed, 'that's good, isn't it?'

Beneath him she nodded into the pillow.

'I am just going to rub against your back for a bit. That's OK, isn't it?'

Silence.

'Zairah. My queen. You want to give me pleasure like I've given you pleasure, don't you?'

Silence. Then, ever so quietly, 'Yes.'

She felt the insistent stroke on her skin, which was becoming somehow electrified. She began to twitch and jolt. Fabrice edged between her buttocks. She was wetter than she had ever been in her life before.

'Say yes, Zairah.'

She could feel the tip of his cock pressed against her anus.

'Please say yes. It would mean so much to me if you just say yes. Say yes please.'

The gentle yet steady pressure caused her to open under him. She wanted him inside her. She wanted to feel pleasure, the same pleasure she had felt in the shower, which was volcanic in its intensity, utterly life-changing. She pushed up onto her elbows, perspiration bathing her face.

'Yes,' she said and even as the word was out she regretted it and her muscles contracted.

'Say yes, please,' Fabrice directed, the tip of his cock boring into her. He would wait. He could wait. He waited as she gradually opened to him, a ripe and stinking flower.

'Yes. Please.'

He might even forget his lighter tomorrow; leave it on her table as a happy souvenir.

XXX

'And my tongue will bring you to tears of ecstasy . . .'

Xanthe held the phone unsteadily in front of her face. In her other hand the last few measures of gin slopped in the bottom of the bottle. They had been texting all evening, while she slipped in and out of consciousness. His texts promised the fuck of a lifetime: to drive her to extremes, beyond reason. She knew he was capable but . . .

Xanthe struggled to open her eyes. Her lashes were glued together. Mascara streaked her ashen cheeks. It was not even midnight yet. She was losing all sense of time. She launched herself like a silver ball towards the kitchen sink, where she poured a glass of water.

The letter was still on the table. It shone luminously against the dark background of her empty flat.

'You fucker,' Xanthe muttered, although to whom it was unclear.

She drank the water, which pooled in the cavern of her gut. She felt its sinister swirls and eddies and bashed her forehead on the corner of the cistern before hunching over the toilet to vomit.

It was not a serious injury but when she tapped out the words to Fabrice, *'my head is broken,'* it felt like the truth.

'Watch out Xanthe – I think you need to stop all the

booze . . .' He had phrased it kindly, respectfully, the way a concerned friend might. Xanthe snorted and tossed the phone from her.

Nobody had the right to tell her what to do. Not any more. What did he know, the teetotal shit? She lit a cigarette, picked up the letter and went to her open window. Holding the results in front of her face she knew what was written without having to read.

Negative.

Negative.

No HIV. No hepatitis C.

The viral screening had given her the confidence to go for a full STD check-up. Also no chlamydia. No syphilis. She knew she did not have herpes or crabs. She was clean.

The news shocked her. It was a bolt of lightning rooting her to the earth.

The sickness was all in her head.

'Forget your head. Forget my head?' Would that make her free?

Xanthe was staring at the wall outside her window, the plague cross marked on the plaster with a hundred cigarettes. For eight years she had been Paul's dirty whore. He had fucked her when he liked, how he liked; the same way he fucked all the others. She had not deluded herself about them. It had happened gradually. He was always popping out at odd hours. She accepted that. It was how he paid the rent. She never had to give him money. He would not even let her pay when they went to a café together. But the longer she stayed – the more abuse she accepted – the more driven he had been to defy her. He started coming home without showering; jammed his fingers – redolent of some other cunt – in her mouth. Eventually she listened to his tales with a quiet detachment, comforted by the thought that he always returned to sleep in their bed. She was Paul's top bitch. The rest came and went. The black sun on Xanthe's back was just an imitation of the malign force that guided him.

She had always assumed . . . No, not always . . . But she had assumed that whatever was in him was a part of her also. They were clasped together in their dizzying fall from grace. Paul, for Xanthe, had been happy death.

The blood test changed things.

The message alert beeped on her phone.

'ARE YOU FUCKING?'

She looked at the words, the capital letters, and replied, 'No, Fabrice, I am not fucking fucking.' Her voice was pure in the chill calm. She would make him wait.

She decided to run a bath. She uncorked a bottle of wine, poured a generous glass – being sick had sobered her up – and relaxed into the suds. From the other room came the sound of a whispered conversation. As if she had left the radio on. Xanthe did not strain to hear what they were saying. The hum of human voices was comforting. It helped her feel connected.

In bed with her phone Xanthe wondered what to write. There were almost no words left.

'. . . *x* . . .'

Fabrice was tired and irritable. *'What's that? A magic formula for me to recapture the time I've been wasting?'*

'No, silly,' Xanthe sighed into her hand. With her thumb she typed, *'its a kiss goodnight.'*

His reply came: *'goodnight . . . miss x'*

She was smiling as she fell asleep.

XXXI

'Joseph Roth drank himself to death here.' There was a plaque on the wall. Fabrice had looked him up.

They were sitting in the window of the Café Tournon. It was one of the few cafés in Zairah's area that Fabrice could tolerate: shabby and simple inside, with worn linoleum and fake leather benches. Although he knew that its day too would come, the inevitable renovation, ripping away the patina of history to make the place more appealing to paying customers such as Zairah.

'Who's Joseph Roth?'

He looked at her lips, plump with gloss, and felt almost nauseous. 'How many years did you spend at university?' He smiled.

She shrugged. A tiny cardigan was draped over her bare shoulders, its top button – a delicate pearly thing – done up. Thus attired any child could make believe they were a superhero. 'Was he a lawyer?'

'No.'

'Well, then. How am I supposed to know?'

Fabrice considered spinning her a line. Not an alcoholic writer but a hero of the Resistance, a man every self-respecting Frenchman and woman was in awe of. He shrugged. It was not important.

Fabrice was burning with curiosity to see how far she would go. He could not understand it but he suspected she might love him. He had held her gently through the night, whispering, 'Nine, at least a nine.' He had not had a nine for ages. She deserved it: her blood; his alien tentacle ripping her open. She had curled against his body and slept like an exhausted infant. In the morning they had made love again, and while she was in the shower he had stripped the stained sheets from her bed and stuffed them into the washing machine. She had even thanked him for that.

'I'll walk you back to your building,' Fabrice offered.

'Walk me back? You're not staying?'

'I can't. I have an early client tomorrow. I need to be ready.'

She reached across the table for his hand, stroked it thoughtfully and raised it to her cheek. 'I won't let you oversleep.'

She was trying to cajole him, to manipulate him into staying.

'I have said I can't, Zairah.'

She should have been with her parents. When Fabrice suggested they spend some time together she had accepted without hesitation, even knowing how hurt her mother would be that she was missing another meal. Zairah looked at her watch. Her father would be sliding plates into the dishwasher by now; the Sunday film would be on in the background. She was hungry. No dinner. No second serving of dessert spooned into a plastic tray for her to take home and greedily eat in bed, then throw up again later. She had thought she would be in bed with Fabrice. With Fabrice, she did not need food.

Even just holding his hand Zairah felt the charge of connection between them. He had touched her more deeply, more profoundly, than anyone else in her life. She had wondered at it for days after: the change he had wrought. Zairah had never imagined herself as the kind of girl who would . . . the sort of woman who would . . . She could not even say it to herself. She had never suspected that such pleasure were possible. And it was the pleasure she remembered: coming in the shower with the scent of mangoes, not the cold, hard, mechanical sodomy later in bed. Fabrice was her guide in a new world. She trusted him.

He extricated himself from her grip and took her face in both hands.

'What?' she asked, her perfectly plucked eyebrows tilting.

He said nothing, knowing what was expected at moments like this.

'What?' Her voice sharpened as she reared away.

Fabrice folded his hands on the tabletop. He gazed at her steadily, but dropped his head to one side so that she would not perceive him as challenging.

'Zairah, I could tell you that you are beautiful.' He watched her face fall at the conditional. He paused. 'You are beautiful.' She smiled. She had good teeth despite the issues with food. 'But that is not enough. I need to show you how beautiful you are, so that you feel it, so that you know it in every cell of your being: I am Zairah and I am a beautiful woman.'

He had begun to whisper. She leaned closer.

'Beauty shines from within, Zairah. It is a light. Men see this light, they do not see the little roll of fat on the belly or the dimpled thighs.' He pinched her playfully under the table. She jumped to feel his fingers through the flimsy fabric of her skirt. Immediately she thought: I must do more exercises for my thighs.

'I want you to see yourself as I see you, Zairah. The way I see you . . .' Hooyah! Heard Understood Acknowledged!

The coffee machine screeched in the background. A queue of cars idled at the lights nearby. The man at the next table banged down his beer glass and angrily chomped handfuls of peanuts. Zairah watched Fabrice's lips moving and as he spoke she sensed her whole world contract.

She was concentrating so hard her upper right canine nipped her lower lip.

She had been listening but she did not hear everything he said.

'Did you hear what I said?' Fabrice demanded, his voice grown loud in the almost empty room. Had she heard what he was going to do to her – humiliation after humiliation on the long road to self-discovery? The revelation that she was nothing, a cipher, so empty that he could fill her up with any shit he chose?

Zairah nodded. It was a reflex, the desire not to appear foolish.

He seemed satisfied. Fabrice stood. The bill lay on its plastic saucer between them. Until now he had always paid. It was what she expected. Zairah stood too.

'Oh!' She suddenly realised.

Fabrice strolled towards the door, turning to say goodbye

to the *patron* as Zairah produced coins from her purse. She followed him out.

The dusk air was soft as they walked towards rue Palatine. He kept his hand on the back of her neck, feeling the way her body moved under his direction through the spotless marble arcade opposite the Sénat. Crossing rue Garancière, he deliberately did not look for traffic. She stepped off the pavement into the road ahead of his outstretched arm. A moped squawked and swerved on their left.

'That was close – you should look where you're going,' Fabrice advised. Zairah was leaning against him, her breath coming in anxious puffs.

She nodded into his chest.

'Shall we circumnavigate the church?'

Zairah nodded again. She had slung her arms around his waist and was bumping awkwardly against his side. She did not want to let go of him.

At the foot of the steps leading up to the great door of Saint Sulpice, they stopped. The honour guard of beggars twitched their cups optimistically. Fabrice ignored them and turned to kiss her. His tongue in her mouth, his lips sealing hers, Zairah felt faint. She pressed her groin against his. He did not respond but continued to kiss her deeply, his fingers cradling her skull.

In due course he pulled back.

'I want to take your picture now,' he whispered as he pulled his phone from his pocket.

Zairah's eyes were black. Her lips were swollen and smeared. She was about to rub her hand over her immaculate hair but Fabrice grabbed her wrist. He kept hold of her as he raised the camera and composed his shot.

She was hot and wet for him. He wanted that to show.

'Am I beautiful, then?' Zairah asked, craning over his shoulder to take a look at the screen.

Fabrice quickly saved and closed the file.

'What do you think?'

She twirled her body like a prepubescent ballerina, one Tod's loafer planted on top of the other, ankle tilted as she swung her hips. Zairah nodded.

'Good girl.'

He entered the code for her when they reached the gate to her building.

'Are you sure you don't want to come in?' She hooked her fingers into the belt loops of his combat trousers, tugging him towards her.

Fabrice shook his head. 'Work to do.' He sounded regretful. Eventually she let go.

XXXII

Zairah had drifted off to sleep but the phone beside her bed chirruped. She reached for it with hungry hands, knowing it would be Fabrice.

'I can't stop thinking about your body . . . so correct in the café today . . . so suddenly transformed outside the church . . .'

Zairah hugged her knees to her chest. A fist of pain – hunger, desire – was jabbing her in the guts.

'So why did you go?'

In the shadowy silence of his bedroom, Fabrice deleted the irritating question. They asked so many questions. It was arrogant to assume that he would answer. He opened the picture file again. The image was blurred; he had been standing too close. Zairah's wet lips were parted. Her eyes shone. He had managed to capture that hint of the obscene in her, editing out the perfect clothes and grating, whiny voice. It was not quite what he was looking for, but it would have to do. He regretted now not keeping some of Yoshiko's little efforts. One cunt looked much the same as another.

'I have a painter friend I would like you to meet . . .' he texted Xanthe, although he did not expect an immediate reply. She usually contacted him around three o'clock in

the morning. Perhaps she went clubbing and needed to wind
down.

After his exercises Fabrice woke Zairah up again. Ignoring
her question he typed, *'Zairah remember . . . salt, sulphur,
mercury . . . THREE . . . the secret of transformation . . .'*

In her bed, head full of sleep, she could not understand.
Her thumb hovered over the keypad.

A few moments later another message arrived.

*'Zairah . . . I want to give you pleasure . . . drive you
to ecstasy . . . beyond reason . . .'*

Her breath came heavy in the fragrant room. She did not
know how to respond. His words reached her as if from a
dream, portentous. Her grip slackened on the open phone.

'Three,' she murmured into the pillow. Something slipped
snakelike under cover of her consciousness.

XXXIII

*'Xanthe remember . . . salt, sulphur, mercury . . . THREE
. . . the secret of transformation . . .'*

Xanthe was smiling. She knew for sure now it was a
game they were playing. Fabrice's texts, though full of
promises, invariably contained devices to deter the unworthy.
Porn films, anal, threesomes: she doubted he ever went
through with it, unless the girl was keen. He was not a
danger to her like Paul.

The smile faded from her face. Fabrice was handsome
and charming; he could bend women to his will. That was
the danger . . .

'It's only a game if both people know they are playing,'
Xanthe decreed. A cat in the courtyard looked up, listening.
Xanthe continued her lecture at the open window. 'If not,
it's just sadistic. And I don't like that.' Her voice became
hard. Her eyes narrowed. The cat dashed towards the
stairwell.

Xanthe lurched over to her fridge and extracted the bottle
of Old Lady's. She took a pull of gin, the empty glass waving
in her other hand.

'I don't like that at all,' she repeated threateningly. The
glass skittered in the sink, where she tossed it. 'Sadism.
Cruelty.'

Xanthe flopped face down and naked on her bed. She was singing 'Three is the Magic Number' but her neck hurt with the effort of keeping her head up and, anyway, the song reminded her of being young, summer, clubbing. Big beats. Before Paul. Big beatings.

She let the crumpled sheet press against her mouth and nostrils. It would be so easy. She was tired. She was old. Older than she had ever imagined possible. Why wait? It was a stupid idea anyway: time to die. Everything she needed was in a plastic bag beneath her pillow.

A giggle erupted from her.

'Patience is a virtue,' she quoted, heaving herself onto her back. She rested the bottle between her legs and held it there, a hard smooth implacable erection. She began to caress its cool neck, furthest away from her skin. 'I can wait. I am patient.'

Xanthe had the sense that everything was connected: Paul, the past, Fabrice, the present, the black sun that shone on her like a giant eye observing everything she did. The end of the year would be the right time, just before Christmas, red and green everywhere. It would be a storybook ending. *'(And Sylvia shot herself. She died instantly.)'* No one would get hurt. There was no one to miss her.

That gave her almost five more months.

She reached for her phone.

'You still want to play with me?' she texted in English.

'Hooyah!' Fabrice slapped the thigh of his second-hand army fatigues and pressed send.

233

XXXIV

Fabrice sat listlessly in the torpid heat. His black shirt was sticking to his armpits. His trousers grated against the hairs of his legs. He had just had a shower. He felt like he needed another. He was irritable that work was keeping him in Paris this August. Usually he would be elsewhere. The city was unbearable at this time of year. They tried to make a beach of it, dumping sand boxes, deckchairs and palm trees down by the Seine. What a joke. As if people were too stupid to notice the difference between ozone and exhaust fumes.

He opened his phone and clicked on one of several pictures of Zairah. It was very nearly touching, the way she gave herself to him, imagining they were experimenting together. Trim trim in close-up. Sitting naked, bony knees tucked under chin, brittle smile. Boyish chest bared. Fabrice wondered which image would most appeal to Xanthe. He knew she was not teaching any more. The school was shut for its annual holiday. Xanthe seemed to sleep most of the day and be up all night. She had said it helped her keep a cool head. Perhaps she was right.

Fabrice passed his hand over the sweaty stubble that covered his skull. 'Magic and liberation,' he whispered as he pressed send. A little frozen moment – Zairah kneeling up in bed clutching a white sheet in front of her – was broadcast.

The night Zairah had agreed to meet Xanthe he had made her cry. His pursuit of her pleasure had been relentless.

Fabrice's phone buzzed: a reply from Xanthe straightaway. She must have liked what she saw of his 'painter friend'. The dirty bitch. Xanthe needed next to no coaching. She had obviously seen it all before, her jaded green eyes bloodshot with booze. Fabrice opened the file.

A gothic clock tower – he recognised it from somewhere – showing just after five. In the foreground was a blurred arm, a riot of colour in motion. In perfect focus her middle finger jabbed the skyline in a gesture of defiance.

'Fuck you, Fabrice,' Yoshiko had cried in English as she sent her message. And she meant it. What a useless creep. Rape was the wrong word; she had come to accept that. But what a lying, manipulative bastard. He had taken advantage of her, her youth, her naivety. Well, Yoshiko had realised, it was the first and last time something like that was ever going to happen.

Fabrice absorbed the insult writ large on the impassive face of Big Ben. He swiftly deleted the image. However, as he sat in the silence of his studio, it continued to niggle at him. How many years did he have left to attract young girls like Yoshiko? He was acutely aware that time was a tricky sod, his implacable foe. He was getting older. He locked the door; turned away angrily, the pot-bound bamboo scratching the bare skin of his forearms. He had to take another shower. Cool water, caressing his fevered brow like a mother's hand in the night. Then more exercise, a carapace of muscle to overlay the soft mess of organs within.

Yoshiko was loving London. Paris was an old city; London was new. She saw where she had gone wrong last time. She did not take the serviced room her father had arranged for her. Instead she was staying in a hostel near Covent Garden, where she met people her age from all over the world. She worked Saturdays in an accessory store. Everyone there thought her accent was as cute as the Hello Kitty merchandise. The boss paid her in cash, which she was saving up for more tattoos: a flurry of multi-coloured butterflies over her thighs, buttocks, stomach, hip and breast. She knew exactly what she wanted this time. She would get them done when she went home at Christmas.

XXXV

'You just come here for one thing, don't you?' Xanthe screamed. Her hair was stiff with sweat. The T-shirt she had been wearing for the past three days was yellowed with stains.

Work meant that she had to sleep at night because she had to get up in the morning; she had to bathe because she had to spend all day in a stuffy room with other people; she had to stay sober some of the time because if not someone would notice and maybe ask her what was the matter, and then she would have to try to answer.

No work meant this: cloud covered sky that could have been six a.m. or six p.m. She had no idea.

The neighbours' big ginger cat had slunk over the threshold and was rolling around on her sofa displaying his belly. His presence infuriated Xanthe.

'I didn't ask you in. You're not invited here. Let a vampire into your house and you lose all your power.' She was trying to screech but as she had not spoken to anyone for days her voice had grown small. The cat bolted towards the bedroom rather than the front door, which was now closed. Xanthe followed. He leaped onto the bed and burrowed beneath the sheets.

'Fuck off! Get out of my fucking bed! It's clean!'

Xanthe felt powerless. She did not bend over and simply pick up the cat. It never occurred to her that she might do so. Instead she stood on the threshold and watched him. And as she watched him a transformation took place. Xanthe screamed at the cat to get out, leave her in peace, but she was deaf to her own entreaties. She heaped abuse on the poor beast's idiot head. She accused him of terrible things, of crimes and cruelties beyond his comprehension. She reminded him of exactly what he had done to her, not just the bruises and blood, but the damage no one could see. She would never trust, never love another human being again. He had destroyed that in her.

The words were summoned from a black hole deep inside, an inky and cankerous abyss. She spewed invective the way some people can write, a dark and powerful stream of consciousness. The cat's ears lay close to his skull; his body was hunched, ready to spring the moment he saw a chance to escape. The woman's voice was terrifying. His yellow eyes blinked. Her body, however, was perfectly still. Her arms hung at her sides. She did not look likely to hit him.

Xanthe was exhausted. She sank to her knees.

'You fucking fuck,' she hissed at the cat, who observed her crumple to the floor. She was sprawled across the doorway, barring his exit. She felt purged, peaceful. The words had to be said. She was beginning to find them, a lost script that would connect her to her pain.

The cat watched her sleep until nightfall. His stomach was empty and he wanted to go home. He jumped off the bed and approached her face. Her hair, which was spread all around her, smelled sour. He crept forward. Xanthe's lips were still working; she was still saying all the things that had remained unspoken for almost a decade. Claws retracted, he stretched out a pink velvet forepaw. Ever so gently. Gentle.

Xanthe screamed.

Gentleness scared her.

A gentle touch would tie her to this world.

They both raced towards the door, cat skittering under the sofa, Xanthe bumping into it.

'That's right. Fuck off. You're not welcome here. I live here. I live on the second floor.'

She slammed the door. It was now dark. Xanthe found her phone. There was another unreadable message from Fabrice. Her mobile belonged to another era, pre-photographic. She deleted the blank page before replying, *'dont get it.'*

Her wilful obtuseness irritated Fabrice. What was there to understand? He was sending her a picture of the woman she would fuck in front of him. '. . . *you will* . . .' He had moved his drawing board from the shop counter to the kitchen, where he was trying to work on a new design of interlocking carp. The guy who ordered it had a massive fat-slabbed back. Fabrice had taken the job out of boredom but knew that he would not enjoy it. With a soft pencil in his hand and only the whisper of its tip on paper for company, he tried to concentrate.

The air was stifling.

'. . . *hot* . . . *bored* . . .*you?*'

Xanthe wanted to play. Fabrice considered his phone and eventually put down the pencil. *'What do you propose?'*

She had a good imagination. He was willing to be entertained.

'*all windows open wide . . . bare skin . . . slightest of night breeze . . .*'

Fabrice allowed himself to enter into the narrative she was unfolding. '*And?*' he texted.

'*and my nipples stiffen like stars . . . white tiles cool under your bare feet . . .*'

He thought about it a moment before responding. '*Tiles cool as you kneel . . .*'

Xanthe was in bed, glass phallus in one hand, phone in the other. '*i take you in my mouth . . .*'

Their breathing was slow and regular. He was pacing her. She was pacing him. Although they were so far apart that they did not know it.

'*Your lipstick on my cock . . . my fists closing in your hair . . .*'

And something burst in Xanthe, a dam of loneliness and desperation. She was writhing on her bed, about to come, quick and shallow. An empty orgasm. An orgasm that left her empty. Both the phone and the phallus were flung from her as she curled into a tight ball like the cat that had so recently left.

Fabrice waited. He could tell their rhythm was broken again. '*What do you want Xanthe?*' He picked up the pencil, began making more confident marks on the page.

At first she ignored the incoming message. All the wine, the beer, the gin had been drunk. Tomorrow she would have to get up when it was daylight, take a bath, wash her hair, get dressed and go outside. It would be good for her. Summer was passing. The people she knew from work had all gone away. She was here wasting time. There would never be another summer like this one.

Xanthe took a glass of water back to bed. She swallowed a couple of pills for the pain.

'What do you want?' She read the message from Fabrice out loud. 'What do I want?' Her first answer was gin and lime and lots of ice. This, however, she did not bother to communicate. Fabrice did not drink. He would not understand. She repeated the question over to herself until it grew in significance. It seemed as if, for the first time in her life, somebody cared enough to enquire after her desires, her hopes, her secret wishes. It was a question that looked to the future.

The future.

In a daze, Xanthe's thumbs danced over the keypad: *'I WANT YES EXCESS FUCK FORGET SUNSHINE FUTURE YOU.'*

Fabrice tutted. There was no need to shout. He was a good listener. He always heard what they were trying to say. He even heard what they were trying not to say. The drawing was finished. He returned the board to the studio, washed his hands and switched off the lights.

'*Yes, excess, fuck, threesome, sodomy, wine. Three points* . . .' Seven plus three equals ten – the goal of the Greater Work.

The black sun blazed on Xanthe's back as she slept, oblivious even to dreams.

XXXVI

A chrome electric fan beat the air. The needle droned. Wiping blood from the outline of the carp, Fabrice was able to think.

So Yoshiko had taken her diseased cunt to London as if nothing had happened. That should have been him giving the finger to Big Ben; he was a citizen of the world, without borders or boundaries. She did not fuck with time; he did. His hand slipped on the sweaty back. Fabrice wished he had kept some of her pictures. Her tattoo was one of the best he had done in years, not like this abomination. The customer was grunting in distress.

'Be a man,' Fabrice mouthed as he laid his left hand on the moist mound of shoulder. Nine times out of ten men made more fuss than women anyway. 'OK?' he enquired. The body was just a slab of meat to him, a great pig carcass laid out on his chair.

Victims. Why did they have to be such victims? My daddy doesn't respect me; he doesn't listen to a word I say; all my boyfriend thinks about is sex; he doesn't understand my needs . . . I said no . . . With my mouth I said no but my body was burning with yes . . .

Dissolve the ego like melting lead and gold will appear. Truly, that was Fabrice's goal: gold. He had tried the

242

experiment over and over, had been refining his method for years. Sometimes they came close. He was hopeful about Zairah. He could fuck her any way he liked, or not fuck her at all. He remembered her prim little reaction to the lighter. Ego, for her, was not just about sex, though. She was genuinely close to her family; she loved money. Over time Fabrice was sure he could separate her from both. It might be worth the effort. They could pop into Prada, just near her apartment. He would allow her to buy him a gift. He needed a new bag.

Of course, when he got the two of them together – Zairah and Xanthe – then the magic would really begin. Fabrice imagined two lithe bodies locked in front of him, under his direction. Zairah's tan fingers parting Xanthe's cadaverous thighs. Long blonde hair contrasting with waxed pubic rectangle. One white dress, one black dress, discarded by the bed. And if they said they would allow him to film . . . Would they actually allow him to film? The gloved hand shook. Another scale went down wrong.

One way or another they would both see themselves as they really were. When you strip away family and money and self-esteem and clothes, there is nothing left but a nothing for fucking.

It was not that Fabrice hated women. He loved them, he told himself. Always had. Their natural scent, their taste, the way they opened to him, body and mind: would a misogynist notice that? He had made a life's work out of being an excellent lover. (Give a woman a good orgasm and you can snap on the leash.) But there was always something dark at the heart and they had to be made to see it. No point whining afterwards about being hurt, being drunk, being too stoned to say no, no, no. They had to take responsibility. After all, they invited him in. They were hungry for him, with his bad-boy charm. They shuddered and moaned and came with him. What happened next was up to them, how they chose to see things. The important thing was not to be a victim. Consider yourself a victim and that is exactly what you will be.

Semen was a necessary part of the experiment. It was written in the book, the *Sylva philosophorum,* the way in which base substances may be brought to lasting perfection. Is there any more base substance than a woman? Salt, mercury, sulphur: the trinity could be animated by semen. Sulphur is solar, hot, male. Mercury is lunar, changeable, female. Salt is the secret fire, a dry water that burns without flame. Fabrice was risking his dick every time he commenced his Greater Work, as the brush with Yoshiko proved. He always favoured the Wet Way over the Dry because this was thought to be the noblest method. In the Wet Way the work is carried out at body temperature and it can take a long time. He had read of another way, the Lightning Way, but for that he would have to be sure that his body was incorruptible and capable of withstanding tremendous forces. Maybe one day he would try. Enter her life like a bolt of pure destructive energy. His hand twitched on the trigger. To see the life drain out of her eyes, too drugged to wonder why she was being strangled by this stranger . . . Hooyah.

It was not that Fabrice was on a delusional quest for power. His experiments were spiritual, metaphysical, he told himself. As above, so below. He needed to fuck with their body in order to free their mind. These women who came to him with their botched tattoos: their raw confusion was written on their perfumed skin. In alchemical terms they were the *nigredo,* the black stage before any labour is undertaken.

In order to work on them he had to work on himself by cleansing, fasting, and other abstinences. No alcohol, no meat, no refined sugar; controlled ejaculation once every ten days. It was a trial that he endured alone. He knew of no other engaged in such an activity and therefore remained silent, self-employed in rue Biot, just as Magnus decreed. This was the second stage, the *albedo,* or whitening.

Both stages together – the imperfect women and his preparations to transform them – were the Lesser Work. What followed – the fucking and beyond – was the Greater Work.

The climax of the Greater Work is red, *rubedo.* He wondered at the blood that had dripped unbidden from Xanthe's nose. The sight of their blood on the sheets generally made him tender. It was the point at which he knew they were conjoined, king and queen at a chemical wedding. To continue further took all his intuition. He wanted to unite Xanthe and Zairah, to watch them snarl and snap at each other like dragons.

'Time out,' the thing beneath him snorted. A puddle of perspiration clung to the coarse hairs in the pit of his back. 'I need a fag.'

Fabrice set down the gun. His spine cracked as he stood. The two men leaned near the door together smoking, their eyes narrowed against the glare.

'My girlfriend didn't want me to do this,' the man confided.
Fabrice raised his eyebrows.
'Fuck her,' the man guffawed.
'Fuck her,' they echoed.

XXXVII

'Don't you want a truly decadent weekend? Don't you want to offer yourself to your rogue monk and his perverse assistant? Alternating deep baths, massage, licking, fucking, varied and multiple orgasms, our sweat mingling . . .'

Xanthe had nodded off with the phone in her hand and was unsure if she had already answered. When Fabrice wrote in the negative – don't you want, don't you think – her brain only ever registered the positive: I want, I think. It was confusing. The way Fabrice used words confused her. His texts flitted around her head like hummingbirds. They had not seen each other since the beginning of June. Although they communicated daily, he had come to seem unreal, priapic under his modern gothic uniform.

She was lying on the floor, bright lines sectioning her skin into tile-sized chunks.

'thank u not really,' she texted in reply. She studied the phrase on screen before pressing send. What she was trying to say was that she no longer believed in the world his words conjured up for her. There might be a threesome but it would be as real as a threesome acted on camera, her instinct told her, and how real is that?

Xanthe rubbed her back against the gritty tiles. Sometimes

she felt as if all that ink had poisoned her brain. She rolled and arched and was vividly reminded of the cat.

The answer came quick as a teenage boy: *'I knew you weren't as decadent as that . . . only words . . . as so often . . .'*

She wondered now whose idea the threesome had originally been. Surely not hers? She tried to trace its evolution. She had begun to suspect he was seeing other women that week when he was supposedly climbing. She did not care, but the way he had written about offering her – the mountain – his sweat and respect had reminded Xanthe of their night together. She remembered the concentrated look on his face, the grunts of effort. Had she written something flippant – *'u must introduce me 2 her'* – as he picked his way back down the slopes?

Xanthe's brain was still churning song lyrics like a washing machine stuck in mid-cycle. She did not want another kind of love. She shook her head to try to clear it.

Decadent.

She hated the word.

She went to the bathroom to look at her back in the mirror. As if decadent was about threesomes and sodomy. Decadence is a screaming fall, beyond words. And all falls end in the shattering of bones, and blood.

XXXVIII

Everyone else had gone away. The building was empty. Xanthe's windows were open wide and the lugubrious voice of Leonard Cohen echoed over the courtyard. The days were hot so she was naked.

She had been listening to the title track of 'I'm Your Man' for over an hour and had become lost in a reverie. A man had written that song and therefore such men existed. Was Fabrice responding to her? Was he being the kind of man he thought she wanted him to be? Another Paul, with his hands round her throat and his boot in her liquefying cunt?

The message alert sounded on her phone. Xanthe went to it gratefully, waking out of a trance.

'Hello Miss X . . . what are you doing this evening?'

It was lunchtime and Xanthe was glad she had not been drinking. She ran her tongue over her dry lips. Apart from supermarket and off-licence employees, she had spoken to no one in over three weeks.

'nothing'

She sat on the floor with the phone in her hand. Her breathing was shallow.

'Then perhaps we could attempt the fusion of salt, mercury and sulphur . . . look at it this way . . . if we are inspired

. . . in a flaming triangle . . . and summer evenings in st germain are so sweet . . .'

'Fuck it!' Xanthe raised her phone in a toast as she sent the message that confirmed their meeting. Fabrice and his games were not a danger to her. What could he possibly do to harm two consenting adults? She might even have fun.

She went to the pile of clothes in her bedroom.

'Black, black, black,' Xanthe snickered.

Disregarding the need for underwear, she pulled on a dress and stuck her feet into flip flops.

'Black at the root.' She scraped her hair off her face and secured it with a wide scarf that covered the regrowth.

Lipstick. Dark glasses.

The woman in the mirror looked almost presentable.

It was a Tuesday. She had forgotten that Tuesday was market day. She wandered up and down the stalls. Her hand trailed over displays of fruit and vegetables. She inhaled the pungent scent of olives. Somebody sliced an apricot with a sharp small knife and offered her its sweet flesh to taste. Other women brushed against her bare arms as they stood in a queue for flowers. And then, a conversation about something but she could not think what.

Xanthe had left her phone to charge. There was another message from Fabrice.

'So we will be by the chateau around 9 p.m. Do you want us to come to your place or shall we have a drink first in a local taverna?'

He would probably think she had deliberately kept him waiting for an answer. Xanthe texted back the name of a bar.

She found a glass jug for the lilies she had bought. Their heavy heads drooped. Xanthe's skin was stained with pollen as she stood them in water and carried them to her bedroom. She pulled her new dress out of its bag and laid it over the end of the bed. Then she lay down to sleep.

XXXIX

'Yes . . . This evening . . . We can get a cab. You know how vile the RER is . . . That doesn't matter, it's a small price to pay . . . Something white . . . Yes, you look perfect in white . . . I don't know . . . Yes . . . One thing . . . Don't bother with underwear . . . Zairah, who's going to know? . . . Yes, I will. That's the point . . . Zairah . . . For me . . .'

Fabrice sighed as he hung up the phone. He was tense. He composed another text for Xanthe.

'And so it is that you have made a date . . . opposite the chateau, noble regard in public before animal lust in a private place . . . God Save The Queen . . .'

He was thinking of Zairah. She was his queen this evening; mercury to his sulphur, moon to his sun. He had a flash of inspiration.

'Yes . . . It's me again . . . I'm working too . . . This is important . . . I thought that moon boots would look good with your outfit . . . You know: the contrast . . . Great big boots and nothing underneath . . . Think about it . . . Don't you want to please me? . . Zairah, I want to please you . . . Moon boots . . . Please.'

He wondered what Zairah, 'my friend the painter', would make of Xanthe, 'my friend the actress'. It was a way of flattering their ego prior to its dissolution, but in truth there was only one artist among them and he was working in breath and flesh. Fabrice hoped that tonight might be his best work to date, even if they did not get as far as Xanthe's apartment. He remembered the pristine white box at the top of the red and green stairs, which contained all her dirty dreams. She might just charm Zairah.

They had to say yes, of course. They had to consent to their own fall. There was no magic otherwise.

If Zairah went along . . . If Zairah allowed Fabrice to direct Xanthe to part her thighs . . . Then God save her. His power would be absolute. He would be her sun and the stars in her sky. She would sleep when his rhythm allowed. She would be a rich seam of gold for him to mine until she lay dry as dust and exhausted. Who knows? She might even lose the will to live. Stranger things have happened.

As for Xanthe, Fabrice was certain she was fucking other men. She behaved like a bitch on heat. At the beginning she had said no to the film, so that was their ultimate goal. And an uncomfortable thought struck him.

Which done, a Wonder to the sight, but more to be rehearst;
The Toad with Colours rare through every side was pierc'd;

XL

'I know what you fucking Frenchmen are like.'

The ginger tom sat with his paws curled under his body, tail swishing. To Xanthe he seemed to nod, inviting her to continue.

'You fucking kill your queen. Off with her head.' She made a dramatic slicing gesture across her own throat. 'But losing your head, losing your head . . .' Xanthe struggled for the words that would complete her thought. She smiled. 'That'll make you free.'

She was leaving wet footprints all over the floor. The clock on her stereo told her she was going to be late, but she knew they would be late too so she felt no need to hurry. She tried to imagine what Zairah would smell like. What kind of girlfriend would Fabrice choose? Pretty. Dumb? Compliant? Xanthe pattered back to her bedroom and sniffed the lilies, which were beginning to fade already. Their sickly fragrance hung like the heat. Her brain switched track to 'Like a Virgin'. An age ago.

Xanthe sat on the edge of her bed and ran her hands over her new dress. The shop assistant had told her it brought out her eyes. They had both smiled as they studied Xanthe's reflection in the mirror. She only ever wore black and most of her clothes did not fit her any more anyway. She was wasting away. The green dress was to see things fresh, a new start – like the lilies – begin again. But when Xanthe had turned so that her back was revealed by the halter-neck top, the assistant had taken an involuntary step away from her.

The message alert sounded: three sharp pips that elicited a physical response in Xanthe. It was not that she drooled exactly. She was not one of Pavlov's dogs. Rather perhaps the human female equivalent: increased heart rate, shallow breath, dilated pupils.

'It will be delicate of you to forget my first visit between your walls . . . This evening I will step foot inside your home for the first time . . . and my hand in your hair . . . if the harmony is chromatic . . . and I don't doubt that it will be . . .'

So Fabrice wanted to begin again too.

It was dark by the time Xanthe left her building. Blue lights illuminated the worn bricks of the chateau; orange lights shone over the pavement tables. She had never noticed the bright colours before. Fabrice and Zairah were waiting for her at the bar. Xanthe went straight to them.

Zairah stood first. She towered over Xanthe, laid her slender hands hesitantly on Xanthe's shoulders, and kissed her on both cheeks.

'Hello,' the women said in unison.

Fabrice stood and also greeted Xanthe. He could hardly believe the dress she was wearing.

'What happened to your customary black?'

Xanthe shrugged. She glanced at Zairah's white muslin slip, which was being stirred by the breeze sweeping in off the terrace. 'I fancied a change. And anyway, there will always be black.' She turned her shoulder so they could see her bare back.

Fabrice nodded. He worked hard to conceal his disappointment, to quell the flames of anger that threatened to engulf them all. Colours are important in alchemy. Black, white, green, red: they are actual and symbolic. Green had been right for Yoshiko; he had even thought of Xanthe as green at the beginning. But not now. She was ruining it.

Xanthe took a chair and sat opposite the couple. She wanted to see how they looked together. Zairah began to talk. Xanthe watched her glossed lips move. She heard the words and understood them but could not always grasp their sense. Suddenly they were discussing Mickey Mouse.

'I used to be such a big Mickey fan. Mickey clock, Mickey watch, Mickey pens, I even had a Mickey tattoo – that was where Fabrice came in – but I guess you change, don't you? I used to draw him – well, Mickey and Minnie – over and over. My mother hated it. She's a real artist. My father's a lawyer, by the way. I'm following in his giant footsteps. Yes, I used to love drawing Mickey. I could draw one for you now.' Zairah reached into her bag but her hand came back to the table empty. 'There was a problem with my Mickeys, though. They always looked sad. Yes! Mickey! Sad! Can you imagine?'

Xanthe shook her head. She continued to ponder the problem of the tragic Mickeys as Zairah's monologue proceeded unabated. Fabrice stared into the middle distance.

Zairah was nervous, which always made her talk too much. She was desperate to make a good impression tonight, even though the words were punching air out of her lungs. Fabrice needed her to get on with Xanthe, for there to be good chemistry between them. It was the first time he had introduced her to one of his friends and she knew he was worried about it too. He had phoned a hundred times during the day to check on little details. It could have been annoying but it made Zairah love him all the more: like he said, they were both perfectionists. Fabrice and Xanthe had known each other for years, apparently. Been travelling together. He had warned her not to be jealous but Zairah wondered about their world. It seemed so much more adult than hers, somehow. Fabrice had stressed that he did not want Zairah to do anything she was unsure about. He was so sweet like that. He had finally found a girlfriend in whom he had confidence, he had whispered; a fierce and exceptional woman with whom he felt secure enough to confide his darkest fantasies. He had not dared to tell his ex about the threesome – the one who broke his heart – perhaps it was why they separated? A lack of openness. Zairah wanted to be as open with Fabrice as he was with her.

'How long have you two known each other?' Xanthe asked Zairah. Fabrice mastered a twitch.

'Four – almost five – months. Fabrice is a lot older than I am. My mother has a bit of a problem with that, actually. I'm twenty-three, only a baby.' Zairah laid a conciliatory hand on Fabrice's thigh. 'I don't even notice the age gap. Thirteen years. Do you think it's important? Fabrice is thirteen years older than I am. He's hardly an old man. I don't think it makes any difference.'

Xanthe looked at Fabrice. He was wearing a black shirt and waistcoat with the combat trousers. A thought clicked in her head.

'No plumber's outfit this evening?'

Fabrice blushed. He could not help it. That bitch could not possibly know, could she? Dissolve the ego . . . like melting lead . . . He turned to Zairah and explained. 'My dungarees. Xanthe likes them but they're in the wash.'

'Those things? They look ridiculous. I wish you wouldn't wear them. Most plumbers don't even wear them. At least, not the ones I've seen.'

Xanthe sensed a spark of anger from Fabrice, a little warning signal before the horrific conflagration. Zairah had criticised him in front of her. His ego was too brittle to ignore it. Xanthe experienced a sudden wave of sympathy for the woman, knowing instinctively that she was going to pay. Somehow. With a man like Fabrice, you always had to pay.

'Are you cold?' Xanthe asked. Zairah's dress was tissue-paper delicate, and the braziers had not been switched on.

Zairah shook her head and rubbed her right forearm

261

with her left hand. Paradoxically she answered, 'I'm always cold. Mum thinks it's because I should move to the island, but my work's here, my boyfriend's here.' Xanthe noticed the thick dark hairs: the bony hirsute limbs of an anorexic. Fabrice did not respond when she referred to him as her boyfriend. He was scared that any minute one of them would realise what he actually wanted to do – the humiliation and psychological torture – and start screaming. Then his game would be over.

'He had a bright idea earlier. Wanted me to wear moon boots. Moon boots! Can you believe it? In the mountains in February, yes. In Paris in August, definitely not. That's just absurd. And anyway, what does he think I am? His living doll?'

'I thought the contrast would be interesting,' Fabrice interjected.

Zairah turned to him and laid a hand on his cheek. They gazed into each other's eyes.

'My lickle lamb.' She kissed him tenderly.

Fabrice turned to Xanthe. He explained, 'She thinks I'm a bit aimless, like a sheep. Zairah works ever so hard. She makes a good living to pay for her beautiful home and lots of lovely clothes. She doesn't know how the rest of us get by.'

'You're doing what she asks you to,' Xanthe stated, with a shrug. Her head was a receiver for every nuance and detail. Zairah required a gentle boyfriend, so that was what she thought she was getting. Impressions were rushing Xanthe's brain in a flood of information. She tried to organise her thoughts. Fabrice had no intention of fucking them tonight. How did she know that? The trousers. Of course: the dungarees. He dressed as a plumber when he wanted to work with lead. They were the lead: women: base matter to be transformed. So all this was symbolic. Tonight was symbolic.

They were ready for another round of drinks and Fabrice asked to see the menu. He ordered a large pizza and a bowl of green salad. When the food came he placed the steaming Margherita in front of Zairah. He sliced the pizza, took a quarter for himself and nodded.

'Go on – eat. It looks good.'

Zairah swallowed hard. She did not want to eat in front of this other woman. Fabrice was not making Xanthe eat.

Xanthe sensed her distress. She reached over and hooked a slice of pizza.

'I can never be bothered to cook on my own. Of course, when I lived with my partner it was a different story. He liked his dinner on the table,' *and if it wasn't on the table in time then it would be up the walls or all over me.*

Zairah and Fabrice were looking at Xanthe. Her sentence hung between them, seemingly incomplete.

The pizza reminded Xanthe of something, but she could not tell why. Words came tumbling out of her mouth.

'They set fire to a million pounds. In a cave. On an island. And filmed it. I remember the orange flames.'

Zairah interrupted. Xanthe tried to explain again. 'A million quid. The KLF. You saw security. The wads of cash being unloaded from briefcases. A million pounds is a lot.

It was stacked up everywhere, great piles of it. And it doesn't burn easily. It wasn't easy to set fire to that lot.'

Fabrice leaned across and whispered a question in Zairah's ear.

Zairah replied, 'I have no idea. The IMF? I think she mentioned the IMF.' They were both bewildered.

'But they shouldn't have filmed it. If they hadn't turned it into art, then it would have been decadent, revolutionary. A million pounds. Fuck! What a fantastic waste, if only it wasn't a clip now on YouTube. True decadence is hard work. Did Van Gogh chop off his painting arm? No. He took a knife to his ear. Real decadence goes against instinct. Against our nature. Because we are hard-wired to protect ourselves. Most of us. And it's ugly. How can you make something good out of something so unspeakably ugly that even you can't bear to look at it? What people call decadence is just mucking around. They're playing. Like dressing up or wearing a mask. And you call that another kind of love.' Xanthe raised her eyebrows and looked at Zairah, believing she had asked a question.

When Zairah did not reply, Xanthe fell silent. A heavy calm suffused her. She knew what she had to do. The black sun was in her. There was no escaping. Game over. Time up. Cut!

'If you have established the principle yourself, then stick to it,' Xanthe told Fabrice. She wanted to communicate something but her head was full of quotations not thoughts. She saw him. She saw him for what he really was. Manipulator. Control freak. Fabricator. Fucker. She wondered if he saw her. She doubted it. No one could see Xanthe: Miss X. And as she told Fabrice to persevere, it was as if she were speaking to herself. She had established a principle. It had become the one illuminating idea after Paul. 'Die at the right time.' Not at the moment of his choosing, to suit him and his frustration and fury and hands round her throat, but the right time for her, Xanthe. She was the master now. *Time to die.* She was the saviour of her own lost soul.

Xanthe rubbed the back of her neck.

'Let me see,' Fabrice murmured, moving his chair towards her.

Xanthe felt his breath on her bare skin.

'Good work,' he congratulated himself, but something was not right. 'It's still there.'

Zairah's face was sour. Xanthe's tattoo was immense and beautiful. It had to be unique. How much time had they spent together on that? She must have been topless, at least. Had he asked her to pay? Whatever job Xanthe did – an actress? Really? – her salary was probably even less than Fabrice's. How could she possibly have paid for the work he had done? Zairah had always suspected she had been overcharged for her tribal, which now looked pretty ordinary in comparison. Tribal tattoos were everywhere these days. Common.

Fabrice tucked a finger inside Xanthe's dress and pulled down the top to reveal the whole of his design. With a hand flat on Xanthe's shoulder blade he turned her towards Zairah. He could tell Zairah was suffering, squirming with jealousy and self-doubt. Zairah wanted him to stop touching the dirty blonde. Fabrice was her boyfriend, after all. Then she remembered why they were there: magic and liberation. Didn't she want to be free?

Zairah was not impressed. The dark roots. Smeared lipstick. Xanthe was not what she would call finished. She might have a disease, anything. No. Zairah loved Fabrice but she could not do it. With her. Tonight. She just could not.

'What you don't see is that she was giving him her heart. Holding the still beating heart up to the sun. Like a sacrifice. But she willed the sacrifice. She wanted it.' Xanthe's voice had an unsettlingly childlike quality.

Zairah shivered and leaned into Fabrice, grabbing him and turning him towards her. Xanthe sat back in her chair and observed their hushed conversation.

'I think it's time for us to go,' he stated.

'Us.' Xanthe tried the word in her mouth but it felt strange. There was no *us*. Never had been. It was a relief. To be *us* would attach her to something in this world. She would not be able to go if she was *us*. 'Goodbye.' That felt right. It was everything she had to say.

Fabrice nudged the bill in front of Zairah, who reached into her bag to extract a credit card.

'You pay and you pay.' Xanthe tried to smile at Zairah as she spoke.

They ignored her. Zairah folded the receipt and tucked it away in her wallet. Fabrice stood and dipped his head in Xanthe's direction. Now he was sure: she was a druggie.

She hid it well – probably when she had to for work – but tonight she was all over the place and her pupils were like full stops. He suspected she knew about the Rohypnol too, and did not care. Slut. Lucky escape. Leave it at seven.

Zairah stood and bent to kiss Xanthe goodbye. She felt sorry for her. Fabrice's friend was wasted.

And White appear'd when all the sundry hues were past:
Which after being tincted Ruddy, for evermore did last.

XLI

Xanthe raised her arms. She was reaching up to clasp Zairah's shoulders. She could smell her perfume. A light, floral scent. Zairah was wearing a white dress. She was pure and innocent. Zairah rained pity on Xanthe's head, but having seen Fabrice – really seen him for what he was, a cold hard user of women – Xanthe felt sorry for Zairah. She wanted to warn her, wanted to save her eight years of pain.

Xanthe sat up straight in bed, her eyes wide and bright with the light of understanding.

'You fucker,' she whispered tenderly, 'you wondrous man.'

And now Xanthe saw what Fabrice had done for her.

'You really were making a film.'

Xanthe shook her head, amazed.

'On the twenty-third of August 2005, you made a film for me to see.'

It was three o'clock in the morning. The bag of pills was under the pillow, untouched. Xanthe gazed at the blank wall opposite her bed.

Zairah had insisted that Fabrice was older than her. She had mentioned more than once the thirteen-year age gap between them. Had she said she was twenty-three, the same age Xanthe was when she met Paul? It was too much of a coincidence. Xanthe therefore concluded that Zairah was an actress, playing a part. She had told Fabrice that Paul was thirteen years older than her. Fabrice had given Zairah the line to say so that Xanthe would see.

The whole evening was nothing more than a symbol. Sitting opposite Zairah and Fabrice, Xanthe had been watching herself as she was when she met Paul. Twenty-three and clueless. Wearing white because she was innocent. Fragments of the conversation drifted back to Xanthe. Zairah had tried to smile and be perky but on the inside she was dying; she could hardly catch her breath. She did not know. The white dress symbolised her ignorance: she did not know what this man was; she loved him even though he hurt her.

Xanthe looked at herself from across the table and down the years. She had not known. She was innocent. She was not a filthy whore fit only for kicking. She was not a stupid cunt who deserved to die a slow and painful death. She was not a self-pitying bitch who had to stand still and shut the fuck up if you know what's good for you. It was not her fault, everything that happened: that's what the white dress meant.

Seeing herself from the outside freed something terrible in Xanthe. She did not want Zairah to suffer. Enough pain.

Xanthe began to cry.

She had stopped crying years before. It had been pointless.

Tears fell in the dark, soaking her pillow.

Her eyes streamed. Her face became red. A howl of anguish grew in her chest. It escaped and tore through her hushed home, releasing more noise in its wake.

Xanthe sobbed and gasped. She wept steadily, letting the ancient pain leach out of her body. Gradually a new day dawned. Xanthe's tears continued to flow. She had never cried for herself. She had sometimes cried from physical shock in the beginning, but never for the damage that no one could see. It had happened so slowly over the years, the attrition of everything there was that made her human. Her mother, a wealthy widow, irrevocably estranged from her perversely imaginative only daughter. Xanthe's connections to friends, her independence and personality, worn away by the storm of loving Paul. Every attachment she had to life had crumbled silently into the sea.

And still Xanthe cried. From outside her bedroom window came the increasing grumble of cars. High heels like Morse code. The blur of a skateboard.

Her stomach and chest ached. Her face stung with salt.

'This is work. I'm at work.'

At eleven a.m. Xanthe decided it was time to clock off. She had put in a full eight-hour shift. She had grieved for herself and for Paul and for what they had been together, a dead baby in the bed between them, its face black and its half-formed limbs shrivelled like lily roots.

It was done. Now she could get some sleep.

XLII

Slippery glossy red. Warm tight walls. Vertiginous. A sheer drop. Plummeting downwards, something liquid greasing the slide.

Feet first. Hands in the air. Waving. Like on the helter-skelter at the end of the pier. No breath to scream, though. Exhilarating. Some force pushing.

What the fuck?

The red changes to peachy flesh tones, globs of off-white. Still something pushing. Still falling. Breath still stopped in the body.

And – ! Something onomatopoeic but no word exists. The light hurts her eyes and she is exhausted. The bed is soaked. She has been working hard. Shit and piss and sweat and tears.

Xanthe lies, safe and alone amidst her tangle of scarlet sheets. Feet first: breach birth, like the first time thirty-odd years ago.

When she wakes again she thinks it is night. The light has a navy blue quality that reminds her of old school-uniform knickers. She gets up and goes through to her living room. She can see her things – the stereo, her CDs and books, the ashtray.

'Smoking kills,' she announces.

She bursts into uncontrollable laughter. It kills, but it does not kill quickly enough. A slow and painful death.

The blow comes swift and sudden and totally unexpected, as the best ones do. She is knocked to the ground, dazed. Taking advantage of her weakness and stupidity, he grabs her by the ankles. Can't breathe. Again.

She is hanging upside-down. Her long blonde hair – the hair she chose to go with her name – sweeps the floor. There is nothing to do but submit. She wants to plead, wants to scream – 'I have no ego' – but the sentence is a paradox. Everything must go. Even the sense of words. No *I*. She feels strong hands circling her ankles, easily bearing her weight. The flesh sags from her cheeks. The hands move apart, spreading her thighs. There is nothing to do but hang there and allow the world to be inverted. Arms at full stretch. If he let go now, her brain would be annihilated on the cold, cold tiles.

Upside down. And just as suddenly, right way up and staggering. Stars are bursting in front of her eyes.

'Shooting stars.' Xanthe's head bobs as she tries to follow their trajectory. 'Make a wish. What do I want?'

Night turns into day, or maybe it is just the starlight, intensely white and bright. Before Xanthe has time to catch her breath it is dark again and she is held captive, upside-down. Upside down. Right way up. She could never do cartwheels, was never an agile kid, but her head is spinning now. Something is wrong with her world. The next time she is twirled, arse up, she begins to feel sick.

Upside down. Right way up. Nausea. Something, like a semi-digested pizza slice, locked deep in the dark of her body, is threatening to irrupt. She swallows hard, patient. If she just submits quietly, all will be well. Puking will not be tolerated. She knows that. She is sweating. If her ankles become too slick she will smash her brains out on the floor. It will be her fault.

'I'm gonna turn your world upside down,' the voice in her head declares.

The smallest of whimpers escapes and scampers away. She wants it to stop, this sickness.

Xanthe, naked, lurches around her flat, rebounding off the tight white walls that hold her like a mother should; like hers never did. She smells. There is the odour of an animal in agony. She does not mean to but she begins to plead.

'No more. Please no more.'

But there will always be more pain to bear. In her rational mind she knows that. Now she hates herself, her teeth and tongue and lips, for bringing those sentences into being.

She wrestles with herself. Not figuratively. She thrashes her arms against her sides and rakes her broken nails into the black skin on her back. She wants it gone, even though it means destroying herself in the process. She gets a knife. She digs its point into the part of the tattoo that reaches her shoulder. As she is trying to work the blade under the beautiful sun, she has an inspiration. She sees the woman, head peeled back like the top of a tin can. Xanthe carefully puts the knife back in its drawer. Aware that she has lost a lot of liquid, she pours herself a glass of water. She looks at it for a long time before she takes a drink.

Time passes, as it must, but Xanthe is unaware. Sun. Moon. Man. Woman. Fixed. Volatile. Sulphur. Mercury. Xanthe's mind skips like a stone on a lake of language. The naming of pairs soothes her. She continues until her head droops to her chest, her back leaning against the cupboard beneath the sink where she keeps her cleaning things. She leaves a bloody mark.

She wakes to a flash of lightning. She has never been struck by lightning before. She has been lucky up until now. The pain is unbelievable. Her bare feet are rooted to the floor. She has jumped up but her spine is a blasted tree. Her teeth grind. She hears them. She clutches her hands to her head. The force of the fork feels as if it has split her skull.

'The Lightning Way,' she tells herself as she crawls back to bed. 'The Lightning Way.' This is the Lightning Way to transformation: only an exceptional body can survive its exceptional force.

Xanthe jolts into consciousness. She imagines she has been talking in her sleep again, maybe screaming. She does that sometimes: screams herself awake. Not because of nightmares. She does not have nightmares. She screams at nothing. There are no words, just black in front of her face, and when she opens her mouth wide in total terror more black spews out of it.

Blue eyes. How she hates blue eyes. The blue eye of her phone is watching her now. He is watching her now. Xanthe fights to regulate her breathing. She wants to appear relaxed and normal. She does not want to draw attention to herself, particularly if he is watching her now.

With exaggerated calm she gets out of bed and decides she must act as if she is doing something normal. She is Xanthe the actress, after all. But what is normal? What in her past did she used to do that was normal?

Xanthe goes to the coffee pot. She adds water to the reservoir and slips the jug into place. She pulls out the part that holds the filter. She bends double. What she sees almost makes her puke, but not quite. The used paper filter is not brown and dry but green and purulent.

'Slut.'

She shakes her head. She does not want him to see that she keeps such a filthy house because that would make him right. She bangs the filter into the sink. The stench is overwhelming, rotten, sulphurous.

She no longer has the heart for coffee. She goes to the window, although she suspects he is watching her. That is probably him, on the top floor of the building across the way, pretending to smoke but really on surveillance. He has got the place bugged anyway. That much is obvious. She cannot even take a shit without him listening in.

'Fucking pervert,' Xanthe whispers under her breath. She has the sense that she needs to build up her courage.

She lights an American Spirit. The sky is sort of nothing coloured. Everywhere is quiet. It could be six in the morning or six in the evening. Xanthe stubs out the cigarette on the wall, as usual, but she sees as if for the first time the plague cross she has made there. Tears spring to her eyes.

'No,' she tells herself firmly, 'I'm done with crying. I put in a full day's work and it's over. I can go home now.'

She feels better. She moves to the other side of the window, away from the X. She likes leaning here. She is protected by the walls of the courtyard but can still enjoy her patch of sky with clouds trailing across it. She looks up. She looks down. Down two storeys to moss-covered cobbles. Falling. Head first. Arms outstretched. No time enough to scream. Skull smashed. Bits of bone and blood flying everywhere.

Xanthe looks at the bins, in their usual place to the left of the door to the street, and she smiles.

'To be or not to be,' she intones seriously, 'That is the question.'

And it is the central question right now.

On the top of each plastic bin – there are two of them – the number of her building is written in indelible black pen. She lives at 2B. Xanthe fetches her bag of pills. The fungus in the filter stops pulsing. She turns the hot tap on it. The stench makes her want to retch. She tips the pills out of the clear plastic bag onto her bed. On the roof opposite a crow walks. She hears its terrible claws on the aluminium. She begins popping the pills out of their packs. Blisters. Green threads and black dots swirl and separate in front of her eyes. Her face is bathed in steam as she bends to her task. The crow watches. He watches too, from his top-floor window, as disinterested as God. X marks the spot. Her thumbs are getting sore from popping all the pills. Her mouth is dry. 2B or not 2B. She takes a washing-up brush and scrubs the filter, knowing she is not a slut, not really. Symbolically, yes, perhaps, in the film of her life, but not really. She taps the filter dry on the draining board. There are so many pills. She straightens the sheet. She begins to arrange the pills. This is not life, this is art. The crow is marching up and down. He is impatient. He is waiting. I am waiting. Her hands shake as she spoons coffee into the clean filter paper. It is hot in the bedroom. It is cold in the living room with the window wide open onto the fall two storeys to the courtyard. At first she tries lines she makes a line that stretches right across her bed as wide as a man is tall and hard but the line is not right so she tries a curve a beautiful curve that swirls into a circle and there is something aboriginal in the flow of the white dots on the plain ground this is not life it is art fuck art the crow says and flaps away disgusted and Xanthe is left with her hundreds of pills as the coffee machine belches next door this is it this is what she has lived for the moment is now the black sun is smiling X is also what you sign if you do not know who you are I do not know who I am any more the lightning tore off the top of my head and everything is getting mixed up but the white pills are clear against the red sheet and then the black descends and this is perfect because Dirty wears the red of swastikaed flags.

White pills. Red sheet. Black sun.

Xanthe's mouth is dry. She swallows the brackish water beside the bed to keep her throat from closing up to protect her.

When it comes, it comes quick.

.

Black. Like a full stop. But a full stop the size of the world.

XLIII

Wake up and smell the coffee.

Wake up and smell the coffee.

'Wake up and smell the coffee.'

Xanthe's throat was raw from misuse. The words meant something both literal and symbolic. She was urging herself to start a new day in full cognizance of reality.

And, of course, there was coffee; the dark blend that she loved.

Xanthe untangled herself from the damp and filthy mess of her bed. Pills stuck to her skin like buboes. She brushed them off and shook the sheet. She would have to vacuum later. She walked through to her living room and the white tiles looked clean and bright. She poured a mug of coffee and sat on the sofa to drink it.

The phone rang.

Xanthe jumped. She must have changed the ring-tone because it sounded like her old landline in the flat with Paul.

The ringing continued.

She was not allowed to pick up. If the call was for her, he would tell her.

The ringing stopped.

The sky was blue over her neighbour's house. Fabrice

was still up there, watching. He had organised all of this to help her. Xanthe was glad she had done the right thing and not touched the telephone. Paul would be pleased. Or at least not angry when Fabrice told him.

She finished her coffee and lay down on the sofa to sleep. She was exhausted.

The phone woke her. Xanthe scrambled to get upright. That was him. Paul. Paul was calling. The moment had finally come when he would confront her with her desertion.

Fear. Paralysing.

'You deserve to die a slow and painful death.' The words were real. Someone had said them.

Xanthe was glad to black out. It happened sometimes. It was a relief.

'Wake up and smell the coffee.'

Xanthe could smell the coffee and she smiled. She sat up. The phone was on the floor beside the sofa. She looked at it. She looked at the house across the courtyard. No one was on duty. She could pick up her phone if she wanted to. She stretched out her hand. It was dirty. There was a black rime under her broken nails. She stretched out her hand as if attempting to pet a cougar. Very shaky. No sudden movements.

'The important thing is not to be a victim.' The words were real. Someone had said them. She had just said them.

Xanthe knew what she had to do. She had to call Paul and tell him. She was not a victim. She still had his numbers in the phone's address book. She selected the first: ten digits: how decadent. She read it out loud to steady her voice. She watched her thumb move over the keypad like it was no longer part of her. The thumb, a fat maggot, dialled Paul. Xanthe's breath froze. Her hand spasmed, hitting the cancel button.

Not ready. Not yet. Xanthe mastered her breathing. She took a deep, calming breath in and held it a heartbeat. Then she let the breath out to join the morning breeze. Just breathe . . . In . . . Out . . . With me . . . Xanthe felt herself becoming very relaxed, very sleepy. Sleep was good. She loved sleep. She curled up on the sofa, the phone pressed to her cheek, her respiration regular.

B.P. normal. Vital signs good.

'Paul . . . Yes . . . You know who it is . . . Why? Why? Because I've got something to say to you, you sadistic fuckwit. No. You shut up. You listen to me . . .'

Xanthe's lips were moving as she got to her feet. Her eyes were closed, the phone held to her ear. She was rehearsing in her sleep. When she had said everything she had to, she let out a sigh and lay back down.

It was night when she awoke again. There was no smell of coffee. Faint light filtered in from the courtyard. Good. She would not be a target for the snooper over the way. She concentrated on her breathing. In . . . Out . . . When she started to speak she did not want her voice to sound stupid or childish. Her words would resonate in him. Xanthe stood. She shook out the ache from her arms. She exhaled. Dialled. It was ringing.

'Hello?'

Paul. Paul's voice. She had not heard that voice for eight months.

'Who is this? Do you know what the fucking time is? What do you want?'

The day after Xanthe left, he had deleted her number from his address book and chucked what remained of her stuff in the bins. Then he had gone out and hooked up with an American tourist who had been hanging around the fountain at Place Saint-Michel allegedly waiting for friends. She was a natural blonde. He had got her drunk, taken her back to the flat, got her stoned, fucked her, emptied her wallet and turned her out in the middle of Montrouge ten minutes after the last Metro. Call that an education.

He was trying to keep a civil tone: might be business.

'Paul.'

Silence.

Xanthe pictured him, his face crumpled and cross, blue eyes shining in the intimate dark of their bedroom. She saw the knots of muscles in his arms, the stubbly fair hair. The sheet would be folded back over his hard flat belly. She saw his hand on the phone, the square fingertips and short clean nails. She saw it all, and her love for him a puny thing and stillborn.

'Xanthe, is that you, you cunt, what do you think you are doing waking me up at this time of night?'

'I have something I need to say.' Xanthe heard her own voice echo from miles away.

'Something you need to say? Who the fuck do you think I am?'

But Xanthe could not hear him; she could only hear herself growing louder and stronger.

'You miserable bitch. So you miss me, huh? You want to

come crawling back with your tail between your legs? Let me tell you what we're going to do . . .'

Paul told her. Guffawing, he described the torments she would suffer, then he hung up. Xanthe did not consciously listen. She did not notice when the line went dead. Her mouth formed the words that had gestated in the heart of her and after it was done she felt a fleeting joy.

The exhilaration did not last. A light flicked on in the other building. The tattooist stood at his top-floor window, smoking and observing, and Xanthe knew it was not over yet. She lit a cigarette too. In the middle of the night, in their separate worlds, their breath came in unison. Smoke wreathed around their heads like dragons.

'Miaou!'

Xanthe jumped. She was shocked. Her lips were moving. She wanted to form words. What came out: could it be the truth? She mewed plaintively and dropped to the floor in front of the window. She crawled backwards and forwards, rubbing her naked side against the smooth pane. She raised a paw to scratch at the glass, straining to get his attention. She could not see if Fabrice was still watching. She mewed and paced, shaking her head to clear the flies. She rolled on her back, exposing her soft stomach to the blows that would inevitably fall.

'Miaou!'

Xanthe glimpsed herself from above, as he would see her. She knew then that she had lost her mind.

Not cats but dogs fuck like dirty dogs dogs know what's what dogs are born cynics you wouldn't find a dog slave to a man but what about a bitch stupid bitch cunt whore.

Xanthe crawled naked across the white tiles, trailing her animal stench of terror. When she awoke again she knew it was time to confront her fear. She had to bark at those who displeased her.

'I know what I've got to do,' she said into her dead phone, 'I've got to face him, haven't I? And this . . .' She waved the Nokia. 'This is just a symbol of communication. It's important to connect with other people. That's what I'm telling myself.'

Xanthe's mind became distracted. She scrolled through her address book. She began calling friends, acquaintances, and former employers to tell them she loved them and she was going to be OK. She saw the calls like narrow ribbons connecting her to the world.

'You've let him in downstairs, haven't you? He couldn't possibly be upstairs. The top floors symbolise my head. He's not there. He's downstairs, like I can feel him in my guts. You've let him in. He's here.'

She was screaming. It was too much. His hands on her throat. He would surely not hold back this time. Striking the match that set fire to her bed as she slept. Tangle of sheets. Tied. An acrid smell. Pounding her head into the floor until her nose ran red.

'Just breathe . . . In . . . Out . . . With me . . .'

Xanthe struggled to get control. It is important to have control. She looked down at her body; all bruises and bones. How did that happen? She had let that happen. She was a victim. No. Not any more. When this was over she would cook a great meal and sit at the table with the radio on and the windows open, and she would savour the fresh vegetables she had chosen at the market and cooked quickly in the black wok, tossing them out, a riot of colour and goodness, onto her plate and straight to her heart.

She would. But now it was time to go downstairs. Xanthe was hyperventilating. Her vision became charred around the edges. She put a hand to her front door. She pressed on the handle. She stepped out into the red and green hall.

'Fuck!'

The stairs were worn and rough to the soles of her feet. She realised she was naked. Xanthe dashed back into her flat and put on her red silk Chinese robe, prudishly buttoning it to the neck.

She counted as she went down. Ten steps. The counting soothed her. On 'Ten,' she stood at the red door to the property below hers. The ceiling was low – not much higher than her head – and there was no bell, just the closed slot of a painted-up letterbox.

He was in there, she knew.

She tapped lightly with her fingertips.

The whole house was bugged. From over the road Fabrice was laughing at her, goading her on.

She made her hand into a loose fist and rapped three times with her knuckles on the wood.

No answer. Paul was definitely inside. He had to be. She would have to work harder to get his attention.

Xanthe tightened her fist and drummed against the door. She felt it judder in its frame. Her left hand, also balled, rose. She pounded out a rhythm that echoed through the empty building.

'Behold, you fucker,' Xanthe started to shout, 'I stand at

the door and knock. I stand at the door and knock!' She kept beating. Her right hand caught on the jagged metal edge of the letterbox and was cut open. Blood ran up her arm but she did not notice. Drops of blood splattered the floor and the moss-green walls. Xanthe continued to thump and scream until there was nothing left inside of her. He was in there, for sure. He had heard her. She did not have to see him to know. Paul was too intimidated to answer. You do not mess with lightning: you crouch low as a dog and keep out of the way. Even Fabrice would be shielding his eyes.

'Ten, nine, eight, seven, six, five, four, three, two, one . . .'

Xanthe counted backwards slowly, out loud, as she climbed the stairs to her flat.

'And you're back in the room!'

She chuckled.

XLIV

'John. Saint John.'

Silence on the other end of the line.

'I can call you that, can't I?'

'Er . . . if you want.'

Xanthe knew she did not have to explain. Fabrice had got John the Baptist from work to call her, to remind her she was not alone. John had once lost his head too and obviously survived. He would understand.

John had had a few calls and texts from people who were still away, wondering what was wrong with Xanthe. He continued, 'You're still up for it then – Rock-en-Seine? Got your ticket? What time shall I meet you?'

Xanthe racked her brain to find the appropriate number. 'Three?'

'Three's fine. OK. I'll see you then.'

He would, Xanthe knew, he would see her, for John was a good person and a saint. 'John?'

'Yeah?'

'What time is it now? I'm afraid I've lost track.'

XLV

'You would try the patience of a saint, Xanth! You know that? We're going to miss Queens of the Stone Age if you don't get a shuffle on.'

It was almost six o'clock. Xanthe had found it impossible to get out of bed. She was exhausted, but every time she fell asleep she had vivid dreams. She knelt naked in the courtyard, worshipping the midday sun. She went looking for Fabrice in Saint Germain. She had an important message for him, something about being a victim, or not being a victim. It was a game of dungeons and dragons they were playing: get this code; hold on to that key; enter this passageway; follow the cat's footprints in the concrete; bark like a dog; use the right words and the door will spring open. Fabrice had found the right words; she would too.

He had got all her friends over – even people she had not seen for years – and directed them to walk up and down the street outside her bedroom. She had watched, her eyes glistening, mouth agape. They had all played their part brilliantly. No one looked up. No one broke the reality of the scene. They were letting her know they were out there, waiting. It meant a lot to Xanthe. She was reminded just how much she would be leaving behind: all those other lives contiguous with hers. She could not bear to go now.

It was no longer the right time to die. Her life was only starting.

'Wait for me by the traffic lights.'

When she got there, alarm bells were ringing but Xanthe managed to ignore them. She would be with John. She would be safe with him.

'Put your seatbelt on,' John said, glancing across at his passenger, who looked even more shot than usual. 'Tell me, what sort of a holiday have you been having?'

She was totally wired. Everyone knew she had a drink problem, but she did her job well and was easy to work with. She had had a hard time. That much was obvious, with her dodgy boyfriend who would not even let her answer the phone. It was understandable that she had finally lost the plot. Anyone would have.

Xanthe watched the road whip away beneath them. She had the sensation of being in a play or a film. She did not want to let the cast down. They were all putting in so much effort to help her see things as they really were.

She chatted with John as they drove towards the Parc de Saint Cloud. Miraculously, he got a parking space close to the venue and they joined the hordes of people streaming towards the gates. Teenagers wearing Pixies T-shirts.

'Of course, I remember them first time round,' said John, eyeing one of the girls.

'Me too, pretty much,' Xanthe replied, and the sudden scent of lilies made her sick.

The dream feeling overtook her again. John asked if she was hungry. She did not know, could not tell him the last time she had had something to eat. He bought chips and beer and found them a place to sit. Xanthe tried to make some more calls but her phone was not working. That was just Fabrice's way of getting her to talk to the people around her. He knew she kept everyone at a distance and was encouraging her to change. She wanted to tell him she could see what he had done: all of it; his experiment turning lead into gold.

Xanthe talked. John disappeared. She wandered over the beaten grass towards the main stage. She was shivering and cold. She needed somebody's arm around her. The sky began to change. The colour faded. Something happened to the air. It became electrified. When the band walked out on stage, Xanthe held her breath . . .

Flashing lights pulses of colour red and green clashing and it hurt Xanthe's eyes to watch and her brain shrank in shock from the sides of her skull as a white fork of lightning split the tree she was hiding under and she dropped to the ground to protect herself and wondered why nobody else did but the tree remained and she reached out to touch its bark it was a survivor not a victim the opening chords and still she was unable to catch her breath because she did not want to hear any more it would be too painful perhaps they would whisper not shout no more shouting not loud quiet loud but quiet quiet quiet and then Xanthe was able to let out a deep sigh it was a miracle Frank Black was whispering whispering just for her 'Wave of Mutilation' no more mutilation she wanted to see his arms what did he know about mutilation did Van Gogh sever his painting hand no he did not this was a song this is art not life *the refuge of art* and Frank continues to whisper and Xanthe is weak with gratitude that finally everybody sees and knows like reading a book *books are where things are explained to you life is where things aren't* and she does not have to suffer her teeth clenched together or her lips prised open sickness hard as his cock down her throat and she has Fabrice to thank she recognises the opening of 'Where is My Mind' and starts laughing and there are people swaying all around her and she is part of them and they are part of her and the black sun is diminished because it shines on them all and John is back and places an arm across her shoulders and whispers in her ear are you OK and Xanthe replies yes I'm OK are you OK and it could go on all night but they are both OK and a man she does not know tucks a blanket around her because she is wearing the green sundress and she must be freezing B.P. low then Xanthe's jaw drops this is the most amazing thing anyone has ever done for her 'La La Love You' cameras swoop on the figure at the drums a man in a white short-sleeved shirt with a shit-eating grin and she recognises those beautiful brown eyes and the shaven head sweet as a monk and her brain is trying to tell her something as she watches Fabrice on the giant screens beating pounding thumping out the rhythm 'La La Love You' working on her and all the others and he looks so happy to be centre-stage beating *batteur* in French drummer in English hitting the drums and singing his head off *idiocy is singing its head off I HAVE PREVAILED!* And someone gently catches her wrist . . .

'Let her stay! Look at her! She's loving it!' John shouts at the ambulance man on the other side of Xanthe.

He is young and glad to be out of the emergency tent and at the front of the audience.

'Are you sure she hasn't taken anything?' he bellows back.

'Not while I've been with her.'

. . . 'La La Love You' he loves her enough to save her life rather she loves herself enough to save her life and Xanthe drowns in the thought that she is not going to die not yet it is not the right time not any more not with all the effort that everyone has gone to to create this glorious fiction . . .

There is a hand on her back to steady her. Xanthe whispers, 'I don't think I feel very well.' She is full of life. She has been reborn. Music continues to crash from the stage. She is weak as a baby, fragile and strong, her skull soft and split open. She sees that they are getting older, Frank and Kim, a good thing. Xanthe's head lolls against John.

'Time to go, I think,' says the ambulance man.

. . . It begins with the bass low notes that go straight to the reverberate like two fingers jammed in her cunt and Xanthe fears she will puke hunches over and dry heaves . . .

'No. I'm OK,' she says, straightening up. 'I want to hear this.'

'*Hey Paul, Hey Paul, Hey Paul, let's have a ball*' and she is smiling as she sings because she loved him and she chose that life but now she does not love him she loves herself in this moment and Xanthe is transformed . . .

Then of the Venom handled thus a Medicine I did make;
Which Venom kills, and saveth such as Venom chance to take:

XLVI

'Did the drummer look weird to you?' Xanthe was sitting up in the ambulance.

'Drummers always look weird,' replied the man who was taking care of her.

'Not weird – different? What's his name?'

'David, I think. David Love-something.'

'David?' Xanthe was disappointed. It was not the name she wanted to hear. 'What kind of a name is David for a star? Fabrice. That's a star's name.'

She pressed her palms together in front of her heart and raised her fingertips to her chin, then bowed her head.

'*Namaste*. The god in me sees and honours the god in you.'

The ambulance man applied gentle pressure to her upper arm. 'Best lie back. We'll soon be there.'

'Is it OK if I make a call?'

'Not yet. You'll have to wait until we arrive.'

Xanthe nodded. There was time. She could wait.

XLVI

A silver thread of perspiration worked its way down Fabrice's neck. He had performed the asanas until his body caught fire and his breath was a living thing in the room with him. He leaped upright and went to look at himself in the mirror. He inhaled . . . In . . . and held it. Could it be that his midsection was thickening? Time, like bloody Big Ben, looming over him. The breath came out and with it his anger. He went to the phone on his bed.

'Zairah, I can't make it tonight – duty calls – you do understand, don't you?'

Zairah was going to be cooking supper. She had been texting him all day with updates on the baby aubergines she had found, the buffalo mozzarella, the fragrant green fistfuls of fresh basil.

Fabrice went to shower. She had not replied by the time he returned to his bedroom.

It was still early. He rubbed his biceps. Could it be that the skin was slackening? Fuck Yoshiko. Diseased cunt. Fuck her youth.

Fabrice flung himself down on the bare floor and repeated his exercises. He took another shower, letting the cold jets soak him like a dirty dog. Who was that slut who had called him obsessive-compulsive? The accusation remained, even though the face and name to which it was attached had long since disappeared. He was tingling. He hopped around his bedroom, gathering his clothes.

He never brought women back here. It was just an empty shell. He always suspected that if he let them through the green door they would see what was beyond as a reflection of him, just as he read the music on their shelves and the food in their cupboards.

The shutters were drawn, the window wide open, but no breeze came from the street. Sweat broke out through Fabrice's pores. He settled to his breathing, sitting cross-legged on the ancient linoleum.

In . . . Out . . .

Repetition and purification.

It was sacred work that he was engaged in. They did not understand, the brainless bitches. They could not possibly appreciate his choice of the hermetic existence. The genuine alchemist possesses the following qualities:

He is discreet and silent. Check, Fabrice told himself.

He resides in an isolated house in an isolated position. Check. Fabrice opened one eye and glared at the window. When Starbucks came, he would have to sell up and move, he reflected, not for the first time.

He should choose his days and hours for labour with discretion. Hooyah! Fabrice allowed himself a moment of self-congratulation.

He should have patience, diligence and perseverance. How long had it been now with Zairah? Four? Five months? How patient is that?

Fabrice's hands lay on his folded knees. They were dirty.

He went and washed them, shook them dry and held them in front of his face, unable to recognise their use for a moment.

Repetition and purification. An idea, intangible as a wisp of steam from a beaker: the work would never be finished. There would be no end to it.

His phone rang. Fabrice was smirking as he picked up, expecting Zairah's whining voice. Tears and pleading.

'*Namaste.*'

'Xanthe?' An ambulance siren died in the background. 'Where are you?'

'Here. Now.'

'What do you mean?' Fabrice was curt. 'I haven't got time for this.'

Xanthe sat snugly tucked into her wheelchair outside the hospital. The medical staff understood how important it was for her to communicate, and would fetch her when she was finished. 'That's true, Fabrice. We neither of us have time, and yet–'

'What do you mean? What's the matter? What's happened?' Fabrice was sweating again.

'I'm positive, Fabrice. Positive. I didn't think I was but I am.'

'What? What the fuck are you talking about, Xanthe?' Positive. HIV Positive? Panic amplified the words coming from his mouth. Blind panic. Something dark at the heart, in the blood, in his blood, circulating through him, not rich red life but black death. The forces of evil. Fabrice's tongue was dry as bone and heavy as lead.

'Oh, Fabrice,' Xanthe soothed, as if talking to a child,

'you know what I mean. You helped me see it. Before I met you I was plagued with doubt. Zero.' She paused and shook her head, then whispered because it was a miracle. 'Positive.'

Nothing but a nothing for fucking. Base matter to be transformed.

Fabrice stood, limbs tensed, ready to fight. His knuckles around the phone were white. His gorge rose. A bilious tide was threatening to irrupt. He fought the urge to vomit. Puking like a girl was intolerable.

'The important thing is not to be a victim,' Xanthe continued, examining the blanket keeping her warm. She thought of Zairah, with her hungry heart and white dress. So cold. Always cold. Because there was no warmth to be had from the sociopath she snuggled up to. She would be saved, as Xanthe was saved. They would survive: it is no sin to be innocent and to love the wrong man. But there has to be a point when you stop yourself from falling and scream, 'Yes!'

'Victim!' Fabrice croaked. It was not possible. No, no, fucking no. What had she done to him? What had she done? He was careful. They invited him in. He had rules. How had it gone so wrong? All he wanted was to pursue his experiments. He had been honing his method for years. There was nothing wrong with the method: it was her, Miss X, the unknown element. She had infected his life with her black poison. It was flooding his veins. 'You're sick, Xanthe!' he almost shrieked.

'Yes. I know. I'm at the hospital. Someone's here for me now.' Xanthe smiled at the ambulance man, who had come back to check on her. 'Would you like to talk to him?'

'No! Of course I don't want to talk to him! What have you done, you whore?' Dread had Fabrice in its claws. Terror at his own mortality gnawed at his chest. His T-shirt was soaked with women's tears. First blood, his own, when his skinny body was pure, drawn by his mother in the heat of her delirium. Fabrice felt the dead weight of a serpent around his neck, a serpent eating its tail.

'What have *I* done, Fabrice?' Xanthe murmured. 'I didn't do anything. We were in it together, weren't we? You. Me. *Us*.' She savoured the word. 'My flat that night. Mingling our fluids like a scientific experiment. It's only a game if both people know, isn't it, Fabrice? We both knew, didn't we? You did all this to help me.'

'No,' Fabrice moaned. 'I didn't know it was a fucking game for you. This is life or death, Xanthe. What the hell are you playing at?'

She sounded so calm, so serene, it was driving him out of his mind. Fabrice spat. He could not help it. A mossy clump of phlegm stained the floor. He bent forward, examining it for blood. Decadent! She had wanted to die all along, he realised that. And she was taking him down with her.

'I'm not playing at anything, Fabrice. I'm deadly serious. But if it aids you to think of it that way, then let's call this my little game.' Xanthe smiled as she plucked at a strand of fluff. She did not know how to act. But the words were coming that erased her pain.

An implacable green tide rose from Fabrice's guts. He cut the call and threw the phone on his bed, where it bounced off the new Prada backpack, scattering condoms and a foil-wrapped square. He had to lope to the bathroom, banging into the doorframe, and when he was done heaving he rested his head against the cool, unforgiving shoulder of the cistern. Where had he gone wrong? He should have been meeting Agnès tonight: Agnès, with her long pale throat and sad tired eyes. He was going to help her revise; had told her he knew a bit about chemistry. She was younger than Yoshiko.

In a daze Fabrice went to his typewriter in a corner of the bedroom. Automatically, he ripped a prescription off the stolen pad and rolled it into the machine. He knew the formula. Tabbed to the right place. Beat the words into being. Hepatitis C: negative. HIV: negative. It was a lie. He saw it now. Fabrice foraged for the envelope that he showed them to gain their confidence and trust, dumped its contents all over the lino. Lies. Lies. Lies. He started tearing at the sheets, ripping them to shreds. His diseased blood coursed. His face was blotched and scarlet. He wanted to turn back time. More than anything. Had to get back to that safe place before he'd started fucking with the dirty blonde called Xanthe.

Fabrice yanked the counterfeit sheet from the roller. The words were there, tattooed on the yellowing paper. Fabrice held them up to the fading light, examining the way the ink was stabbed into the skin. He ripped off a corner. Rolled it into a pellet. Placed it on his tongue. It stuck, ugly as the body of Christ. The muscles of Fabrice's throat worked. Eventually saliva came and eased the wafer down. He swallowed, shuddered, and tore off another piece. He heard his own voice from far away. 'Eat,' it said.

The ambulance man laid a hand on Xanthe's shoulder.

'Ready?' he enquired. He could not leave his patient out here all night, chatting to friends as if nothing was happening and she did not have a care in the world.

'Yes,' replied Xanthe smiling, 'I'm ready for anything. I've been ready all my life. I just didn't see it until recently.'

'Then let's get you to Doctor Decup.' He released the brake and began wheeling her towards the sliding doors.

Xanthe sniggered.

'What?'

'D-cup? Really? Can't wait to meet her.'

'Him.'

'Oh.'

XLVIII

'You have to eat, baby girl. Eat to live.' Zairah's mother glanced down at her ample belly swathed in swishing golden layers of silk. 'I didn't even know you could cook. This smells divine. Is that fresh basil?' Bending carefully over the stove, she dipped a wooden spoon into the cooling pot of sauce. 'Let's add some more herbs. And oil. Where's the olive oil?'

Zairah rested her forehead on the cool surface of her table. No oil, she wanted to yell. Don't add oil. The mozzarella was in the bin, glistening and wet like afterbirth. She was terrified her mother would find it.

'I can't remember the last time we were here together. We should do this more often. I like being here with you. It makes a change from being at home with your father. We knew something was wrong. You haven't been yourself for months. Daddy misses you when you're not there for Sunday dinner. A darling-shaped hole, he calls it.' She could not stop talking. 'You keep a beautiful home. It's so perfect. I don't know how you do it, keep everything so tidy, go to work. And all your friends. My life wasn't like that when I was your age.' She was about to say, I was already a wife and mother. 'A tattooist, Zairah! You can do better than that! We didn't bring you up to throw your life away on

305

someone who doesn't even have a proper job. Thank the Lord that it's over now. Better to find out sooner rather than later. Look at you: you're beautiful and clever and talented; you can have any man you want.'

'I wanted Fabrice,' Zairah murmured mutinously into the crook of her arm.

'Tattoos! Almost everybody has one these days. Even your father's secretary. Such a pretty girl, and with this permanent bracelet on her wrist. It's a nice enough tattoo for a young woman, little flowers and leaves, but it's there forever. What happens when she changes? That tattoo is always going to be the same.'

Zairah sniffed. She sat up straight, her trembling hand on her right hipbone.

'He doesn't deserve you anyway. A man like that. We tried to warn you, Zairah. Older men always have baggage. It's not like you don't have friends your own age. Whatever happened to Simon-Pierre? He was such a lovely boy. I bumped into his mother the other day in Printemps. She was asking after you, too. He's just finished his Masters. Going to get a job at Sciences-Po. You should give him a ring. Is this what you got to go with it? Rigatoni might have been better.' There was a clatter as a saucepan of water was placed on the hob to boil.

Zairah watched her mother in her kitchen. When she had called just to say hello after Fabrice cancelled their date, without really meaning to, Zairah had broken down in tears. Fifteen minutes later her mother had been at the door.

'I'll do it,' Zairah said.

'Look at you, baby girl! Sit down. Let Mummy do it.

Let's have a glass of wine. Where do you keep the corkscrew?'

There were two tumblers on the table, one for her and one for Fabrice.

'He doesn't drink,' Zairah whispered.

Zairah's mother extracted a bottle from the rack and began noisily hunting through the cutlery drawer. She sighed as she gripped the Bordeaux between her knees and pulled out the cork.

'In those?' she asked.

Zairah looked at the water glasses. Then she looked into her mother's face, her round high cheeks, a few faint lines scored into the pouches of fat beneath her eyes.

'Baby girl, are those the glasses you want us to use?'

No, Zairah screamed inside. No. No. No.

'Let me see if I can find the proper ones we gave you for Christmas.'

'No, Mother.'

With her head at the back of a kitchen cupboard, Zairah's mother replied, 'What?'

Zairah pulled down the waistband of her skirt. Clink of crystal. Her mother turned towards her.

'No, Mother. No wine. Not for me. Not tonight.'

Her mother huffed, placing the glasses on the counter. 'Oh, Zairah!' she exclaimed in such tones of hurt and disappointment when she saw. 'What did he do to you?'

'Oh Zairah nothing!' Zairah spat. 'It's my tattoo and I love it. It's fierce. I'm not your baby girl, not any more. Look at me! I'm twenty-three years old. I have a job and a home and a life. Stop calling me that. I'm not a baby.'

Zairah's stripling body shook. Her mother's eyes grew moist, her lips compressed. 'Don't tell me what to do. I've had enough of that. I'm not a doll for all of you to play with.'

'We can do something about it. Lasers. They can burn them off with lasers these days. I'll find out.'

'NO!' Zairah shouted. 'No,' she repeated softly.

Zairah went up to her mother – who, even in heels, was a few centimetres shorter than she was – and threw her arms around her shoulders. They were wearing the same perfume. 'There's no need, Mum. They hurt, lasers. They burn you up from inside. I don't want that. Not at the moment.'

Her mother laid her head against Zairah's shoulder and stroked the downy hair at the nape of her neck.

The tomato-shaped kitchen timer pinged.

'And I don't want any of that either.'

They stood locked together, swaying slightly. Zairah felt her mother's warm breath on her skin.

'You will, b–' She managed to stop the words coming out. 'One day, Zairah, you will.'

XLIX

It was three a.m. Dr Decup leaned forward in his chair, a limp grey forelock of hair dangling into his eyes. It had been a long day. The strip lights hummed overhead. He had just written, 'Pixies???' and was about to light another cigarette. He was trying to get the patient's history into some kind of order. He offered her the pack.

Xanthe shook her head. 'No thanks. I don't want to die a slow and painful death, even if they are Lucky.'

He smiled grimly and his lighter rasped.

'He was up on stage, you see. The drummer. Fabrice. And I know Fabrice is not a drummer. He's a tattooist. But I saw him. Beating the thing with a huge smile on his face.'

Dr Decup's eyebrows nudged upwards, inviting her to continue.

'He beat me. I was nothing to him, a hollow thing. For eight years.'

'You've known Fabrice for eight years, and he abused you?'

Xanthe gazed at the items on the doctor's desk. Each one told a story: the pottery ashtray, the Banania tin full of blunt pencils, the back of a framed photograph. 'No. Not Fabrice. Fabrice doesn't beat women, not with his hands. But they lose, they lose something important by being with him.' Xanthe saw Zairah in her mind's eye, and she saw herself as she had been. 'It was Paul. Paul hurt me. So much. I couldn't take it any more. He was right here.' Xanthe turned her bare shoulder towards Dr Decup. She could show him and he would understand. She did not need to be ashamed. There was no need to cover up her suffering. He would help her see far back, beyond Paul, as far as her Father, whose death when she was twenty-three had left a dark world of words unsaid.

'That's some tattoo!' The doctor's daughter had recently got her first tattoo. He was thankful it was just a little rose on her ankle.

'My black sun.' Xanthe's voice splintered around the terrible truth.

'It hurts, yes?'

'It hurt.' Xanthe shook her head. 'It hurt so much it was killing me, but it doesn't hurt now. It's just ink and skin. My ink. My skin.' Xanthe glowed with the wonderment of self-possession.

'We'd better get that cut looked at.'

Xanthe continued, 'Fabrice didn't beat me, not like Paul. But he saw I was empty inside. Like he is. I was an experiment for him. It was work. He even wore dungarees.'

Dr Decup gave a light laugh.

'I know! It's ridiculous. But he did. Like a plumber. Plumber. Drummer. Tattooist. Alchemist. That's what he was up to: the art of transformation.'

'You know, Xanthe, there is no such thing as alchemy? It's a discredited science. Turning lead into gold! If only!' Decup laughed again. He saw tears spring to the patient's eyes and immediately regretted it. In more measured tones he explained, 'It's what we call magical thinking. You believe there is a causal connection between symbolic actions and real events.'

The doctor crushed out the cigarette and got up from behind his desk. He crouched in front of the patient's chair, tired knees tutting, and held out his hands, palms down. Xanthe stared at them, their code of veins and liver spots, trying to decipher the gesture.

Communication. Human warmth. She slipped her fingers underneath his. Symbol and reality. Not time to die: time to live.

Dr Decup's blue eyes sparkled like the sea. 'You are suffering from Post Traumatic Stress Disorder, Xanthe. You need to rest. Enough of these men! Enough of suffering! You survived. There's no need to feel guilty. Stay here with us, take the medication. You'll be feeling better soon, I guarantee.'

'What about work?'

'Taking care of yourself is a different kind of work, Xanthe.'

L

It was still dark outside. Fabrice stubbed his toe on a packing box as he shuffled towards the locked door of his empire. The studio was cold. He bent stiffly to pick up the post. It was there. Friday morning. As usual. Every week since the end of August.

Fabrice placed his mug of tea on the counter and pulled his new glasses from the map pocket of his combats. The correction was minimal: slight short-sightedness in the right eye. The optician had advised him that it was not worth bothering about. Fuck her. What did she know about seeing things clearly?

He ripped open the envelope. The first few times his hand had shook and nausea drained the colour from his face. However, with repetition, his confidence grew. The weekly AIDS test had become part of his purification ritual. It reassured him that he was still on the right track. There would never be another one like Xanthe. Write it up to experience.

Fabrice whispered the magic words, 'Negative . . . negative . . .' He rolled his sleeves, chucked the gaudy brochures for toys and tinsel in the bin, and settled in the client chair to send a text to Diane. Christmas shopping instead of college. How could she resist?

In twelve hours it would be over. He would be on the train heading south. She would be snivelling into a pile of useless presents. Fabrice's back cracked as he climbed out of the chair to tidy a carton of books. He rubbed the sore spot. Maybe he was overdoing the exercise. But he could not stop now. If he abandoned his Work, what would he be?

Glory be to him the granter of such secret ways,
Dominion, and Honour both, with Worship, and with Praise.

LI

The artificial tree on Marthe's desk was festooned with scarlet baubles the size of eyes. Xanthe stopped to look at it on her way out of the school. Lessons had finished a few hours ago but she had stayed behind to catch up on paperwork.

'Why don't you come and spend the day with us? The more the merrier. My son will be here with his three kids. Frankly, it will be pandemonium, but there's always room for one more.'

'That's so kind, Marthe,' Xanthe replied. Since the summer, with John and the people at the hospital afterwards, she had felt all the kindness in the world. 'But I'll be fine.'

'It's Christmas! You can't be on your own at Christmas,' the older woman continued.

Xanthe stretched out her hand and laid it gently on Marthe's upper arm. 'I'm OK, Marthe. I'm not alone.'

Marthe stood. They hugged awkwardly. She kissed Xanthe on both cheeks. At least after the three-month break she did not look so skeletal. She had changed her hair colour as well. That harsh bottle-blonde never did go with the black parentheses of her eyebrows. 'If you insist, dear. You know, you are looking so pretty these days. Like a silent movie star.'

Xanthe's hand went self-consciously to the back of her bob. 'Louise Brooks,' she admitted.

'Take this.' Marthe held out a card. On the back of the envelope she had written her name and address. 'We're almost neighbours. I'm at Cergy, the other end of Line A. The trains will be running on Sunday as usual. If you change your mind, just turn up. No need to call ahead.'

'Thank you, Marthe.'

Marthe watched Xanthe push through the plate-glass doors.

'I almost forgot.' Xanthe's cheeks were flushed as she paused on the threshold. 'Merry Christmas!'

'Merry Christmas, Xanthe.' *Bless you*, Marthe added, to herself.

The early evening air was refreshing after the dry heat of Xanthe's classroom. The lights were already on. Hundreds of people swarmed mothlike beneath the multi-coloured Chinese globes strung over the pavement outside Galeries Lafayette. Shoppers surged into the road; traffic had to stop to let the mass of festive humanity pass. Xanthe walked with them. She did not even have to watch where she was going because they were all apparently heading for the same place. A multitude of languages bubbled about: French, English, Italian, Japanese . . . A wondrous sea of words and warmth that Xanthe breasted, head held high.

'Fabrice! No!'

Had she really heard that? A woman's voice, urgent and pleading, somewhere in the scrum around her. Xanthe shook her head. No more hallucinations. She knew what was real.

No more magic. During those first days in the hospital she had tried to phone Fabrice a hundred times to say that she had seen what he had done. He had blocked the calls. Eventually she let it go. Anyway, Fabrice was a common name.

The human tide stilled in front of the first grand display. Xanthe's eyes were as wide and shining as all the others on her side of the glass. Parents edged their little ones forward, to where fluffy pink poodles cavorted on the oversized furniture. A pack of glistening black ceramic bulldogs stood by, soft white collars around their necks. Sticky fingers stretched out to try to touch.

An anxious whisper, 'You can't do that! Not here! There are too many people.'

And there he was, right in front of Xanthe, the delicate fingers of one hand resting on the tattooed neck of a young girl as his other hand snaked forward and tugged at her coat. She was naked, or at least topless, underneath. The crowd pressed around them, uncomprehending.

Fabrice had lost weight. The contours of his skull screamed sickness through the jaundiced paper of his skin.

'You said you wouldn't do anything like that,' the girl complained. 'You said only you would know.' She had a nest of scarlet hair, heavy silver rings in her ears, and studs on her nose, chin and eyebrow. She was trying to shake him off.

With some difficulty, Xanthe manoeuvred herself in front of the couple and turned round to face them. The girl glared at her and prised the open folds of her coat from Fabrice's grasp. Her nipples were pierced as well.

'What's it to you?' the girl demanded. She was up for a fight. Women like that, with all their money and poise, they made Diane want to spit.

Xanthe looked over the girl's shoulder. There was a ghost of a superior smile about Fabrice's lips and he was wearing glasses. Xanthe had not seen him wearing glasses before. But she was sure it was him. Some things never change.

Remembering Zairah and what she had instinctively felt that summer in Saint Germain, Xanthe addressed the girl in measured tones. 'That man, the one with his hand on your neck, he thinks you're a victim.' Xanthe nodded in Fabrice's direction.

The girl snorted. Her piercings clinked like armour. She was about to tell this supercilious stranger to fuck off. Most people on the street were too scared to even look her in the eye.

'He says the important thing is not to be a victim, but that's not what he means. Every time he says it, he wants you to hear: the important thing is to be a victim. That's how he sees us. It's an experiment.'

The girl's painted mouth dropped open in recognition, revealing a black bolt through her tongue. He said that a lot, Fabrice. Diane thought it was because he appreciated how fierce she was. 'How do you know?' The girl's brain was whirling. 'Look at me! Do I look like a victim to you?' She tried to lean backwards into Fabrice's arms. He was old enough to be her father, but he was cool. She was learning a lot from him; maybe she would become a tattooist one day, just like him. He jerked smartly to the side of her, facing Xanthe.

'*Namaste.*' It was awkward for Xanthe, bending her arms to make the gesture of acknowledgement.

Diane's anger flared. Something was going on. She did not understand it fully. She buttoned her donkey jacket, jabbing some pensioner beside her in the ribs, and squared her shoulders. She was not stupid. There was some kind of complicity between them; it was obvious. But Fabrice was her bloke now and she was not prepared to share him, no matter how much he drooled on about having a threesome. 'Who the fuck are you? What's he to you? That's my boyfriend you're trying to pull.'

Fabrice was surrounded by shopping bags. He sagged under their weight: the useless things he had encouraged Diane to buy for him. It was boring, middle-aged, middle-class, to pay bills and rent, he had said. Let's blow it all on chocolate and champagne! Her grubby roll of Euros had positively flown out of her hands in the heady rush of irresponsibility. She would think back on that moment come January, facing eviction alone: call it an education. She should have stayed in school.

Fabrice did not return Xanthe's greeting. He could not possibly know the beautiful woman standing in front of him. There was an assurance about her. Her glossy black hair and red coat reeked of a confidence that repelled Fabrice. Somebody's mother? Older sister? Outraged aunt? He wanted to dismiss her from his mind.

'Fabrice? Who's the madwoman? Do you know her?' Diane's voice came shrill and accusatory. A few people tore their eyes off the animatronic display, sensing something more interesting happening in their midst.

'No. I don't. Let's go.'

Xanthe looked from Fabrice to the girl to Fabrice again, her eyes alive with understanding.

'Xanthe,' she stated.

'Xanthe!' Fabrice blushed. He could not help it. But how? Where was the raddled blonde, dying of an incurable disease? Where was the dog on a leash? She was so different, Fabrice was incredulous. His tongue darted out to wet his dry lips.

'Hey! You!' Diane was becoming increasingly heated. She did not care what people thought of her. Discretion was for saddos who lacked the balls to express themselves openly. 'You make me go Christmas shopping topless. Topless! My tits are like fucking lead weights! And we just happen to bump into your ex-wife, or whatever she is. It's not on!'

Those nearest the altercation – a mild group of Burberry-clad tourists – started to inch away, glancing in Diane's direction and muttering in Japanese. A young guy, shaven head, ornately pencilled facial hair and a single chain-store diamond earring, focused his attention on the weird little man in specs. Creep. Hanging out with young girls with tattoos and piercings. No wonder the fit-looking one had left him.

Xanthe took advantage of the space that opened up, and edged between the couple to lean closer to Fabrice's ear. There was no need to shout. Her words would resound in the hollow space of his heart. She laid a hand on his shoulder. He tried to flinch away but Diane was there, roiling fire and fury. She was making a scene. He hated that. Fabrice's heart was hammering. People were watching. He had to get away. He felt Xanthe's breath on his skin, dark droplets of water vapour from the core of her, polluting him, making him ill all over again.

Full of tenderness, Xanthe whispered, 'The Lightning Way, Fabrice. You did it. The Lightning Way. Base matter into gold. You can stop working now.'

Fabrice's lungs were paralysed. It could not be true: the Lesser Work, the Greater Work in Saint Germain that summer. Is this what it had come to? How he had suffered, was still suffering. Why wasn't she dead? Breathe, he told himself, breathe in . . .

Fabrice looked at his empty hands in horror and amazement. His Prada backpack slipped from his shoulder, stuffed as it was with Christmas treats the girl had bought at Lafayette Gourmet, imagining they would be sharing them in bed together over the weekend. Some hoodlum he had never met before gave him such a look of disdain, and sucked his teeth, that Fabrice was mortified.

'I'm not going to carry all this stuff alone.' Diane's voice, her face, faded into nothing. The dogs in the window display mocked him, heads nodding in unison. The crowd turned. Fabrice sensed it. They knew. They saw. All he wanted was to go home, take off the dungarees and be quiet and still. But where was home now? The lease was signed on rue Biot, and Fabrice was tired. Terminally tired.

Xanthe was still shaking as she stepped onto the escalator that carried her down into Auber. She popped a little white tablet out of its Friday blister and swallowed it. She was not mad, though. Not now. She knew exactly who she was and was taking the medication properly. It helped. She had thrown out the pick-and-mix when she got back from hospital. She no longer had to batter herself into unconsciousness. Dr Decup had said she would probably not be on Abilify forever, as long as there were no further psychotic episodes.

Xanthe was looking forward to going back to her flat. It was much more homely these days. John had given her a plant to tend, which she placed by the door. Its fat green fronds were thriving. And the cat was waiting. Her neighbours had asked her to look after him while they were away for Christmas.

'Yes!' Xanthe said to herself, looking at the poster for her school as she got onto the train.

About the Author

Louise Black was born in Devon. After a Masters and a PhD on Georges Bataille she moved to France, where she currently lives. Her short stories appeared in *The Erotic Review* for over a decade. *The Tattooist* is her first published novel.